SALOME AND OTHER

DECADENT FANTASIES

SALOME AND OTHER

DECADENT FANTASIES

BRIAN STABLEFORD

COSMOS BOOKS · MMIV

Published in the US by **Cosmos Books**, an imprint of **Wildside Press**
P.O. Box 301, Holicong, PA 18928-0301
www.cosmos-books.com
www.wildsidepress.com

Hardcover ISBN: 1-58715-407-2
Trade Paperback ISBN: 1-58715-408-0

CONTENTS

INTRODUCTION

The artistic notion of Decadence was first defined by Theophile Gautier in
the introduction that he wrote to the third edition of Charles Baudelaire's
Les Fleurs du Mal, which appeared not long after Baudelaire's death in
1866. According to this celebratory essay, "the style of the decadence" is
"no other thing than Art arrived at that point of extreme maturity that
determines civilizations which have grown old; ingenious, complicated,
clever, full of delicate hints and refinements, gathering all the delicacies of
speech, borrowing from technical vocabularies, taking colour from every
palette, tones from all musical instruments, contours vague and fleeting,
listening to translate subtle confidences, confessions of depraved passions
and the odd hallucinations of a fixed idea turning to madness."

Such a style, Gautier argues, should be "summoned to express all and to
venture to the very extremes." Baudelaire's work recalled to his mind
"language already veined with the greenness of decomposition,
savouring of the Lower Roman Empire and the complicated refinements
of the Byzantine School, the last form of Greek Art fallen into deliques-
cence; but such is the necessary and fatal idiom of peoples and civilizations where an artificial life has replaced a natural one and developed in a
man who does not know his own needs."

Gautier goes on to say of Decadent style that "contrary to the classical
style, it admits of backgrounds where the spectres of superstition, the
haggard phantoms of dreams, the terrors of night, remorse which leaps
out and falls back noiselessly, obscure fantasies that astonish the day, and
all that the soul in its deepest depths and innermost caverns conceals of

7

darkness, deformity and horror, move together confusedly."

This was written before the humiliating collapse of France's so-called Second Empire in 1870, which seemed to lend further credence to the notion that the nation and the civilization it represented were in terminal decline. Gautier's analysis of Baudelaire, in combination with Paul Verlaine's study of other "accursed poets," was taken up as a manifesto by a number of prose writers in the 1880s, most prominent among them Joris-Karl Huysmans, Jean Lorrain, Rachilde and Remy de Gourmont. Their work became definitive of the *fin-de-siecle* period, and it had a considerable, if somewhat muted, influence on the development of fantasy fiction in England and America. Its influence in England—very evident in the prose fiction of such writers as Arthur Machen, M. P. Shiel and R. Murray Gilchrist—was swiftly curtailed when the conviction of Oscar Wilde strangled the English Decadent Movement in its cradle. American "Bohemians" like Ambrose Bierce, James Huneker and Edgar Saltus fared only slightly better in a moral landscape constricted by the Bible Belt and easing its way towards Prohibition.

As second-rate comedians are fond of pointing out, no one was ever hurt by a fall, however steep; it is the abrupt halt at the end that does the damage. Since the invention of the parachute it has been possible for the adventurously-inclined to make a sport out of free-falling, to savour the aesthetics of descent. This, in metaphorical terms, was the strategy of those artists we now call Decadent. They decided that in spite of (perhaps even because of) its obvious technological achievements their Imperially-ambitious society was in a state of irrevocable cultural decline. They elected, therefore, to explore and advertise the peculiar aesthetics of cultural free-fall.

Decadent art is not representative; it does not reflect commonplace conceptions of "Life" or "Nature," which it despises and makes every attempt to de-mythologise. Decadent literature points instead the way to an opposite ideal, wherein life and nature would become entirely subject to every kind of clever artifice. Because this ideal is incapable of attainment in practice, Decadent literature is essentially pessimistic, and sometimes brutally horrific, but this makes it all the more ruthless in demolishing the pretensions of rival philosophies. It mocks these rivals mercilessly, taking delight in questioning or overturning all judgments that are ordinarily taken for granted.

Decadent artists are eager to make their fantasies as gorgeous as possible, but they know well enough that anyone who undertakes Odysseys in Exotica will encounter all manner of chimeras. Such artists, knowing the futility of taking refuge in the commonplace, desire to confront these chimeras, to see them clearly even though no understanding of them or reconciliation with them is possible. Decadent artists have an avid hunger for sensation, which can sometimes override the overly simple distinctions which are normally drawn between the pleasant and the unpleasant, they know that horror is a stimulant. They also feel that there is some essential truth in horror: that the world is sick at heart, and that even the most obvious of evils—pain, death, and disease—may require aesthetic re-evaluation.

Decadent literature is, intrinsically and proudly, a literature of moral challenge; it is sceptical, cynical and satirical. It recognises that everyday morality does not work either in practical or in psychological terms, and is therefore a sham, but that ideal morality is—not necessarily unfortunately—unattainable. The moral of a Decadent prose-poem or conte cruel, if it has a moral at all, is likely to recommend that we should make the best compromises we can, recognise that they are compromises, and refuse to be ashamed of them. Decadent art is, however, dedicated to the smashing of all icons and idols, and it is always ready to attack stern moralists of every stripe; it is fiercely intolerant of intolerance and revels in the paradoxicality of such a stance.

The fashionability of literary Decadence was brief even in France. It faded away with the birth of a new century and the steady advancement of the rival philosophy of progress. That rival philosophy has achieved such a dominance over human thought in the twentieth century that the idea of civilizations slowly and contentedly crumbling to dust seems hardly tenable. Notwithstanding T. S. Eliot's judgment, the overwhelming majority opinion during the last hundred years has been that the world is far more likely to end in a bang than a long-drawn-out simper. To the extent that Decadent prose has survived in the twentieth century it has lived a fugitive and marginal existence, whose most adventurous produce was consigned to the absurd environment of the American pulp magazine *Weird Tales*, where H. P. Lovecraft and Clark Ashton Smith took some of its preoccupations and mannerisms to a new limit.

Most modern writers of Decadent fantasies have little alternative but to work within the Lovecraftian tradition, most of their publications emerging from small presses; notable exemplary practitioners include

Thomas Ligotti, Jessica Amanda Salmonson and Jeff VanderMeer. This collection assembles some of my shorter works in this vein; others can be found in the Necronomicon Press collection *Fables and Fantasies* (1996). Longer stories in a similar vein include *The Hunger and Ecstasy of Vampires* (Mark Ziesing 1996) and its two sequels, thus far only published in abridged form as "The Black Blood of the Dead" (1997) and "The Gateway of Eternity" (1999)—although I hope that a portmanteau version will one day appear as *The Gateway of Eternity*. Many of my science fiction novels, most obviously *Firefly: A Novel of the Far Future* (Borgo 1994) and *Architects of Emortality* (Tor, 1999), also have significant Decadent elements.

SALOME

When Salome the enchantress danced, she was beloved by all those who watched; she made them drunken captives of her art. Her silken costumes were sewn with crystal shards, which glittered in the light of ruddy lanterns like the scales of many-coloured serpents, and the gliding movements of her body were like the swaying of an asp in thrall. When she leapt up high with her white arms thrown wide, she was like a creature in flight: a lamia with frail wings, or a delicate dragon's child.

When Salome the enchantress danced, she stirred the fires of Hell in the hearts of those who watched; she made them willing slaves of her passion.

* * *

Salome was never taught to dance; hers was a spontaneous art born of inspiration and nurtured by an altogether natural process of growth. She danced because dancing was the most precious aspect of her nature, and she began to express herself in the rhythms of dance as soon as she began to know who she was.

Her earliest dances were witnessed only by the female slaves into whose charge she had been delivered when her mother died in bearing her. She first danced for her father, who was Herod the Magician King, when she was seven years old. He immediately commanded that the tongues of her slaves should be cut out, so that they could not speak of it, and that their eyes should be scored with thorns, so that they would never again see anything clearly.

In the seven years which followed, only Herod and his brothers in blood were permitted to watch Salome dance, and to watch the magic grow within her as her art grew to perfection. She obeyed her father's command to reserve her gifts for his own delight, and for the seduction of his noble friends.

Herod used the spell which Salome's dancing cast to increase his power over his brothers in blood. He took advantage of the state of intoxication into which she delivered them to bind them to his will, and paid them for their servitude by granting them the privilege of watching Salome dance. The greater privilege, of slaking the lusts which Salome's dancing excited, Herod reserved to himself.

Herod believed that in taking carnal possession of Salome's unripened body he was protecting himself from the kind of sottishness which she inspired in her other admirers, but he was wrong. Although his eyes had never been scored with thorns he saw unclearly, and although he was a Master of Magicians and not a slave, he was captive without knowing it to the magic of his daughter-wife.

* * *

When the mother of Salome had died in bearing her, Herod had used his magic to procure the death of his brother Philip. He did this in order to make a widow of Philip's wife Herodias, so that she would become his property under the law of his people. Herodias was very beautiful then, and well pleased with what Herod had done in order to possess her, for she knew the worth of a Master of Magicians, and was ambitious to be his mistress in every possible way.

Inevitably, with the passing of time, Herod became bored with Herodias, and left her alone in her apartments for months on end. There she played perpetually with her magic mirrors and her cards of fortune, by which means she sought—hopelessly—to discover a way to rescue her ambitions. Herodias never saw Salome dance, nor heard any trustworthy report of the artistry of her dancing, but she divined in the end that it was Herod's infatuation with Salome which had obliterated any trace of affection for herself which had ever lodged in his heart.

For this reason, Herodias grew to hate Salome with a very violent passion. She tried to hurt her niece with curses and maledictions, but her own magic was not powerful enough to prevail against Herod's protectiveness and the armour of Salome's maturing art. She was therefore forced by circumstance to be patient, although she could barely contain her rage against the irresistible pressure of time which leached away her glamour.

Herodias was chafed and teased by her frustration for seven long years, but she never despaired. She knew that there would come a day when Salome ceased to be a child and became a woman, and she knew that when the day came, Salome would be ready to be made captive in her turn by the savage grip of infatuation.

* * *

As the fourteenth year of Salome's life drew to its culmination, there appeared in the borderlands of King Herod's petty empire a man named John the Prophet, who preached to the common people whenever and wherever they could be induced to listen to him.

John the Prophet told his hearers that those whose mastery of men was achieved by command of magic, wealth and privilege were doomed to burn in Hell for all eternity, but that the common people might acquire a kingdom of their own beyond the grave, if only they were virtuous and humble and hopeful. This kingdom beyond the grave was named by John the Prophet Heaven; he told his hearers that there was no suffering there, and that no man had power over another, because all were equal in the eyes of God.

Herod was glad when news of John the Prophet's teachings reached his ears. He was a clever statesman, and knew that it was always to the advantage of rulers when prophets appeared to promise the common people fabulous reparation for their current misery. Such notions helped to make his subjects content with their subjection, by deferring the promised settlement of all their grievances to an imaginary life beyond death, and deflecting their ambitions away from rebellion and revolution.

Like all petty emperors, Kng Herod loved to see his subjects confirmed in a determination to be virtuous, humble, and hopeful.

Although Herod was very pleased to have John the Prophet wandering in his kingdom, he knew that he would eventually have to destroy the preacher. It was in his interest to make it seem that he feared such men, and that he did not want their message to be heard. For this reason, he followed the methods of all wise rulers, making it his habit to imprison, torture and ultimately martyr all the prophets who came to his attention.

This way of dealing with prophets invariably brought rewards to all who used it. It lent careful emphasis to the sermons which they preached, and made their teachings all the more precious to those foolish and unlucky persons who had found hope in them.

In his dealings with John the Prophet King Herod was careful and methodical as he usually was. His first move was to have his quarry hunted for a while without actually being caught. He sent out instructions for the arrest of the prophet, but made sure that rumours flew ahead of his instructions, so that John would always be one step ahead of the officers who came to take him. Then, at his leisure, Herod closed in. He issued a public proclamation banning John the Prophet from entering the gates of his Capital City, thus making sure that the preacher would be all the more enthusiastic to carry his message within the walls. Finally, he had the man seized as publicly and as violently as possible, and brought before his fully-assembled court to be mocked, scorned and condemned.

* * *

When John the Prophet was brought to stand before him, Herod deemed it desirable that as many people as possible should be looking on, so as to create a proper sense of occasion. He had summoned all his brothers in blood, and he had invited Herodias to descend from her apartments in order to appear at his left hand. At his right hand he set his beautiful daughter Salome.

When everything was ready, Herod asked John the Prophet to repeat all his heresies, in order that they might be debated by the wise men of the kingdom.

John the Prophet stood up bravely, in spite of the bruises which had been inflicted upon him at he time of his arrest, and stated the items of his faith. All magic, he said, was evil; those who owned and used it were impure and ungodly, and would be condemned to the flames of Hell for all eternity. All men who exercised power over others, whether by right of birth or wealth or strength of arms, would likewise be punished for the abuse of their power. Only the meek, the virtuous and the pure in heart would be rewarded after death; they would be taken into the kingdom of Heaven, where they would dwell eternally in peace and harmony, without want or pain.

Herod's brothers in blood then stood, one by one, to ridicule the preacher. With clever sophistry and cunning logic they demonstrated the fatuity of his claim that there would be a further life beyond death for anyone save those gifted in magic, whose souls were immunized against extinction. Then they charged him with sedition, saying that his ideas were an insult to the honour and station of King Herod. Then they proceeded, each in his turn, to offer suggestions as to the particular way in which the false prophet might best be put to death.

While all this was going on, John the Prophet stood as straight as he was able, apparently quite unafraid. He was a young man, not more than twenty years of age, and very handsome. He had fine dark eyes of an unusual clarity, and neatly-shaped eyebrows. He never looked at his would-be tormentors or answered their gibes; instead, he alternated his gaze between the two women seated on either side of the Magician King who sat in judgment upon him. He looked long and hard at Herodias, and he looked longer and harder at Salome; to them and to them alone did he present the argument of his eyes.

Although it might not have been his intention, what John the Prophet's eyes said to Salome was: I am a better man than any you have ever seen before, and were you to dance with me, we might discover a sweeter rhythm than any you have ever felt before.

And although it certainly was not his intention, what John the Prophet's eyes said to Herodias was: Here is an opportunity to serve your own ends, by persuading Salome to loathe her father-husband.

* * *

When the great debate drew to its close, Herod promised to think upon the matters brought to his attention, and to deliver his verdict the next day. The purpose of this delay was to allow the rumour of what had occurred to spread to every nook and cranny of the city streets, and to take wing even beyond its walls. Thus, everyone who cared to do so might have the leisure to discuss the justice of the case and the deliciously particular cruelties of all the methods of execution which had been proposed.

During the night, however, Herodias tricked one of Salome's half-blind slave-girls into carrying a letter to her, representing it as a message from John the Prophet.

The substance of the message was this: You are the most beautiful woman in the world. It is not permitted to me to love you, nor can I recant a single word of what I have preached. I am doomed to die for what I believe, but the hours of life which remain to me would be immeasurably enriched by one more sight of your wondrous face. My one regret is that I will never see you dance.

Herodias was careful to express these sentiments as artlessly as she could, in the cause of authenticity. She trusted to the logic of the situation to ensure that Salome, in spite of her own extraordinary artistry, would not see through the deception.

* * *

Salome was not allowed to leave her chambers unsupervised, but it was an easy matter for one of her abilities to dupe her half-blind guardians and the soldiers who stood watch over the prison where John the Prophet was held. She entered his cell without difficulty, and woke him up.

"I can save you," she said to him. "Only do as I instruct, and you will win free of the castle, the city and the nation."

"The truth dare not flee from persecution," John the Prophet told her, "else men would know it for falsehood."

"Do you prefer to die?" she asked him.

"I do," he told her. "Only by dying for his beliefs can a man hope to persuade others that they are worth dying for."

"You can say that," Salome marvelled, "even though you have looked upon my face, and found it the most beautiful in the world? Can you really refuse to love me, now that I am with you?"

"Certainly," said John the Prophet. "I am a virtuous man, and must remain so if I am to persuade others that the highest rewards of all are reserved for the virtuous."

"You will not think so highly of virtue," Salome promised, lewdly, "when you have seen me dance."

There and then, she danced for him.

She danced upon the floor of his cell, despite that it was moist with stinking excrement. The cell was narrow, with walls of filthy stone, and it was illuminated only by the light of a single tallow candle, but Salome did not need a huge space or a polished floor or a bright light in order to display her art. She was full to overflowing with enchantment, and magic radiated from her body as soon as she began to move.

She lost herself in her dance, and was carried away by the tide of its bewitchment; she was as much its captive as she intended him to be, and it held her in perfect thrall as its rhythms thundered in her eager blood.

When it was over, she said to him: "Will you refuse to love me now?"

"I cannot refuse to love you," admitted John the Prophet, not entirely unhappily. "But still I must die, for the sake of what I preach. Even though my soul has been sullied by affection for a witch, I must be a martyr to my cause. My flesh might betray my heart, but my lips cannot betray the truth."

During the hour that she danced for John the Prophet, Salome had ceased to be a child, but she was no wiser now than she had been before. She did not know the real reason why Herod was determined to kill John the Prophet, and could not tell him that the acceptance of his "truth" by the common people was what Herod most devoutly desired.

Even if she had been able to tell him, it might not have changed his mind; he was, after his own silly fashion, an extraordinarily sincere and virtuous man.

"You are a fool," Salome told him, "but that will not prevent my loving you, as you love me."

* * *

On the next day, with all his court assembled before a crowd equal to that of the the previous day, Herod pronounced judgment upon John the Prophet. He found him guilty of sedition, and announced the following plan for his execution: first, his tongue was to be cut out and he was to be castrated with shears; then, he was to be trussed from shoulder to ankle and placed breast-deep in a great urn full of oil, which would be slowly heated to boiling point; then, his head was to be struck from his neck and placed on a spike atop the city gate, so that passers-by might judge from the expression on his face whether or not he had really gone to a more pleasant place.

"Better to be boiled alive," John the Prophet said, before they cut out his tongue, "than to burn in Hell for all eternity."

Salome watched while her lover was ungently castrated, knowing that what he was sacrificing was nothing that he needed. She watched slaves wind the ropes tightly about his body, and lower him into the huge bronze urn whose broad belly was filled with cooking-oil. Only his beautiful head projected from the narrow neck. She listened to the macabre music of his attempted screams, which rose to an ecstatic pitch as the oil, warmed by a roaring fire set beneath the oil, came gradually to its boiling-point. She watched them detach his head from his body, carefully studying the unspeakably horrid expression which agony had graven upon his features. Then she rose from her place, and went down to take the head from the man who held it; he was too astonished to refuse to part with it.

Herod was also taken by surprise, but when he saw Salome take the head of John the Prophet from the soldier he came swiftly to his feet and ordered her to return to her place.

She ignored him.

Instead of obeying, she began to dance.

* * *

Whenever Salome the enchantress danced, she enraptured all those who watched; it made no difference that thousands watched her now instead of a few. She made them instantly drunk with the sight of her; each and every one—man or woman—was captive to her art.

Her courtly attire was modest enough, though sewn from silken and golden threads, but as she whirled and cavorted across the arena, passing the head of John the Prophet from one hand to the other and back again, she shed her cloak to reveal a filmy chemise decorated with a thousand crystal shards, which glittered in the light of the morning sun like the scales of many-coloured serpents.

Her flowing movements held the whole vast crowd in thrall. No one moved once the dance had begun; only the expressions on the watchers' faces changed.

In the beginning, Herod's eyes were wide with alarm and wrath, and his mouth was wide open in protest; but as the dance continued the alarm and the wrath faded from his eyes and his lips came together in a curiously wistful smile.

In the beginning, Herodias bared her teeth as she permitted herself a mockingly triumphant laugh, and leaned forward in anticipation of satisfaction; but as the dance progressed her lips came together, pursed with anxiety, and she tried unsuccessfully to draw back.

In the beginning, the dead prophet's eyes bulged out of their sockets, bloated by the pain which he had suffered, and the bloodied stump of his tongue was visible inside his mouth; but as the dance went on the eyes softened into an expression of adoration and the mouth relaxed into a curiously ironic yet loving smile.

When she leapt high into the air with her slender arms thrown wide, Salome was like a creature in flight: a lamia with frail wings, or some delicate dragon's child. As she tumbled and soared, she stirred the fires of Hell in the hearts of those who watched; she made them willing slaves of her unleashed passion.

At first, only poor dead John danced with her, but as the dance became wilder and more insistent she drew Herod from his throne and Herodias from her lesser seat, and they moved as though to join her in the paces of a tarantella, partners to one another as John the Prophet was partner to Salome.

Herod and Herodias now opened their mouths again, as though to cry out the gladness of their ecstasy, but their tongues were unkindly ripped out of their mouths and hurled—writhing like earthworms cut by a spade—to the ground.

Then the King and his former mistress reached out to one another as though to embrace in the heat of passion, but their clothes caught fire and the skin came away from their flesh as if it were no more than a kind of clothing itelf, and the flesh melted from their bones.

Still they danced. Even when there was nothing left of either of them beneath the neck but a wrack of bone and sinew they danced on, avid with excitement, fervent with the furious ecstasy of Salome's magic.

Meanwhile, Salome drew the head of John the Prophet tenderly to her breast and cradled it there, protectively. She continued to dance, but her arms were no longer flung wide and she slowed in her paces for a little while.

The severed head seemed to melt into her breast and become part of her; it was lost amid the shimmer of tiny sequins. Then the dance grew wild again, and wilder and wilder . . .

In the end, all three of the dancers came together, in a riotous tangle of bleached bones and many-coloured scales, and vanished into a whirlwind from beyond the world, which carried them away.

* * *

All the people who had watched the dance were freed from the spell which had been put upon them.

The commoners went swiftly away, to spread the news of the miracle which they had witnessed. They were convinced that Herod, Herodias and Salome had all been carried away to Hell, but that John the Prophet was in Heaven.

Herod's brothers in blood fell to fighting among themselves to determine who might take his place, and eventually settled the matter. The Magician King who came after the one who had been taken was every bit as cunning and cruel as his predecessor had been, and there was no perceptible change in the condition of the kingdom.

In time, the new king's wife bore him a daughter, whom he loved very dearly. The careful disposal of her favours helped him to extend his power over his brothers in blood.

In time, another prophet came to the kingdom, to preach to any who would condescend to hear him. This prophet, inspired by the glorious example of his predecessor, told his hearers to be humble and virtuous, to love one another, and to wait with patience for their reward in the Kingdom of Heaven.

The new king was suitably grateful for this gift of circumstance. The new prophet was eventually crucified.

* * *

Meanwhile, in Hell, Salome danced.

While the dauhter of Herod danced, in her peculiarly demonic fashion, before the courtly host of Hell, she delighted all those who watched her. She excited them almost beyond endurance with the magic of her art. Her silky skin was covered now with a million crystal shards, which glistened beneath the fiery sky like the scales of many-coloured serpents. Whenever she leapt up with her lovely arms thrown wide in rapture, she was like a creature in flight: a lamia with frail wings, or a delicate dragon's child.

When Salome the enchantress danced in Hell, she stirred the fires which breathed life in the hearts of all those who watched; she made them willing slaves of her passion. But one and one alone was privileged to dance with her, and share the burning heat of her inmost soul, and that was John the Prophet.

Once, and once only, Salome asked her lover whether he would rather have enjoyed the cool pastures of Heaven, from which he had been excluded by his love for her.

"Only the meek and virtuous and pure in heart," he told her then, "could ever believe that the flames of passion are naught but pain and punishment. Those who know the ecstasy of true enchantment could not possibly endure eternity, were they not perpetually bathed by such fire as ours."

O FOR A FIERY GLOOM AND THEE

La Belle Dame Sans Merci was kin to Jack A-Lantern: a whim o' the wisp alloyed from light and shadow, air and dew. Such contradictory beings cannot long endure; their warring elements long for separation and their fated dissolutions are rarely quiet, never without pain. How should such a being look upon a man, save with wild wild eyes?

La Belle Dame Sans Merci could not stroll upon the mead like any earthbound being for her footfall was far too light, but she had the precious power of touch which earthbound beings take overmuch for granted. She could not be seen by light of noon, but when she did appear—bathed by the baleful moon's unholiness—there was magic in her image.

Salom, the enchantress knew how to dance, and stir the fire of Hell in the hearts of those who watched, but La Belle Dame Sans Merci knew how to lie as still as still could be, and ignite the fire of Purgatory by sight alone.

La Belle Dame Sans Merci was a daughter of the faery folk, but it is not given to the faery folk to know their fathers and their mothers as humans do. It is easy for faery folk to believe that they owe their conception to the fall of the dew from their father the Sky: from the dew which never reaches mother earth but drifts upon the air as wayward mist. That, at least, is the story they tell one another; but what it might mean to them no merely human being could ever understand. Humans are cursed by the twin burdens of belief and unbelief but the faery folk are no more capable of faith than of mass; they have the gift of touch without the leaden heaviness of solidity, and they have the gift of imagination without the parsimonious degradations of accuracy.

The earliest adventures of La Belle Dame Sans Merci were not concerned with warriors or princes but with men unfit for oral or written record—mere passers-by on the rough-hewn roads of myth and history—but she always felt that she was made for the Royal Hunt and for the defiance of chivalry. She always felt that she was made to tempt the very best of the children of the Iron Age, to draw the users of arms and armour from the terrible path of progress. Because she had no human need to transmute her feelings into beliefs she had no human need to ask *why* she was made that way—or whether she was made at all—so she followed the force of her impulse with all blithe innocence, her eyes as wide as they were wild.

* * *

Like the rough-hewn roads of myth and history, the many roads of England were not at this time wont to run *straight*. The Romans had come but the Romans had gone again; their legacy remained only in a few long marching-paths, and it was more than possible that the few would become fewer as time went by and Rome became but a memory.

Made for men a-foot and horses poorly shod, the older roads of England wound around slopes and thickets, ponds and streams, always avoiding places of ill-repute, always preferring the gentle gradient and the comfortable footfall. In poor light such pathways become mazy and treacherous and there is no cause for astonishment in the fact that far more travellers set out in those days than ever arrived at their destinations.

These older ways were the roads that the faery folk loved—not so much for their actual use, but rather as a means of design and definition: a map of the world whose interstices could provide their home and habitat. The faery folk had hated Rome, and they hated echoes of Rome with equal fervour. They hated arms and armour because arms and armour were the mechanics of empire, and they hated knighthood and chivalry because knighthood and chivalry were the ideals of empire.

When the Romans had gone, there still remained in the population they left behind the idea of a *Great* Britain and a concomitant cause of fealty and fellowship. The idea of that Great Britain was the property of petty kings ambitious to be Once and Future Kings, and the guiding light of counsellors ambitious to be Magi. There was more than one Arthur, more than one Merlin and more than one Round Table—but they all became one in the labyrinth of myth and history because they were all bound into one by the idea of empire and the notion that all roads should run straight, cutting through slopes and thickets, filling in ponds and bridging streams, and frankly disregarding matters of ill-repute.

The idea of Great Britain and the dream to which it gave birth would probably have come to nothing, had it not been for the Church, but Rome was replaced by Christendom, and Christendom returned to the England the Romans had abandoned. The actual empire of Rome was replaced by the imaginary empire of God, which was all the more dangerous to the mazy roads of England and myth by virtue of its ingenious abstraction.

Christendom gave the knights of England a Holy Grail which none of them was good enough to touch, and made them mad with virtue as they strove for worthiness. The idea of chivalry had never quite contrived to extinguish lust from their hearts, but the idea of the Grail was all the stronger for its manifest absurdity; it forced the minds of knights and princes into straight and narrow paths, so that their vaulting ambition became ever-more-narrowly focused on broad, *straight* highways: highways fit for ironclad chariots of vulgar fire.

Because of chivalry and Christendom it was not easy for La Belle Dame Sans Merci to follow the force of her defining impulse, but she was a creature of paradox from the very start: an amalgam of elements at war. For folk such as her there is no end but catastrophe, no medium but hazard.

* * *

That evening, a knight whose name was Florian had sent his horse to a well-appointed stable and his servants to sleep in the straw. He could have had a bed for himself, a loaf of bread and a cup of mead, and dreamless sleep—but that was not his way. Sir Florian was a chaste knight oft disposed to prayer, to the rapt contemplation of the heavens, and to the frank disregard of matters of ill-repute. Rather than dispossess a doleful but dutiful host of the only good mattress for miles around he set himself to sleep beneath the stars, at one of those mysterious crossroads where the winding paths of myth and England intersect in a tangled knot. He had been warned of Jack A-Lanterns and their kin, but he considered his stubborn virtue to be proof against all temptation.

There are those who say that men see most and best when blinded, but the principle of pedantry defines such persons as fools and poets. The prosaic accuracy of the matter is that men see *most* in gentle sunlight, but *best* when they are no more than half-blinded; it is then that light and shadow have the greatest power of conjuration. The stars shone brightly enough that night, but the autumn air was cold and the mists condensed as soon as the sun had set.

Long afterwards, Sir Florian thought that his ill-remembered visitor might have come from the direction of the lake, perhaps from behind its rampart of withered sedge. In the beginning, however, all he knew was that she was suddenly *there*, her silver hair hanging loose about her shoulders. She was clad in white—or so it seemed against the darkness of the night—and he might have taken her for a saint, had it not been for her wild eyes.

Even though the faery was more beautiful by far than any human woman he had ever seen, without the least trace of a pock-mark on either cheek, the innocent but armoured Florian would have thought her good *had it not been for the wildness in her eyes.*

"What dost thou want with me, Lady Fair?" he asked, abridging the final word as half a hundred men had done before, without quite knowing why.

"I'd like a garland for my head," she told him, as she had told half a hundred before, "and bracelets for my arms. Summer's all but dead, and I must mourn her passing."

For a precious moment, Sir Florian hesitated. The lady stood as still as still could be, and his eyes had never beheld anything so marvellous. He felt that if he turned aside from the vision he would never see anything so lovely in all his life—but a man in search of Christendom's Grail is not in search of loveliness.

"I will not give thee anything," the knight replied, with a catch in his throat. "I know what thou art by the hectic wildness of thine eyes." Saying so—and with considerable effort of will—Sir Florian drew his sword and raised it up before him, so that the hilt and handguard were displayed in the sign of the holy cross.

To his consternation, the lady did not disappear. Nor did she move, for she had the art of lying still even when she stood erect. Had she only moved, the spell might have been broken, but she was as still as still could be and her beauty had all the force of sorcery. She waited for a moment before she replied: a moment sufficient to win the damnation of any ordinary man.

"If thou wishest to be rid of me," she said, in the end, "thou hast only to banish me with a threefold conjuration. Do so, and thou wilt never see me again although thou livest a hundred years and more—but I must warn thee that if uncertainty should cause thee to falter or hesitate in mid-injunction, I shall have the power to trouble thy most secret dreams."

Had Sir Florian been as true a knight as Parsifal or Galahad he would have called upon the name of God without delay, and pronounced the threefold curse as easily as any other feat of simple arithmetic, but he was what he was and the thought that sprang to the forefront of his mind was a question.

Can a man sin in his dreams?

Had the question been followed by an answer the knight might yet have been saved, but it was not. He did not know the answer. Whether his ignorance was folly or wisdom, he did not know the answer.

"In the name of the Lord," he cried, "I banish thee! I banish thee! I . . . banish thee!"

When she vanished on the instant, neither recoiling from his curse nor turning on her heel, nor fading into the mists that dressed the shore of the lake, the knight almost believed that he had won. No sooner had the faery gone, however, than he felt an ache in his heart born of the knowledge that he would never see her like again should he live a hundred years and more—unless she came to him in a troublesome and secret dream.

Again the thought came into his mind: *Can a man sin in his dreams?*

Now, alas, he knew the answer. He knew it with a certainty that charmed and terrified him, in equal and by no means paradoxical parts.

* * *

La Belle Dame Sans Merci could work her wiles in the world of dreams as easily as any other. She preferred the world of mist and stars and mazy roads, but that was merely her whim. There were those among the faery folk even in those days who thought the empire of the earth far overrated, and not worth fighting for, but La Belle Dame Sans Merci was not among them. She loved the air and the dew, the light and the shadow which made her earthly form, despite that they were elements at war which would, in time, tear her raggedly apart.

She went to Sir Florian in his dreams that very night, as he had all-but-invited her to do with a moment's hesitation in his speech. She bade him come to her, while she lay as still as still could be—stiller by far than any human woman could ever have contrived at any distance from the brink of death. She was as delicately pale as a wisp of frosty mist, but she had the gift of touch unspoiled by the contempt of familiarity. La Belle Dame Sans Merci touched the knight as lightly as the forefinger of fever, and set the fire of Purgatory alight throughout his kindling flesh.

Sir Florian gave her a garland for her head, woven from prettier flowers than ever grew in the earthly spring, perfumed more fragrantly than any musk of nature or artifice. He bound her hands and waist with vines and she thrilled to the binding, knowing that every circle was a fortress wall imprisoning his heart. He set her upon his horse so that they might ride together, both astride, so that the rhythm of the stallion's gallop might carry them beyond the reach of any roads, to the jewelled infinity east of the sun and west of the moon and the quiet eternity beyond.

And so they rode, imprisoned both by the saddle and harness which contained them, borne by the power of a tireless mount, from the curving roads to the undulant hills and away into the airy wilderness, where the height made them giddy and giddier, until the subtler rhythm of a horse's sturdy heart displaced the clatter of its hoofbeats and they passed at last into the jewelled infinity east of the sun and west of the moon.

Then La Belle Dame Sans Merci took Sir Florian, in her turn, into the warmer and warmest depths of the motherly earth: to those caverns measureless to man that lie beneath the purgatorial realms of Tartarus. There she sang to him, and sang again, and gazed at him with such apparent adoration that he closed her wild wild eyes with kisses, unable to bear the yearning of her stare.

The knight unwound the binding vines from the faery's helpless wrists while she trembled sightless in his arms, drawing every vestige of intoxication from the pressure of his body upon hers and the congruent pounding of their hearts. She took them from him, and opened her eyes again, commanding him to tilt his head and bare his throat.

There was no hesitation this time, no faltering is his resolve. It was not that he was not afraid, but only that he was content to savour his fear as he savoured every least sensation which still had the power to stir him, all equalised as pleasure.

La Belle Dame Sans Merci wound the vine about Sir Florian's slender neck, and began to draw it tighter. The pressure she exerted was gentle at first, and it was only by the slowest imaginable degrees that it grew more and more insistent.

Now he closed his own eyes, even though there had not been the least trace of wildness in his sotted gaze.

Still it was not finished, for the sense of touch still remained to Sir Florian's dizzied mind, and for the first time since consciousness was born in his infant brain the knight felt as a faery might feel, taking nothing of that sensation for granted. He could never have done so had he been awake, but he was not. In dreams, sometimes, even humans are privileged to forget the follies and fervours of flesh. For a moment and more Sir Florian was well-nigh incorporeal, yet gifted still with the sense of touch.

Had the knight been truly incorporeal, of course, the strangling vine could not have harmed him; but even in dreams, the follies and fatalities of flesh may reassert their sullen shift upon the human form.

When the delicious moment was gone, Sir Florian fell into the sleep within sleep: an abyssal deep as far beyond the shallows of dreamless peace as quiet eternity lies beyond the jewelled infinity east of the sun and west of the moon.

* * *

The story would have ended there but for one thing.

It did not matter in the least to La Belle Dame Sans Merci that Sir Florian had felt, if only for an instant, as a faery might feel. She knew it, of course, but there was nothing in his momentary revaluation of the preciousness of touch to strike a spark of empathy. When she drew back from him, however, and saw him lying cushioned in the earth, *as still as still could be*, she saw for the first time how beautiful he was.

It occurred to her, in a way that no other notion had ever occurred to her before, that he was unusual among his own kind—and perhaps unique.

When she had appeared to the knight by the lake the faery had only seen him in general terms. The wildness of her own eyes has ensured that when she looked at him she saw nothing but arms and armour, holiness and chivalry, empire and progress. When she had first come to him in his dream she had seen even less, for she had been in the grip of her own passion. There is nothing human about a faery's passion, but it is passion nevertheless, fiercer in its own way than the lumpen kind of lust which oozes in a human's veins. It was she, then, who had consented to be tied about the wrists and waist, knowing that the binder is more securely captive than the bound. It was she who had consented to be placed astride his mount so that the two of them might ride from the earth into the sky, to soar beyond the limitations of the air, knowing that the commanded is more securely in control than the commander. It was she, then, who had been caught between light and dark, as between full sight and blindness, seeing so much *more* as to be convinced that she saw *everything*.

It was she, now, who realised with unaccustomed, appalling and massive accuracy that the *best* sight is not necessarily the *most* sight, and that beauty works most insidiously in misty uncertainty.

La Belle Dame Sans Merci touched her hand to her own throat, and asked herself whether she rather than he might have been more securely strangled by the knot that she had made. She closed her own less-than-wild eyes in order to wonder whether *his* consent might conceivably have more power than her command.

And she did not know the answer.

For the moment, at least, she did not know the answer.

La Belle Dame Sans Merci was afraid, and could not count her fear solely in the common currency of intensity, in which all is equalised as pleasure.

She was afraid for herself, and rightly so. Creatures of paradox cannot abide *doubt*. Doubt is the crack which opens the way to destruction.

La Belle Dame Sans Merci might still have saved herself, if she had searched assiduously for the answer to her question, found it and made it fast—but she did not.

Instead, she murmured the words which came spontaneously into her head as she looked down at the pale Sir Florian, who was lying as still as still could be.

"O for a fiery gloom and thee," she whispered, wishing as the words escaped her that the two of them might be other than they were, further elsewhere and further elsewhen than the jewelled infinity east of the sun and west of the moon or the quiet eternity beyond.

Alas, there is no elsewhere or elsewhen beyond infinity and eternity, for any such place and time would be a blatant contradiction in terms—and neither human nor faery can be other than they are, however paradoxical their natures might be.

* * *

Sir Florian awoke with the light of dawn and the warning words of a warrior host echoing in his ears. It seemed to him, although he could not quite imagine why, that kings and princes had come to him, with all their armoured knights in train, with the pallor of death upon all their faces, crying: "La Belle Dame Sans Merci! La Belle Dame Sans Merci! La Belle Dame Sans Merci hath thee in thrall!"

He found himself on a cold hillside far above the lake and its miasmic mists. While he watched the silver light of dawn play upon the clouds clustered on the eastern horizon and a few frail sunbeams flickering in the nearby mists the knight felt a flush of fever in his heart and upon his cheek; but when he rose to his feet the fever died like the vestige of a dream and when stronger rays of the rising sun burst through the clouds a moment afterwards he saw the golden track it laid upon the still and silent waters of the lake as a great straight road connecting earth with Heaven.

In that instant of revelation, Sir Florian knew that it would not matter how many kings were fated to fall in battle, nor how many knights were doomed to perish in hopeless quest of the Holy Grail of Christendom. He knew, without a moment's faltering, that the cause of progress and empire could not be stopped, nor even significantly interrupted, and that Great Britain would one day exist.

He knew, too, that he ought to feel proud of his knowledge, grateful for his certainty. He knew that the gift of this revelation was a token that he had won the greatest battle of all: the battle of right over wrong, of reality over myth, of reason over emotion. Within this knowledge, however, there was the faintest seed of doubt—not doubt that it was true, but doubt that truth was as precious as he had been taught to hold it.

He noticed then that although dawn had broken, there had been no chorus of voices to greet it. No birds sang.

Autumn had not yet given way to winter, but no birds sang.

Sir Florian shivered then, in the cold morning air. A strange thought came into his head, which he could not understand at all but which filled him with a longing more desperate than any he had known before or ever would again.

O for a fiery gloom and thee!

He could not understand at first what it was that he longed for, or why, but the thought persisted nevertheless, as plaintive as the echo of a soul torn apart by damnation, until he began to remember. He never recovered all the memory, but in the fullness of time he remembered far more than enough, with the consequence that the enigmatic thought echoed down his straight bright days—and deeper still in his long and lonely nights—though he lived to be a hundred years and more.

O for a fiery gloom—and thee!

THE LAST WORSHIPPER
OF PROTEUS

When I was a student in Leiden, some thirty years after the death of the city's most famous son, Rembrandt van Rijn, I used to lodge in a third-storey room whose only window looked out over a dark and narrow canal. The canal had no towpath, being used solely to transport cargoes of linen and finished cloth in small rowing-boats, and its waters lapped against the foot of the rear wall of the house in which I lived. All the houses which bordered the waterway were cellarless and very tall, and because the canal was so lacking in width, the space between the buildings was always in shadow, always grim. My window let in hardly any light, even when the sun stood high and bright in a cloudless sky, but the gloomy shadows which dwelt beyond the pane seemed always to be restlessly astir.

The room next to my own was occupied by a man named Clement Folle, who told me the first time we met on the stairway that he was a painter. He struck me even then as the most curious person I had ever met, and I thought at first that his description of himself was mere vainglory, for I could not imagine what light he painted by, if his room were as dim and dismal as my own. Later, when we became better acquainted, I found that he had told me the truth, and was ashamed for doubting him.

I had always thought myself to be a desperately poor man, but Clement was even poorer than I. He too had originally come to Leiden to be a student at William the Silent's great university, but he had discovered—so he said—that he had no more vocation for orthodox scholarship than for holy orders. He told me even before he had cause to trust my discretion that for one such as him the world itself was the only subject fit for serious research, and that the wisdom of fable and legend seemed infinitely greater and finer to him than the stored-up heritage of the theologians and rhetoricians who taught in the ancient colleges. He took a risk in saying so, in the city which had become the heart of Protestant Holland, even though he knew that I deemed myself a tolerant man. He was probably past caring what others thought of him, and the heresy-hunters were far less active then than they had been in earlier and direr days.

Clement's room had only a narrow wooden bed and an unsteady table for furniture. He had but a single wooden spoon and a single polished knife, and possessed no fork at all. The pitcher which he used to fetch water was cracked and chipped, and so were the shallow bowl from which he ate and the cup from which he drank. He owned nothing of any value, save for his easel and his canvases, and his most precious possession seemed to be a curious but commercially worthless piece of dull stone which he kept on the mantelshelf above his cold and empty fireplace. Whatever money came his way he infinitely preferred to spend on paint rather than food, and he bitterly resented the threat of starvation which frequently prevented him from exercising his preference. I never knew him other than ravenous, and was embarrassed by the eager way in which he devoured the crusts and and pastries which I sometimes offered him.

I did not visit his room very often, and in the early days of our acquaintance he was reluctant to enter mine, but poor as I was I could still afford bundles of firewood to keep the winter cold at bay and set my kettle to the boil, so the simple instinct of survival encouraged him to make the most of my hospitality. For this reason, I rarely saw him actually engaged in painting, and caught only glimpses of the produce of his supposed artistry, but I often heard him talk, sometimes for hours on end, about his philosophy of life and the ancient wisdom which he believed to have been preserved in fables and legends.

Although I was rarely in his room, I do remember that his easel was always stationed close to the window. By that means, I supposed, he sought to make what use he might of the feeble daylight—for he was as parsimonious with candles as he was with comestibles. But the images which he committed to his canvases bore not the slightest resemblance to the dull greyness without the window; they were full of the most extraordinary colour.

I had never seen pigments of the particular kind which Clement used, and he explained to me that they had been devised for him by a cunning pharmacist.

"The colours are suspended in a lighter and less viscous oil than those which are commonly used," he said. "Portraitists would consider such a medium worthless because it would not allow them to hold a firm line, and all their fields of colour would become blurred—but there are no clear edges in my representations, and the flux of the paint reflects the flux of the world, which I am not at pains to suppress. Other painters endeavour to freeze time and clarify the boundaries which separate entities; my interest is in change rather than constancy. My own pigments permit greater accuracy in representing the mercurial play of light and colour, and greater scope for the exercise of the visual imagination."

The influence of these ideas upon his work was easy to see. His canvases depicted very fantastic scenes—if they could indeed be thought of as "scenes"—in which no shape was definite and everything did indeed seem to be in a constant state of flux. They were riotously bright, and it sometimes seemed to me when I stood before one of them, struggling to divine some sense or meaning in it, that I was looking through a magical window upon a world illuminated by a sun less gentle by far than the one which shines on our own quotidian earth. There was a sky of sorts in most of his paintings, and ground over which it arched, but the landscapes thus described were always blurred and hazy, and their horizons were always obscured by the strange creatures which cavorted in the foreground. These figures were never distinct, though they did not seem to be surrounded by cloud or mist, and were so intimately crowded together that it was difficult to say where one ended and another began.

At first, I thought that these creatures of Clement Folle's extraordinary imagination might be birds, for there was something very bird-like about them. Peacock-feathered and eagle-eyed they seemed to be, but they were never entirely avian in form, often seeming to be cursed with a curious superfluity of wings, and sometimes having snakelike appendages or almost-human limbs. There were always entities of other kinds mingling with them, as though to accompany them in a madcap dance; their predominant hues were vivid scarlet, bright yellow and startling blue, and their contours somehow defied the logic of shape and perspective. Some seemed to have the texture of living flames; others reminded me a little of the stranger creatures of the sea whose likeness was preserved in some of the books which I was expected to study, but I could not imagine that Clement Folle had ever been a fisherman.

When my neighbour first showed me his paintings I was quite tongue-tied, and for want of any honest or adequate response I muttered about their unusual nature. I dared not request explanations of their composition. But when the painter had gained my confidence more fully, and I had become more curious about him, I began to ask him tentatively why he never portrayed more conventional subjects.

"No doubt I would be better paid," he said, sorrowfully, "if I could paint portraits of stout burghers, and printers' wives, and good Protestant cloth-merchants. A tolerable living can be made, I understand, by those who will condescend to devote their lives to the production of flattering images of the scornful sons and harridan wives of petty noblemen. Alas, I cannot be one of that company, for when I try to copy such images they appear on my canvas exactly as they appear to my eye: flat, false, and devoid of interest."

Eventually, when I had become fond enough of him to want to understand him better, I plucked up the courage to ask him exactly what it was that he was trying to achieve in his painting. At first, though, he shied away from the question, and elected to discuss his aesthetic philosophy in such vague terms that it was difficult for me to discover the relevance of what he believed to what he actually did.

Once, when I knocked upon his door and entered without waiting for an invitation, I found him standing before one of his paintings—but he had set down his brush and his palette, and was holding to his forehead the piece of stone which he kept on the mantelshelf. His eyes were closed and his manner was rapt, and I had no doubt that he was in some way seeking inspiration from the stone.

When he opened his eyes to see who had disturbed him, he seemed at first to be alarmed and annoyed, but his expression soon softened. I think that was the moment in which he decided that I was to be reckoned a true friend rather than a mere acquaintance, and it was not long afterwards—without any undue pressure on my part—that he attempted to explain, step by careful step, the true nature of his artistic quest.

"Do you know the name of Proteus?" he asked me, while he sat before my fire, pulling his threadbare jerkin tightly about his lean frame.

"Certainly," said I, having by then progressed far enough in my education to know more than a little Greek. "He was the Old Man of the Sea, Poseidon's sealherd. Homer tells the tale of how he was trapped by Menelaus after Troy fell; although he changed his shape repeatedly, Menelaus would not let him go until he had revealed the secret of what Menelaus must do in order to win safely home to Sparta."

"That story reduces him in status," Clement told me, soberly. "He is an older sea-god by far than the upstart Poseidon, and not just a lord of the sea, though he came out of its bosom uncountable aeons ago. He is change itself, and the world is not rid of him, despite that we think that we have bound him to our service, as proud Menelaus claimed to have done."

"I know no older tales of him than those the Greeks told," I admitted. "He is in the *Odyssey*, and also the *Georgics* of Virgil, but that is all."

"The older tales were never written down," said Clement, "but they are preserved nevertheless for those who know how to listen. Do you know the western isles, beyond the northern part of Britain?"

"Only by repute," I replied.

"They are inhabited by fisher-folk, who have many tales to tell of the tempestuous ocean from which they make their living—and which they call, in recognition of the price which they must pay for their livelihood, the Great Grey Widowmaker. Many of these tales tell of a group of islands which lies far beyond the western horizon, which the fisher-folk call Mag Mell, or the Land of Happiness.

"In Mag Mell, they say, summer is perpetual, and the trees produce fruit in great profusion, while fine corn is always ripening in the valleys between the warm wild hills. From these isles, it is enviously said, no man need ever set sail in a tiny wooden boat, to submit himself to the mercy of the murderous waves. If they are asked, 'Why do men not set sail for these Isles of the Blest, to make better lives for themselves?' the fisher-folk will answer that many have, and that some have succeeded. They will also say, however, that the journey is extremely perilous because the sea between their own islands and the others is the haunt of a dire demon of the sea, which they call a draug.

"The draug, according to the island people, was once a fabulous dragon of the air, whose scales were coloured like the rainbow and which meant no harm to man. One day, though, the wondrous beast was seized by an old and meddlesome sea-god, who cast it down from the bright blue sky into the cold grey sea. There its scales became silvery and pale, and its glorious wings became mere spiny fins. The gall of these misfortunes made its heart bitter against all creatures, especially the men who might witness its degradation, so that it became an enemy to all those folk who sail in ships. Now, they say, the draug does the dark work of the master who remade it, seizing the boats of all who try to sail to the Land of Happiness, and crushing their timbers in its cruel coils.

"If these folk are asked, 'Why did the old sea-god set this hateful leviathan to do such work?' they will answer that he is vilely envious of any who might find calm and content and peace of mind, for though he has the powers of a god he has none of these things for himself, and by virtue of his nature can never find them.

"There are in the land of the Scots those who keep sheep on the hills, and those who till the ground, and none of whom can truly understand the life of fisher-folk. Men like these have long taken leave to laugh at those islanders who dare to believe that a god might be envious of happy men, and by their mockery have driven the old beliefs into secrecy. Nowadays, fear of heresy-hunters makes the islanders anxious to copy the religious forms of the mainland, but some of the most ancient men and women still remember what was done in olden days. Then, when a brave man set out in his boat and did not return, his family would hold two funeral rites instead of one. In the first they cried their anxious lamentations because the Great Grey Widowmaker had claimed another life with its cold embrace, but in the second they sang and danced to express the hope that the man might have escaped the draug and the envy of the old sea-god, and might have come therefore to his appointed rest in marvellous Mag Mell."

"It is a pretty tale," I admitted, though the mention of heresy-hunters made me shiver. "And you believe that this old and meddlesome sea-god, who could never find calm and peace of mind, was the same as Homer's Proteus?"

"He is the same," Clement assured me. "I know it, for I am his worshipper—perhaps the last worshipper he has in this dull and Christian world—and I am the custodian of one of the seven fallen stones."

I did not immediately ask him what he meant by the seven fallen stones, because I was deeply disturbed by his declaration—even though I did not think he meant it seriously—that he worshipped a pagan god. We live in enlightened times, it is said, but in the days of my youth heretics still burned in their hundreds in many European lands, and none but a fool would ever declare himself a worshipper of demonic idols, even in metaphor or jest. Like the careful young man I was, I closed my mouth whenever I heard the least suggestion of blasphemy or heresy, and it was not until another night, when the cold had driven Clement to my fireside yet again, that he told me the legend of the seven fallen stones.

"There is a very ancient story," he said, contemplatively, "which—alas—is true, that tells how the first god of the sea once cut seven magical stones from the rocks which support the deepest part of his kingdom. He threw them high into the dark night-sky, so that when they fell once more upon the earth, they were scattered far and wide about its surface.

"Many tales have been told of the finding of those stones, by men or by hobgoblins, though none but a few of their tellers had any inkling of where the stones originated, or what their purpose was. Most tales of this kind are tragedies of lives and projects blighted; some few are tales of tragedy avoided by cleverness and self-restraint; but none are tales of fortunes made and power gained, for these dull and deceptive stones cut by the old sea-god were made to sow the seeds of a terrible revelation.

"According to the legend, the unlucky creature which finds one of the seven fallen stones, and takes it in his hand, will find that while he holds it he has a magic power of sight, which shows him in the things which are that which in time they are certain to become. When he looks upon a worm, the holder of the stone might see a bright-winged insect; but when he looks upon a lover, he can only see a corpse mouldering in the grave; when he looks upon an empire he must witness the bloodbath of rebellion which tears it down; when he looks upon the sun, he will see an exploded ember; and when he looks up into the starry sky, he will see the eternal darkness which will reign when the stars themselves have died. By such means, the finder of one of the seven fallen stones is forced to know that there is hope only in the smallest and most wretched of things, while in all that seems glorious, there is naught but the promise of loss and emptiness.

"The tales of which I speak, almost without exception, regard the finding of such a stone as a misfortune to be avoided. This is understandable, for such tales are intended to offer advice to brave soldiers, clever thieves and bold explorers. The moral which they intend to draw is that men should beware of strange dark things which are found, as if by chance, in secret coverts; and that they should not seek to know the mysteries which the future holds, lest the revelation be too much for mortal hopes to bear."

"I presume from your tone," I said, "that you have some cause to disagree."

"I am neither a soldier nor a thief," he told me. "I am a painter, to whom truth is more precious than glamour. I do not fear change, nor seek to bind it to my convenience. I desire to be its celebrant, to perceive it as it is, and to make my perceptions known to other men."

"So you strive to capture the spirit of change in your paintings," I said, proud of my powers of deduction, and anxious to show that I too knew how to declaim in a passably eloquent manner. "You have taken this ancient and troubled sea-god as your spiritual tutor, and it is Proteus which guides your arm when you ply your brushes. You believe that you have come into possession of one of the seven stones which he cast up on to the land to make men miserable, but you seek inspiration in it, not despair."

He nodded his head fervently, and his prematurely grey hair fell untidily about his eyes. "You understand!" he crowed, as though it were a minor miracle. "I am trying to paint the most intimate processes of change. My mission is to confirm and prove the essential *flux* of things, their eternal *becoming*."

What I really understood, of course—or *thought* I understood—was that the poor fellow was entirely mad. Poverty, misfortune and malnutrition, I believed, had so addled his brain that he thought he heard sermons in stones. Nor were they the virtuous sermons of our own blessed Lord, but the ravings of some unholy pagan deity: some vile member of that host which was cast out of Heaven into Pandemonium, but which had returned to earth by the permission of the Lord in order to tempt and torment the sons of Adam and the daughters of Eve. Those who resisted such temptation, I knew, achieved goodness through the exercise of their free will, and thus proved themselves worthy of Paradise—but those who could not were damned by their weakness.

I was a charitable man in those days, as I try to be today, and I believed in my heart than many of those who had been burned in time past as witches and sorcerers were merely harmless lunatics. Because of that belief I did not run to any priest with the rumour of Clement Folle's heretical convictions, nor did I try to keep him from my hearth and my table. I tried as best I could, within my limited means, to be his friend and help him to stay alive. I resolved to try to convince him of the error of his beliefs, but I confess that I did not try as hard as I might have done, for he was impatient with my efforts. I admit that I found his tales quite fascinating in their way, and would have felt myself far poorer had he ceased to relate them to me.

"Ever since I was a boy," he told me, once he had decided that I might safely be further initiated into the mysteries of his strange art and his peculiar religion, "I have been quite convinced that the world of appearances is only that: an appearance. I do not mean that it is an *illusion*—only that the semblance which it presents to the eye depends more upon the properties and limitations of the eye than upon its own inherent nature.

"Even before I found the stone, I was convinced that my eyes might see far more, and very differently, if I could only make them adept and sensitive in an appropriate fashion. Certain other creatures, I am convinced, must look upon a very different and perhaps much richer world than the one which is ordinarily available to our over-precise eyes. Where human eyes can perceive nothing but shadow and darkness, others have light by which to see. Where human eyes are ever avid to select out constancy and order, others surely remain content with the gorgeous bewilderments of change and confusion. Where we see those objects and living beings which are ordinary to us, they might see entities whose colours and properties are dramatically transfigured, among which life and inertness might be very differently distributed.

"It was always the primary mission of my life to learn to see things as higher beings than ourselves might see them—and I did not hesitate to use whatever means came to hand towards that end. I was not always as poor as I am now, but the meagre inheritance I had was soon exhausted by my quest. I sampled many exotic potions which I bought from hedge-wizards and dubious pharmacists, and attempted many magical rituals which I found in certain tomes in that section of the university library which is nowadays forbidden to students like yourself. Nothing served my purpose, until I finally came upon the stone, and realised what it was. Only then could I begin the work of penetrating the veil, of looking into the worlds beyond the world, into the Protean realm of the Ephemeral."

As befitted a humble and pious person, I was properly horrified by the revelation that Clement's madness had led him to dabble in witchcraft and sorcery—but if the truth be told, I found the violence of my reaction to be a rather pleasant and exciting sensation. Far from being intimidated by my horror, I became hungry for more revelations, although I felt it incumbent upon me to make my own reservations perfectly clear.

"I am compelled to believe," I told him, awkwardly, "that we are made as we are for a reason. We are men, made by God, and were made to see as God intended men to see. What you are trying to do, I fear, is to see the world as *demons* might see it, and you may be sure that if you make way within the threads and sinews of your being for Satan to control your sight, he will not hesitate to seize the opportunity to steal your soul. I beg you to abandon this quest of yours, before it leads you to a tragic end."

Clement was not annoyed with me for saying this, but only sorrowful. Needless to say, he entirely ignored my good and heartfelt advice, and his contempt for my opinion renewed the barriers of embarrassment and mistrust which had only recently been lowered. He did not try to shun me, or to hide his paintings from me, but he recovered his discretion, and ceased to speak of Proteus and magic spells. In the meantime, as the harsh winter extended into March, he continued to deteriorate physically. I continued to let him warm himself before my fire, and I gave him the occasional crust or rind of cheese, as common charity demanded, but my own table was by no means so rich that a man might live off its crumbs. I am certain that he had no other resource with which to ward off starvation; his other acquaintances had by now deserted him.

Precisely what happened in Clement Folle's room on the night of his disappearance, I cannot say. I know that I was roused from fitful sleep by a very peculiar sound, which seemed to me to be like the rushing of a great wind or the roar of a tremendous fire. The thought that the building might be ablaze filled me with consternation; I leapt from my bed and immediately put my trousers on. Then I threw open my door, very fearfully—and was astonished to discover that the noise appeared to be coming from my neighbour's room.

Perhaps I should have opened his door immediately, but such was the strangeness of that uncanny sound that I dared not. Nor did I return to collect the nightlight which burned by my bed. I only stood in the unlit corridor and called out to Clement, imploring him to tell me what was going on. By the time my courage was equal to the task of opening his door and entering the room, the noise was already fading—fading to a thin keening which was almost plaintive in its tenor.

When I finally looked inside, I could see nothing at all. The room was pitch-dark—but the noise was still perceptible. It did not seem to be emanating from the place where, as I assumed, Clement lay in his bed, but rather from the direction of the window; and it seemed, although I cannot say exactly how or why, to be horribly menacing.

In spite of my terror I stumbled forward in the direction of the bed, reaching out with my hand in order to rouse the man who ought to have been lying there. But when I found the bed, falling to my knees as I did so, Clement's body was not there.

I groped about the ragged mattress, unable to believe that it was empty. Stygian gloom was all about me, and I was quite blind—until my hand fell upon the stone which ought to have been on the mantelshelf.

I did not grasp the stone or pick it up, but the moment my fingers touched it I felt a horrid thrill travel up my arm, which burst like a Roman candle inside my head. My eyes were suddenly deluged with light. The darkness split, and was instantly dispelled. From the window of Clement Folle's room, which should have looked out into dark and dismal shadow, there fell an amazing blaze of many-coloured light. It was far too bright to permit my startled eyes to see anything *through* the window, but I had the impression of the fluttering of myriad wings, and of a host of dancing creatures made of pure white flame.

I did not take a single step in the direction of the window; indeed, I put up my arm to shield my eyes from the appalling glare, and shrank back against the frame of the bed. I understood then that when Clement had looked out into the void above the black canal, he had not seen what other man would have seen. Whether it was in truth the gift of Proteus, or of Satan, which had transformed his power of sight, I could not tell—but I had no alternative save to accept that his powers of sight had indeed been strangely augmented.

The glazed window which separated the shadowed room from that brilliant world beyond was not open or broken, but I could not suppress a conviction that Clement had somehow been claimed by that other world, and ripped out of the fabric of ours. If he had been among the fabulous host beyond the window I could not possibly have seen him, nor recognised him, but I could not help but wonder whether he might have undergone some astonishing metamorphosis in being devoured and consumed by that incredible cataract of light.

I pressed my arm more firmly across my eyes as I thrust myself up from the place where I knelt. I regained my feet, unsteadily, and staggered towards the door. I found it somehow, and launched myself into the corridor beyond. I closed the door behind me, and only then did I lower the protective arm from my face.

I ran to my own room, which was as darkly shadowed as it had always been. I went quickly to the window, there to stare out into the comforting darkness, which veiled the high, blank walls that men had laboured so hard to build in the cause of civilization.

You may think me a coward, but I told no one what had happened. I dared not speak to anyone about what I had seen, lest they should conclude—as I already had—that I had glimpsed the fires of Hell, and the legion of the damned. Many years passed before I felt able to speak of those events even to my most intimate friends. You will readily understand, therefore, how it came about that several days passed without my making any attempt to enter the room next door to mine. I tried with all my might to pretend that the world was exactly as it had always been: firm; dependable; *fixed* by the indomitable will of God.

During those days I heard no sound from within the neighbouring room, and never saw the door open, until the day when a new tenant moved in.

It was only then that I recovered my lost courage, and I went to bid the newcomer welcome, as a good neighbour should—but when I asked him, belatedly, what had become of Clement Folle's canvases, he replied that he did not know.

Later, I discovered that the landlord had sold the bed, the table and the easel. He had tried to sell the completed paintings too, but having been assured by everyone to whom he showed them that they were absurd and utterly worthless, he had consigned them to the cold, still waters of the canal behind the house. I have no doubt that the mysterious stone accompanied them.

Now, in looking back on that far-distant time, I cannot regret that I made no effort to acquire one of Clement's paintings, and I certainly cannot regret the loss of that infernal stone. I know only too well that had I had such a painting on my wall, I would not have been able to resist looking at it, and wondering, and remembering. Such things have always had a fascination for me, and I am very well aware of the dangers of Satanic seduction.

I firmly believe that it is the divinely-ordained task of mankind to find the clarity and solidity that is in the world, to oppose change and inconstancy, and to strive for certainty and perfection. I understand, therefore, that it is the appointed duty of all God-fearing men to keep Proteus at bay, and I am glad that his last worshipper is dead and gone, and that the world is safe in the sovereign charge of science, truth and certainty.

And yet . . . there was such *luminosity* in that uncertain world which I glimpsed, such awful *glory* in its infinite possibility, that somewhere deep inside me there has ever burned a flickering flame of hellish doubt. Now that I am old, I can no longer believe that it will one day die, but still I dare to hope that it will not prevent my salvation.

THE EVIL THAT MEN DO

The crimson sands of the Cinnabar Desert had always had a mysterious attraction for eremites and cenobites alike. While the cenobites laboured long and hard to ring its deep-set wells with stern edifices of stone and sun-baked brick, the eremites found homes among the caves that pitted the vermilion cliffs, which had been weathered for thousands of years by the simoom which blew from the west.

These holy men served half a hundred different gods, and competed fiercely with one another, on behalf of their solemn masters, to set the most perfect examples of chastity, austerity, humility and self-mortification. There was not a man among them who did not dress himself in a bug-infested hair-shirt by day and lie down upon the cold bare rock by night. None ever slept for longer than an hour, and all but the feeblest in body and soul scourged themselves thrice daily with nettles, thorns or supple rods according to their taste. The hardiest of them were ever eager to inflict themselves with purulent ulcers and festering sores, for their gods were of the uncompromising kind which had put their followers on earth to win purity of spirit by tormenting the flesh; the few old men among them went naked but for their loincloths, in order to show their younger brethren what a beautiful mass of livid scar-tissue a human body might become, with the proper encouragement.

Although they had sought refuge in the Cinnabar Desert in order that they should be as far away as it was possible to be from those sinks of inquity which men called cities, the eremites and cenobites were by no means free from temptation, for the region drew imps and succubi and all manner of other petty demons like a magnet, whose delight was to taunt these happy and innocent folk with terrible nightmares. By day, the Cinnabar Desert was the most desolate place imaginable, but by night it became a battlefield where the forces of Light and Dark fought bitter skirmishes in memory of that long-ago battle which was supposed to have settled such questions forever. But the cenobites and eremites quickly became so hardy that no temptation could shake their resolve.

There was no better place in all the world for the souls of men to be purified. There never was a sinner so great that he could not be turned into a man of indomitable virtue by the fierce heat of the desert sun.

Many there were among the eremites and cenobites who became legends in their own lifetime on account of the extremity of their virtue, but such lifetimes were often, understandably, cut short; the better gods are ever avid to claim their most loyal and self-effacing followers. But there was one particular eremite whose reputation extended not over mere years but over decades, in spite of the fact that he had never shirked his most injurious responsibilities. The eremites who knew him—some of whom saw him as often as once a month, in spite of their devotion to solitude—proclaimed without hesitation that they had never known a man who lived in such a narrow and uncomfortable cave, or who kept it so filthy. Never, they opined, had there ever been one of their kind who contrived to be so lean for so long, or succeeded in maintaining about his person gangrenous lesions which would have killed a lesser man in a matter of days. No one who saw this man could possibly doubt that he suffered intensely and interminably, and everyone marvelled at the fact that he was never silent; prayers of a most devout kind poured from his withered lips without pause or cease.

The name by which this holiest of holy men was known was Nanayakara, though everyone knew that this was not the name he had been given at birth. Many of those who came to the Cinnabar Desert in search of spiritual health had formerly worn other names, and had followed careers which they now wanted to forget entirely. Rumour had it that Nanayakara had once been a very bad man, but the holy men who lived in the desert were all agreed that the evil that men do should not be held to their account eternally. They believed that men should be permitted to repent, and expiate their sins in suffering, and might then become truly virtuous. Even the most vile of men, they believed, might be won to the path of light by a god who was sufficiently generous to encourage him to redemption.

The god whom Nanayakara served was the most mysterious of the members of the Great Pantheon of Light, but by no means the least significant. His true name was very rarely revealed even to his most devout and devoted followers, because it was a name of awesome power whose pronouncement could turn the whole world upside down. His followers were only permitted to refer to him—apologetically—by means of a brief vowel sound like that contained in the middle of the word "but."

Nanayakara's sojourn in the Cinnabar Desert lasted three-and-forty years, and he took a certain very modest pleasure in the fact that it had taken him only a year to forget his former life in its entirety, so that he would not be distracted from his sacred mission of and self-abasement by wayward memories. In time, Nanayakara outlived everyone who had been numbered among his neighbours when he first arrived to claim his miserable cave, and there was no one save for himself who knew how long he had dwelt there. But he knew, for he kept count of every single prayer which spilled from his mouth, and the rhythm of those incessant prayers measured the passing of time with consummate accuracy. He knew exactly how long he had spent in the ragged fissure in the red rock, and every time the number of his prayers reached a particularly significant figure—ten thousand million, for instance, or seven times seven times seven times seven times seven times seven—he wondered whether the moment of his release might have come.

* * *

Because nothing in the world is eternal, Nanayakara's release eventually did come—but it came in a most unexpected way. Nanayakara had long been convinced that his joyous ordeal would end triumphantly in death and transportation, amid clouds of glory, to whatever ultimate reward was reserved for the most faithful servants of his unnamable god, but he was wrong. As things turned out, he awoke one morning to find his surroundings exactly as they had always been—but that he himself had changed. The wounds afflicting his flesh had healed, to the extent that they were capable of healing; the prayers which had flooded from his lips for so many years had ceased in their flow; and he had recovered the memories which he had earlier taken such great care to lose.

Had Nanayakara been able to burst into tears he would have done so instantly, for the knowledge of what he once had been was very unwelcome to him, but he could not.

O great but unnamable god, he moaned, in the awful silence created by the absence of his prayers, why have you allowed this to happen to me?

The unnamable god was one of those who never addressed his followers directly, but he was usually generous in allowing them to leap intuitively to correct conclusions. Nanayakara, uncomfortably aware of the fact that his name was no longer Nanayakara, quickly realised that his memories must have been reawakened for a purpose, and he soon saw what that purpose must be.

He also realised that something else had been put into his mind. He realised that he knew the true name of the unnamable god! The power to turn the world upside down was his.

His first thought, on being confronted with this miraculous intuition, was that he was utterly unworthy; but it did not take him long to conclude that his unworthiness was beside the point. Clearly, he had been given this information for a particular purpose, and it was his duty to carry out that purpose. With that name in his possession he had become a great magician, and it was obvious that the unnamable god did not intend him to be an eremite any longer.

The man who had been Nanayakara for three-and-forty years immediately left his cave, and walked down the face of the rugged cliff to an assembly of stony hovels where the cenobites serving the god Mutisaya gathered together to celebrate the most demanding and esoteric rites of their faith. When they saw him coming they rushed from their dens, crying: "A miracle! A miracle! Nanayakara the Gangrenous is made whole again!"

But the former Nanayakara cried out to them, and warned them to keep their distance lest they should be polluted by him.

"Alas, alas," he wailed, "I am Nanayakara no longer. I know now that the name which was given me at birth was Rumulshah, and that I was a king in my own land. I know, too, that I was a very wicked king—a lover of luxury and vice, and a tyrannical oppressor. For three-and-forty years I have been allowed to do penance for my hideous sins, thanks to the mercy of the unnamable god, but so extemely vile were my transgressions that my redemption is not yet complete. I must now seek out the kingdom which I once ruled, when I was the hapless and hideous instrument of the dark god Xanatos, and make what reparation I can for what I did, as the instrument of a better, kinder and infinitely more generous deity."

The followers of Mutisaya were suitably impressed by this revelation, and they instantly began to pick up stones and hurl them as hard as they could at the former holy man, in order to help him on his way. That night, each and every one of them took care to thank Mutisaya for his mercy in allowing them to find their own deliverance so easily, but there was not one among them who did not give himself a few extra strokes of the lash, lest he had fallen into the habit of treating himself too leniently, and might be sent back to the world in order to make reparation for his error.

* * *

Now that he was Rumulshah again, and no longer Nanayakara, the ex-eremite set his face towards the south-east, and began the long march which would take him out of the Cinnabar Desert and into populated regions. Ultimately, he knew, he would have to go into the Sweltering Lands where the Infinite Forest and the plains which interrupted its infinity, was host to countless petty kingdoms, including that which was formerly his to rule and to ravage. He did not know exactly where it lay, but he knew the general direction, and he remembered that his journey to the Cinnabar Desert had taken three full years.

As he walked, he tried again and again to pray, but he found that his lips—which had done nothing else for three-and-forty years—had somehow lost the knack of it. Rumulshah guessed that he would not be able to pray again until he had made himself truly worthy to utter prayers; not until he had added substantial reparation to his long apology could his heinous sins be properly forgiven. He did not bemoan this sad fate, but put on a brave face.

I have learned to be patient, as well as to be virtuous, he told himself. The unnamable god has prepared me for this task, and I will not fail him.

As the sun set behind him on the third day of his journey Rumulshah came at last to the edge of the Cinnabar Desert, and passed into a region in which thorny bushes grew, though hardly in abundance.

Nomads roamed this region with their sparse herds of goats and camels. He quickly fell in with one such party, whose women took pity on him because he was so old and so nearly naked, and covered in fearful scars. They fed him milk and cheese and sour unleavened bread, and gave him a cloak to wear, all out of charity. Rumulshah thanked them very kindly, and asked them if they had ever heard the name of the city-kingdom of Munimazana, which had once been his but they had not.

"I have heard," he said carefully, "that it once had a very evil king named Rumulshah, who became notorious."

"Alas," said the oldest of the women who had taken pity on him, "we know nothing at all about cities or their kings; we're the wildest of folk, whose way of life is wandering. We have no truck with wheat or gold or writing, and those who deal in such things, whether they be kings or merchants, have no truck with us."

"Perhaps you are better off," muttered Rumulshah. "No doubt your humility saves you from much ill-fortune, and preserves virtue among your people."

"Perhaps so," admitted the old woman, with a sigh. "But it's not easy to be virtuous, even when you have nothing. I'm glad we could help you, but it's not often that folk of our kind find people worse off than ourselves, and thus discover opportunities for charity."

Her kindness would have caused Rumulshah to weep with shame had he been capable of tears, but he was not.

"Alas," he said, in a whisper, "I am not worthy of your charity. I was once a very great villain—but I hope that the cloak which you have given me might help to keep me alive until I have made some reparation for my terrible sins."

"I was young myself once," she told him. "I know how delicious sins can be when the flesh is avid and the conscience calm. Now I'm old like you, and probably just as full of regrets. My advice to you, old man, is to make peace with yourself, and forget about worthiness and reparation."

"I can never do that," he told her. "I am not that kind of man."

* * *

Beyond the thornscrub Rumulshah found more fertile lands, where there were vineyards bearing purple fruit in great profusion, and villages huddled about the huge stone vats where the grapes were fermented to make wine.

There were roads in this region, for where there is wine there are merchants who come to carry it away to distant cities in stone jugs and glass bottles, bringing grain in exchange, and cloth, and pots and iron tools. Rumulshah set his feet upon these roads, but he slept beneath the stars because he had no coin to pay for lodging at the inns, and he had nothing to eat but the sour berries which grew wild outside the fences which guarded the vineyards.

It chanced that in one of the villages through which he passed the wine was just ready for drinking, and its inhabitants were making merry. Rumulshah was taken in by a company of amiable drunkards, who gave him good bread and wine. One of them, seeing that he was so frail, took him to his house afterwards, and let him use a bed of straw.

In the morning, this young man gave Rumulshah a staff which had belonged to his father, now deceased. Rumulshah thanked the young man very kindly, and asked him whether he had ever heard of the city-kingdom of Munimazana, in the Sweltering Lands, or the reputation of its atrocious king, Rumulshah.

"We're not travelling folk," the young man told him. "We're sons of the vine, rooted in the soil. You must ask the merchants for news of cities and kingdoms—it's their business to know the names of distant places, and the prices in their marketplaces. We only know the price of wine. But I suspect that you have a long journey ahead of you, and I can only hope that you have time enough for its completion. I'll give you a jug to take with you, but you must sip it slowly, else it'll make you dizzy in the noonday heat."

"I do not deserve such kindness," Rumulshah told him, sadly, remembering the Munimazana had vineyards of its own, whose produce he had once quaffed in mind-befuddling quantities. "I was once a very bad man, and I only accept your gifts in the hope that they may help me to make reparation for the evil I did."

"I'm not a good man myself," the young man told him, unregretfully. "I was never as dutiful as I should have been, and my father died a disappointed man. In giving you his staff to help support you, I am making reparation for the fact that I failed in supporting him."

"The reparation which I have to make," Rumulshah told him, "is greater by far than that."

* * *

The roads which led south-eastwards from the vineyards took Rumulshah into more prosperous regions, where some farmers planted their fields with grain and some grew dazoes, while others had orchards or grazed sleek cattle. There were many merchants on the roads hereabouts, and many robbers too, but neither the merchants nor the robbers paid much heed to Rumulshah, and the farmers did not deign to notice him at all.

Every now and again he would ask people he met whether they had heard of Munimazana, or the name of its terrible king, but no one had. He was beginning to feel slightly offended by the fact that the great evil which he had done was not better-known in the world. In his own reckoning, he had fully deserved to be reviled far and wide, and he had hoped to find his name made a by-word for all that was vile in human inclination. But he consoled himself with the thought that he was still two years distant from his destination, and that the world had a more than adequate supply of evil kings to revile. Poor folk such as those who would condescend to pass the time of day with him were understandably philosophical about such matters.

It was far easier to find food in this region, though it was sometimes difficult to decide which fruits might be legally picked and which might not. Sometimes labourers who sweated in the fields for a meagre wage would share a little of their bread with the traveller, and sometimes men of that kind would fall into step with him as he went on his way, having tired of one employer and determined to search for a better one.

"I've always kept on the move," one such sun-bronzed fellow explained to him. "If you stay too long in one place, you find yourself anchored down by wife and whelps, and you lose the knack of sleeping in barns and under hedges. A labourer can easily become a bondsman, obliged to his master for the roof over his head and the bread on his plate. Freedom's priceless, don't you think?"

"I am not free," Rumulshah told him, sorrowfully. "Nor can I ever be free, until I have made reparation for the evil I have done."

"What evil was that?" asked the other, curiously.

"I have been the cause of great suffering," Rumulshah said, reluctantly. "There is not a sin you can name that I have not committed. I have raped, I have tortured, I have murdered, I have cruelly oppressed an entire nation."

"I dare say that every man gets away with whatever he can," answered the other, looking at Rumulshah very strangely. "I'm of the kind which never could, and would have judged you to be of the same kind. Mind you, I've managed a rape or two in my time, and enjoyed them to the full. You're harmless now, I hope—or are you perhaps a mighty wizard in disguise, able to raise the spirits of the dead and turn men into toads if they look at you askance?"

"I was once a master of necromancers and sorcerors," said Rumulshah, in a low and mournful tone. "Their guilt is my guilt." He did not confess that he was indeed a great magician, armed with the secret name of the unnamable god. He knew that he had to hoard that name and its magical power most jealously, so that he might use it for its proper purpose.

"Did it ever occur to you," the labourer asked, pensively, "that you might be mad?"

"I am the sanest man in the world," Rumulshah assured him. "I am the only one who truly understands the meaning of sanity."

* * *

In the marketplace of a city called Motshubi, Rumulshah finally met a dealer in amulets and petty magics who had heard of Munimazana. "It's said that its citizens breed salamanders for their venom," the merchant said, "and that no better venom is to be found in all the Sweltering Lands. Also, rumour has it that their snakedancers are particularly beguiling—but that's probably just talk. Wherever you go people will tell you about distant lands where the magicians are much more powerful and the whores much more attractive."

"Did you ever hear tales of a king, more wicked than any before or after him, who ruled in Munimazana?" asked Rumulshah, quietly but expectantly.

"Can't say," replied the merchant, dismissively. "I only listen to interesting gossip. If you believe their subjects, kings nowadays are infinitely more wicked than their forefathers. It's the nature of lesser men to complain about their betters. It'll all be the same in a hundred years time."

"That it will," agreed Rumulshah mournfully, "unless someone, somewhere can begin to make reparation."

The merchant looked at him oddly, and hurried away to be about his business.

In cities like Motshubi it was not so easy to find food. There was always plenty of garbage in the streets, but there was also a legion of scavengers ever eager to derive what sustenance they could from its meagre bounty.

In these city streets Rumulshah met thieves so desperate that they might readily have killed a man for a plain staff and a worn cloak such as those he carried with him, but on the few occasions when someone came close, intending to molest him, he fixed them with his stern eyes—and they invariably saw something there within which made them fall back, and save their avaricious malevolence for another occasion. He was glad of this, for it saved him from having to use his magic to protect himself.

It was the same with constables and men-at-arms who sometimes came across him when they were searching for someone to arrest on suspicion of a crime. Whenever such men came close enough to see the tormented expression in his eyes they fell back in embarrassment, and turned aside in favour of some less disconcerting victim.

Rumulshah never used his magic to provide him with food. He knew that it was intended for a much higher purpose, and must not be frittered away. He was well-used to deprivation, and his needs were scant. He never begged, although he might easily have folded up his cloak and sat near-naked upon it, thus to present an appearance far more wretched than the majority of those who made a decent living as urban mendicants. He was not ashamed to pick up scraps from the gutter, nor to accept charity if it were to be freely and generously offered, but he did not think himself worthy to ask others for alms until he had made reparation for his sins.

* * *

He passed from the more prosperous lands into hotter regions where the landlords used dark-skinned slaves, raided from the depths of the Infinite Forest, to raise cotton and sugar-cane. Here, again, he found food growing wild in abundance—but beyond the cultivated lands there was a further wilderness which was all briny swamps and sullen, creeper-decked trees. The swamps were swarming with crocodiles and biting insects, and there were bandits too; but his limbs were thin and his blood was watery and his pouch was always empty, and so the various predators passed him by.

Whenever he came to a part of the swamp which was impassable, he found fishermen willing to take him across, and they would often let him share their meals.

"Men who love city streets hate the swamplands," a philosophically-inclined medicine man told him, "though the odour of stagnation is pleasant enough by comparison with their sewers. The merchants who carry goods through here curse the necessity of using barges, and they hate our blood-sucking flies, but they have no idea how bountiful the swamp really is, and how easily a man may live on fish and shrimps. You are clearly a more understanding man, for you take no notice of the flies at all."

But the fisherfolk had never heard of Munimazana, and the name Rumulshah meant nothing at all to them.

"It must be one of the kingdoms in the great grassy plain," the medicine man explained. "We trade with the forest people, and sometimes with the slave-merchants, but the plain is very dry and we abhor dryness. We hear rumours occasionally of its disasters and its wars, but no one here bothers to remember the names of distant kings who are no better and no worse than our own."

"Rumulshah was uncommonly bad," said Rumulshah, tiredly. Repetition had begun to make the assertion seem ineffably tedious.

"They all are," said the medicine man. "Better to avoid them, by making a home where kings will let you alone. A man like you or I, too old for hard work or making love, should make a home where it is possible to rest, and forget about the interminably anxious affairs of the greater world."

"Munimazana is my home," said Rumulshah. "There can be no rest for me until I have made recompense for my sins."

"A man who thinks like that can waste his entire life in regrets," the medicine man pointed out.

"While I have travelled the world these last two years," Rumulshah countered, "I have seen wasted lives by the score, and the evidence of a million unrepaired sins. But I learned virtue in the Cinnabar Desert, where the simoom scoured my soul, and I must do what I can to make amends for my former villainy."

* * *

The forested lands beyond the swamps were the most beautiful through which he had passed, but they were also the most dangerous, for their various tribes were embroiled in a terrible war. Rumulshah marched for some twenty days in the wake of a ravaging army whose soldiers he never saw, constantly coming across villages which they had burned and people they had killed or maimed.

Once he found a young girl who had been raped a dozen times, then stabbed in the belly and left for dead. He could not do much to make her comfortable, but he built a fire to keep her warm when night fell, and sat up with her, singing softly to her.

She asked him if his songs were magical, and whether they would soothe her pain, and he wanted to lie to her in case the belief might spare her a measure of suffering, but he could not do it. Three-and-forty years in the Cinnabar Desert had purged his soul of all propensity for lying. He longed to speak the secret name of the unnamable god, and use its magic to heal her, but he knew that it would be wrong. That name had to be saved for a higher purpose.

"Were you, too, made homeless by the war?" she asked him.

"No," he told her. "I was made homeless by wickedness. Once, I too made war, and sent forth my armies to kill and be killed. In the meantime, I kept myself safe and indulged my every appetite, thinking that the dark god Xanatos would keep me safe. But the dark gods are betrayers all, and Xanatos abandoned me. I was fortunate to be committed by chance to the care of that god whose true name is never spoken, who is known only by the vowel sound which marks the heart of the word but. With his help I repented of my sins and became an exile and a holy man. Now I must return to Munimazana to undo a little of the harm I did."

The girl, like almost everyone else he had encountered in his travels, had never heard of Munimazana. "I have not been very wicked at all," she told him. "But I suppose I must have been more wicked than I thought, or the god which was supposed to look after me would not have given me to the soldiers."

"It is because the innocent suffer as you have," he said, "that the guilty must go to such extremes, if they hope to redeem themselves from the burden of their sins."

She did not know what he meant.

"The evil that men do," he said, wanting to explain it to her so that she would understand, "leaves terrible scars upon the world, and yet the men who do evil are ever ready to excuse and forgive themselves. True repentance is difficult to achieve, but even when a man has truly repented of his sins, the scars are still there. Evil should not simply be forgotten; it should be undone. The world is a sick place, and it needs turning upside-down. Even though my name has been forgotten by everyone outside the kingdom which I once ruled, I know what horror that name should evoke in all who hear it. I know, and I must make amends."

Despite all his best efforts, however, she still could not follow the intricacies of his argument.

She died before dawn, and he had to leave her where she lay.

* * *

When he came to the edge of the great plain which sat like a vast green sea in the heart of the Infinite Forest, Rumulshah found men who knew precisely where Munimazana was, and could set him on the right road. "But it is not a good place to go," one man advised him. "Its fields are rich and the hunting is excellent, but the nobles of the land have long grown overaccustomed to luxury, and are notoriously capricious. The city has a bad reputation nowadays, and its king is said to be an uncommonly evil man."

"It has had kings before who were more evil still," said Rumulshah, dolefully. "Surely they still remember the villainies of Rumulshah, and shudder at the memory?"

"I doubt it," said the man. "I never heard that name spoken there. They are too full of their present woes, and their hatred is all reserved for King Guronihar."

The name Guronihar meant nothing to Rumulshah, but that did not surprise him. He had had a dozen wives and half a hundred concubines when he was tyrant in Munimazana, and had never bothered to count his children, let alone to memorise their names. This Guronihar might easily be the fruit of his own loins, or one of his myriad grandsons. He could not suppress a pang of vexation at the thought that his own villainies had been so easily eclipsed, but took satisfaction in the knowledge that whether or not men had contrived to forget the evil that was done by Rumulshah, due reparation must still be made.

"Do they still worship Xanatos in Munimazana?" he asked of his informant.

"The nobles do," he was told. "But the common people have some petty god whose name they never speak."

That petty god is not so petty, after all, thought Rumulshah. He has forged an instrument which will right the wrongs that his people have suffered so long.

As Rumulshah proceeded on his way along the dusty roads of the great plain he encountered many merchants who had traded in Munimazana at one time or another.

"There's a healthy market in exotic animal skins," one told him, "but you have to be careful when buying salamander venom. A few drops of the local brew is easily enough to kill a horse, but there's absolutely no way to disguise the stuff; it turns food putrid in seconds and makes wine stink like rotten eggs. I've sold a few doses in my time, but I've never yet had a satisfied customer."

"There's money to be made there," another said, "if you're clever enough. There are so many semi-skilled sorcerors working for the noble families that you can get a fortune for all kinds of rubbish, especially if you can pass the goods off as dwarfs' work or invent some elvish connection—all that twee stuff sounds wonderfully exotic to people of their kind. If only I could get my hands on a jawful of dragons' teeth next time I'm up north I could make a real killing. Can't think what they see in that snakedancing, though—why should a man pay extra for a whore just because she's kissing cousin to a cobra?"

"I'm never going back," said a third. "The bribes you have to put about just to be able to set up shop! It might be different if they got a new king, but Guronihar simply doesn't understand the rules of the game. What's a king for but to keep the roads safe and to make sure the coinage isn't debased? I don't deny that he does his fair share of mutilating thieves and vagabonds, but last year he had an honest trader castrated for giving short measure. We should all steer clear of the place until he's safely out of the way—though I dare say his successor won't be much better."

As he approached still closer to his destination, Rumulshah finally contrived to discover an old woman who remembered his name. "Aye," said the ancient, ruminatively, in answer to his question, "there was a king in Munimazana who had that name. His army won a battle against the hordes of Arthanyx of Quirillian, I remember that."

"Was he not an exceptionally evil man?" asked Rumulshah, desperately. "Is his memory not hateful to his people, even after all these years?"

"Probably," said the crone. "I've enough to do keeping track of who's related to whom, and who beat whom in which battles. If I tried to remember the crimes people committed I'd be full up in no time. Are you bound for Munimazana?"

"I am," said Rumulshah.

"Got children there?"

"I have," Rumulshah replied, with a sigh.

"Mine don't care much about me neither," she said, mistaking the motive for his sigh. "You spend your life teaching them everything you know, and they call you an old nag and wish you dead. You know better than to expect a decent welcome, I suppose."

"I am not worthy of any welcome," said Rumulshah, miserably. "I have much to set right before I can be forgiven by those I have injured in the past."

"Don't do your children any favours," said the crone, persisting in her misunderstanding of the implication of his words. "They won't thank you for it. They never do."

* * *

At long last the day came when Rumulshah passed through the gate of the city which he had once ruled with a rod of iron. He soon began to recognise the streets through which he passed, and was glad to observe that the people going about their daily business seemed reasonably well-fed, and reasonably well-dressed, and—in spite of their constant complaining—as happy as any people he had seen during these last three years.

They could not have been so cheerful when I was king, he thought, for I was a very wicked king indeed. Time must have eased the memory of my terrible reign, so that people nowadays think this mild Guronihar an authentic tyrant. But that cannot excuse the dreadful things which I did, and reparation must be made.

When he eventually came to stand before the huge ornamented doors of the palace at the centre of the city his heart was possessed by a fierce ache. He had quit that edifice without ceremony, nine-and-forty years before, driven by the awful consciousness of his evil nature. How merciful the unnamable god had been in permitting him to forget for so long his terrible past, and allowing him to find a better way of life among the virtuous eremites of the Cinnabar Desert! What patience the unnamable god had exhibited, in transforming him into a worthy instrument of divine retribution!

Now, although he could not see exactly how he was supposed to go about the task, the time had come when he must put that marvellous training to use.

I am a magician without compare, he reminded himself—but now, for the first time, a hint of doubt crept into his silent reassurance. It occured to him that he had been travelling for three years, and had not worked a single spell, even of the most mediocre quality. But he put such doubts aside immediately, for he had limitless faith in the god who remained nameless to everyone but him.

While he stood there looking at the awesome portal of his former abode the ornamented doors were drawn back, to make way for the gilded carriage of King Guronihar, drawn by six snow-white horses and flanked by a dozen mounted soldiers. It was not the same carriage that Rumulshah had used, and he stared at it curiously as it emerged from the doorway. He was so fascinated by the sight of it that he did not observe the bahaviour of the crowd which had surrounded him only moments before, and was not aware that it had melted away with astonishing alacrity.

Rumulshah was not in any way impeding the path of the carriage or its escort. The entire entourage could have sailed past him with ease while he stood and stared, and for a moment or two it seemed that it would do just that. But while he stood there, erect and solitary, with his pale eyes mesmerized by the sight of the gilded carriage, the horses were suddenly reined in. The mounted soldiers, after a moment's confusion, were likewise stopped in their tracks.

The curtain which hid the interior of the carriage was abruptly drawn aside, and two faces stared out. One was middle-aged, bearded and bloated, with eyes like a vulture's; the other was young, delicately veiled and crowned with soft jet black hair.

Rumulshah ignored the girl, and focused his pale eyes on the face of Guronihar, tyrant of Munimazana. Guronihar stared back, seemingly astonished and mysteriously perturbed.

"I have taught my subjects to be wary of insolence," said the king, lazily. "You must be a stranger here, to stand so boldly before my palace, with every nerve and sinew of your skinny frame giving evidence of treasonous intent."

"I am no stranger," said Rumulshah, softly. "But when I was last within these walls, there was a man named Rumulshah upon the throne, who was, I think, a far crueller and more evil king than you."

Guronihar's bloated face was suddenly contorted with fury. "That is my grandfather's name which you have dared to blacken," said the king. "He ruled as wisely and as well as he knew how, and thousands wept when he suddenly and unaccountably disappeared—the victim, no doubt, of some vile sorcery worked by the followers of that nameless god beloved by the all the riffraff of the city. Captain, seize that man and throw him in the deepest dungeon, until I have time to pass proper judgment upon him."

When he heard this, Rumulshah smiled—and he saw that his smile annoyed Guronihar even more intensely than what he had earlier said to him. At a word from their captain, two of the mounted soldiers leapt down from their horses. They seized his staff out of his hand and threw it away. Then they dragged him to the great doorway, where they passed him on to others of their kind. He was then ungently escorted across the great court-yard, down a series of winding staircases, and along numerous filthy corridors, for half a mile and more. At last, he was taken into a tiny cell, where he was pinned to the wall by shackles placed about his ankles. He was left alone in the cold and dark.

He made no resistance or complaint about this treatment, because he felt in his bones the unshakable conviction that the hour of his deliverance, while not quite yet, was close at hand.

* * *

How long Rumulshah remained in the dark he could not tell. He would have marked the time with prayer if he could, but his lips were no longer permitted to give voice to his piety. That was his only discomfort; he did not mind the darkness, or the cold, or the thirst and hunger which soon began to afflict him. Such deprivations had no power to injure him, who had been the holiest of all the eremites of the Cinnabar Desert.

He had not the slightest doubt that Guronihar intended to have him tortured and killed, but he laughed softly to himself while he wondered what torture Guronihar could possibly inflict upon him one tenth as harsh as those which he had lavished on himself for three-and-forty years.

Eventually, they came for him. His jailers stripped him of his cloak and loincloth, and threw them away, then sent him to stand with a dozen other persons similarly unclad. Under the watchful supervision of a sergeant-at-arms, the entire company was doused down with buckets of icy water, and scrubbed with brushes whose bristles were laden with caustic soap.

Afterwards, the shivering victims were given clean loincloths. It was the first change of underwear Rumulshah had had in nine-and-forty years. He accepted it gratefully, although he knew that his captors' sole purpose in giving it to him was to ensure that he did not offend the nostrils of the king and the nobles of the court when he was brought before them for judgment.

There was a long queue of people awaiting judgment in the great court-yard; Rumulshah's group was merely the latest batch in a long series. The queue included men and women of all ages—the youngest was barely seven years old. They were arranged as neatly as the sergeant could contrive, behind a wall of stout spearmen.

The Court of Judgment had changed little since Rumulshah had sat upon the stone throne; many of the coloured tapestries that bedecked the king's pavilion had been replaced, and the carpet in the nobles' section was now a deeper shade of blue, but out in the open, the terraces where the common people stood were exactly as they had always been, and so was the headsman's dais. The garotte, the rack and the brazier gave every indi-cation of being the same instruments that Rumulshah's own torturers and executioners had used.

There were so many felons to be tried that the court did not linger long over matters of ceremony. When each unfortunate was brought forward a seneschal would read out the offence with which they were charged, an advocate would promptly give the verdict (guilty, in every case), and King Guronihar would immediately pronounce sentence.

Rumulshah observed that the great majority of the crimes were trivial, and the great majority of the sentences were fines. Usually, someone would hurry forward from the crowd to pay the fine in question; if they did not, the prisoner was taken away again. Rumulshah was unimpressed by this demonstration of consistent clemency; he knew that the most serious cases would be saved until the end, so that the occasion might be suitably crowned with a generous measure of state terrorism.

It was not until the man three places in front of Rumulshah in the queue was taken forward that the expectant muttering of the crowd signalled a change of pace. Three ordinary murderers had already been given heavy fines, but the charge against this man was that he had struck a nobleman, and he was condemned to be garotted.

As soon as the sentence had been carried out the next prisoner—a woman—was brought out. She was charged with negligently allowing a nobleman's baby to die of a fever, while she had been wet-nursing it. The crime was trivial enough, the baby having been a girl, but Guronihar favoured the assembled multitude with a brief speech, explaining that an example had to be made.

The woman was set upon the rack, but she broke very easily and did not delay the proceedings for too long.

The prisoner immediately in front of Rumulshah was a boy of eleven, who was charged with a very impressive list of thefts which included several exotic and valuable objects. Because the law of Munimazana specified that each charge had to be separately dealt with, it took rather a long time for the ironmaster to put in place the appropriate number of brands; but the job was done at last, and Rumulshah knew that his hour of glory had come.

He was led out into the open space before the king's pavilion. The seneschal read out the charge against him, which was treason. The advocate pronounced him guilty. The king leaned forward, ready to make another speech while the crowd waited, with bated breath, to hear exactly how the traitor was to be done to death.

But Guronihar was not allowed to begin his speech. It was Rumulshah who spoke instead.

"Do you not know me, Guronihar?" he said—and although he had not spoken very loudly, his words fell into an uncanny silence, and were heard in every corner of the great courtyard.

Guronihar frowned, but he did not seem entirely displeased. He evidently had a certain appetite for debate and discourse, and there was no one else to be executed today.

"I know you," said the king, confidently. "I know every traitor in my kingdom, and it is my pleasure to play with them as a cat plays with mice. No villainy escapes the eyes and ears of my multitudinous agents. I know you, traitor—just as I know the others of your kind who think themselves safe while they watch your ignominious end."

As he spoke, Guronihar glanced sideways at the beautiful woman who sat beside him—who was not the same one that had been in the carriage with him at the time of Rumulshah's arrest. She smiled at him admiringly.

"What, then, is my name?" demanded Rumulshah.

"Names," said the king, negligently, "are unimportant."

"That is a lie," said Rumulshah, evenly. "For he who knows the name of the unnamable god has only to speak it, and the world itself may be turned upside down, so that evil may be undone, and virtue put in its place."

These words brought forth a murmurous, and yet somehow tumultuous, reaction from the crowd on the terraces. Guronihar frowned again, much more deeply than before, but he was angry, not in any way alarmed.

Rumulshah could see that the king was perfectly confident that the implied threat was empty.

"The world is the right way up as it is," said the king. "We have the guarantee of Xanatos—whose name everyone knows—that it will always remain so. If you think that you can overturn it, by all means try."

Then, for the first time in nine-and-forty years, Rumulshah raised his voice. He turned to the crowd, and he cried out: "Is there anyone here who knows my name? Is there anyone here who remembers me?"

There was silence: deep, profound, pregnant silence.

"Apparently not," said Guronihar, with grim satisfaction, after a full minute had passed.

"I am Rumulshah," sad Rumulshah. "For three-and-forty years I was Nanayakara, who lived in the meanest of all the eremites' caves in the Cinnabar Desert, but before that I was Rumulshah the Tyrant, Rumulshah the Vile, Rumulshah the King of Munimazana. Now I am Rumulshah again, but I am Rumulshah the Repentant, Rumulshah the Avenger, Rumulshah the Great. Do you hear me, Munimazana? I AM RUMULSHAH RETURNED TO REIGN IN MUNIMAZANA!"

This time, the silence only lasted for three or four seconds. Then Guronihar laughed.

Then everyone else laughed.

A gale of laughter swept through the courtyard like the simoom of the Cinnabar Desert: hot, sand-laden and scouring.

While they laughed, Rumulshah pronounced the secret name of the unnamable god.

And the world turned upside down.

* * *

The reign of Rumulshah the Great lasted but a few short years, but it was not forgotten for centuries. Rumour of it spread far and wide across the great plain, and into the Infinite Forest. The story was whispered in the swamplands and the great cities of the north-west, and in the vineyards beond them. Even the nomads whose goats fed upon the thornscrub heard of it. In time the news was carried back even to the Cinnabar Desert, where the cenobites spoke of it between themselves in hushed tones, before going forth to tell it to the eremites.

Under the second reign of Rumulshah, the gluttonous noblemen of

Munimazana were immediately cast down, and made wretched. The torturers' guild was instantly disbanded and all instruments of official torture were burned or melted down. All merchants were promptly expelled from the city and the marketplace was destroyed. The breeders of salamanders were unceremoniously poisoned by their own products, and the infamous snakedancers were precipitously thrown out of their gaudy houses of ill repute into the streets.

The army was disarmed but it was not disbanded; it became the people's army instead of the king's army, and under the inspiring command of Rumulshah the Repentant its officers quickly learned to be very zealous in the cause of virtue. There were many deserters in those early days, but those who remained soon cultivated a healthy love of proper self-discipline, and an appropriate taste for subjecting others to proper discipline.

Henceforth, Rumulshah decreed, the people—without exception—would live humble and sinless lives. They would repent of their former transgressions and excesses, and each and every one would discover the inexpressible joy of having a clean conscience.

At first the people were allowed to live in their houses, with all the furniture that they had had before, but Rumulshah soon perceived that this only maintained certain undesirable inequalities, and encouraged the people to maintain certain slovenly and luxurious habits which inhibited their achievement of true humility and true virtue. So he commanded that the houses be gutted, and made more like the caves which the eremites of the Cinnabar Desert had been content to inhabit, and his virtuous army saw that it was done.

Rumulshah the Avenger quickly realised that the salvation of his people was not to be won simply by humbling their former masters. He came to understand that they would never see the light, as he had done, unless they were to undergo an educative process not unlike his own. So he decreed that they must take care to mortify their flesh, as he had so gladly done; and cultivate ulcers and sores, as he had so happily done; and wear hair shirts infested with bugs, as he had once deliriously done.

When these decrees were issued, many of his people tried to flee the city, but he could not allow them to damn themselves in such a fashion, and he sent his zealous soldiers to bring them back, and to make sure that his instructions were carried out to the letter.

For a while, Rumulshah thought that he had done enough to secure the spiritual health of the realm, but in fact the people became astonishingly bitter and quarrelsome, and he was forced to issue further edicts in order to save them from themselves. The Court of Judgment was always busy, but it was no longer an instrument of tyrany and terrorism. The rack, the garotte and the branding-iron were things of the past, as were the punitive fines which were really a form of disguised taxation. All the sentences passed by Rumulshah the Repentant were designed to rehabilitate offenders, and his officers were only required to scourge those recalcictrants who could not scourge themselves with sufficient enthusiasm.

Often and anon some poor deluded soul would stand before the stone throne and declare that Rumulshah the Good was a thousand times crueller and more hateful than Rumulshah the Evil had ever been, but Rumulshah knew that such outbursts were the last and most desperate inspirations of the defeated dark god Xanatos. He forgave everyone who spoke such blasphemies, no matter how deeply they wounded him.

* * *

Rumulshah expected that within a year of his return to power his people would be utterly happy, and was grievously disappointed by the discovery that they were not. He increased his efforts on their behalf, and became sterner still in the cause of virtue when he realised that his exertions were beginning to take toll of his health; he was, after all, an uncommonly old man.

Even when it became clear that that he had not long to live, Rumulshah the Great never relented in the efforts which he made on behalf of the virtue of his people. He never became tired of helping them to discover the benefits of a thoroughly purged soul. He did everything he could, fervently and uncompromisingly, to assist them in their piety. Nor was his crusade entirely without result and reward, for some few of his people—thoose who scourged themselves and starved themselves and cultivated ulcers and sores with the greatest assiduity—did indeed begin to praise him very loudly, and proclaim him a great saviour.

Alas, these faithful and enlightened ones were still in a tiny minority when death finally came to claim him.

While Rumulshah lay on his deathbed he pressed his ministers to make sure that his great work would be continued, and they loyally assured him that it would. In time, they said, the cause of righteousness would surely triumph, even over the awful stubbornness and innate wickedness of the men and women of Munimazana.

"You must be patient with them," he told them, "for they laboured far too long under the rule of very wicked kings, and the evil that such men do cannot be undone in a day, even though the world be turned upside down. Never tire of urging them on in the cause of humility and virtue; though the hand that bears the whip may tire, still must it do its work, as fervently as it can."

When his last moments arrived, Rumulshah wondered if he ought to pass on to some favoured successor the secret name which had been entrusted to him, which he had used to turn the world upside down; but he found to his consternation that he was strangely unable to utter it. He was mildly surprised, because he had certainly rediscovered his ability to pray, but the inability was not without parallel, for he never had recovered the capacity to shed tears.

It does not matter, he told himself. I have done everything I could to make certain that Munimazana cannot be returned to its former condition, and I am certain that a dark god like Xanatos has not the power to turn the world downside up again, after it has once been righted.

He was comforted by this conviction, which was the foundation-stone of his ardent hope that salvation was possible for all men, wherever in the world they lived. One day, he felt sure, missionaries would go forth from Munimazana who would carry his example to the furthest corners of the world. He knew full well how hard a task it was to undo the evil of centuries, even in a single kingdom, but he also knew that it could be done.

Anyone else, he was convinced, could have done as well as he had—anyone, at least, who was armed as he had been, with the secret name of that mysterious god who was known to his ordinary followers by the abrupt and apologetic vowel sound which lies at the heart of the word "but."

EBONY EYES

She was the queen of a an enlightened realm, which allowed women to reign in their own right. Her appointed consort was dead but he had left her with two infant sons; under the law, the elder would inherit the throne, but not until she died. She had no daughter to threaten her reputation as the possessor of the fairest face in all the land.

She fell in love with a very handsome youth, who was poorly born but had the most beautiful body she had ever seen, hair like black silk and eyes whose irises were ebony-dark. She took him for a lover, and at first he was content, but the time soon came when she caught him looking around at her ladies-in-waiting and the prettier servants.

At first she was tolerant of his straying gaze, confident that she was more beautiful than any of those on which his ebon eyes alighted—but ladies-in-waiting and servant girls came and went, constantly replaced by younger kin as they became wives, while she grew slowly older.

She considered the possibility of selecting ugly girls to dance attendance upon her, but dismissed it out of hand. Why should her own eyes be offended in order to guard against the straying of his? Instead, she hired a clever assassin, instructing him to contrive a duel between himself and her favourite, in the course of which he was to wound the youth in both his eyes. Then she instructed her physicians to find them irredeemable, and to cut them out with scalpels, replacing them with identical but unseeing duplicates wrought by the cleverest artificer in the land.

At first, the distraught youth was delighted to discover that his royal paramour still loved him no matter that he was blind, and he took it as kindness when she told him that his marble eyes—whose irises were indeed inlaid in ebony—were no less beautiful than those he had lost. There never was a palace in all the world, however, where a secret could be kept, and he had only lost his eyes. His ears grew keener, as if by compensation, and caught the whispers which told him that what had happened had all been a scheme of hers. He might have wept, but the wellspring of his tears had dried when he lost his fleshy eyes.

By way of revenge, he threw himself into a series of secret affairs with the young ladies-in-waiting and the best of the kitchen-girls—who did not mind at all that he was blind, given that his body was firm, his hair silken and his unseeing eyes so very beautiful. But there never was a palace in all the world where a secret could be kept, and the news of his infidelities soon reached the queen.

When she charged him with his faithlessness he readily admitted it. "And what will you do now?" he demanded. "When I was tempted by the sight of other women you had my eyes put out and replaced by useless duplicates—but you cannot break the fingers with which I feel their lovely flesh without ruining my ability to touch and tease your own decaying body. Steal my pleasure and you steal your own. Let me be, and my fingers will inform me more honestly than my eyes ever could of the widening contrast between your age and their youth. Nothing you can do can hold back time."

She commissioned her assassin to break his fingers anyway, one by one, and to tear away his fingernails in order to redouble his distress. But she left his ears alone, so that he might hear the whispers which circulated even in the dungeons to which he was confined. For years thereafter she took care to send garrulous informants to converse at length within his earshot, so that he might continue to have news of all the lovely girls he could neither see nor touch.

She was, after all, the queen of an enlightened country, who would reign in her own right until the day she died. Whether she possessed the fairest face in all the land or not, she had her pride.

THE FISHERMAN'S CHILD

The man who paused before the broken gate was dressed in clothes which once had been colourful, but now were faded. The dark dust of the roads and the harsh light of the sun had turned the red and yellow tints to brown and ochre. His skin, too, should have been browned and leathery, if he were really what he seemed, but his complexion was oddly clear and lustrous, and his eyes were infinitely deep and grey.

He forced the unhinged gate aside, making a gap just large enough for him to slip through, lifting up his pack so that it did not become wedged there. Then he walked up the weed-infested path, past the gloomy yew trees, to the ancient oaken door of the house. He rapped loudly with the knuckles of his left hand.

The house was large, and one would have assumed that its inhabitants were uncommonly wealthy had it not been in such a poor state of repair. Its grounds were neglected and overgrown. It had quarters beneath the eaves for a dozen house-servants, gardeners and grooms, but the latticed windows of those rooms were grimed and shadowed, and it was obvious that all but one or two were untenanted.

The visitor had to wait for several minutes until his knock was answered, and then the door was opened by the merest crack, through which he was inspected by a wary eye.

"Who are you?" asked a voice, hoarse with age.

"A travelling player," he replied, "come to beg a loaf of bread and a cup of water, in exchange for a song or a tale. Your mistress will be glad to see me, I think, for I have been told that she can no longer rise from her bed, and that the tedium of time weighs heavily upon her."

"My mistress sees no one," the old servant replied—but he opened the door a little further, so that the wanderer could see his wizened face and tired, rheumy eyes. "Whoever it was that told you about her should have told you that. She sees no one."

"But would she turn me away from her door?" asked the man who called himself a player. "Would she begrudge me a loaf of bread and a cup of water in her servants' hall? Is she so fond of her solitude that she could not bear to hear my footsteps in her hall?"

The door opened wider still, but the old manservant did not make room to let the player enter.

"Does she know you?" asked the old man, the tremor in his voice suggesting that he thought it unlikely that the question could be answered in the affirmative.

"She does not know my face," answered the player, "but she would remember the story which I would like to tell her. It matters far more that a tale be familiar and true, than that the face of its teller should be recognised. Let me in, I beg of you. Give me food and drink—and then tell your mistress that I am here. I think that she will see me."

The old man shook his head slowly, to indicate that he could not believe it—but he stood aside in the hallway, to allow the traveller to enter. Then, after making the door secure, he showed the visitor to the kitchen, where an equally ancient woman kept guard upon a stove and a washing-tub. She looked at the newcomer as strangely as her companion had, and repeated all over again what the old man had said, but she brought him bread and a bowl of soup and a cup of seething ale, and made him welcome at her table.

The traveller ate, hungrily but unhurriedly, and slaked his thirst by slow and pleasant degrees. In the meantime, the old man went away, to tell his mistress who had knocked upon the door and why—and when he returned, it was to say that his mistress would indeed consent to see the traveller, and hear the tale which he had to tell.

"But you must not mind," the servant cautioned him, "that my lady keeps the curtains drawn about her bed, and a veil upon her face. She may look at you, if it pleases her, but you are not to try to look at her—do you undrstand that?"

"Better than you know," answered the traveller, calmly. "She need have no fear of me."

"She fears no one," said the cook, sternly. "Despite that she is old and frail, she has no fear of anything. She has no fear of Hell itself." But the way she spoke the words suggested that they were not true.

"I am glad to hear it," said the visitor, calmly. "And you may be sure that I have not come to frighten her."

*　*　*

The curtains beside the bed were made of embroidered silk, and had once been as valuable as they were fine; but they were ragged now, and stained. Like the player's clothes, they seemed to have endured too much of the ravages of time. In the middle, where the two drapes met, they were caught together as though by some insistent hand. There was a narrow crack, through which an eye might have looked out, but the room was gloomy because the bed cut off so much of the window's light, and the shadow behind the curtain was impenetrable to human sight.

The traveller sat down upon a chair which had been placed beside the bed. "I have come to tell you a tale, my lady," he said.

"Do you have a name?" asked a voice from behind the curtains, even hoarser than the old man's, no more than a whisper in spite of the evident effort which produced it.

"I have had many names," he answered, but did not offer one—though he took care to leaven his impoliteness with a certain levity of tone.

"So have I," she said, sarcastically. "But none that were secret. No matter—what could it matter, even if you were Death himself, come to claim my sin-stained soul for the fires of Hell? I am too weary to hide any longer in the silence of my thoughts and the darkness of my dreams. Had you come a year ago, or even a month, it would have pained me to se your face and hear your voice, whatever tale you told . . . but now . . . can you imagine what it is to be past pain, past care, past all anxiety and shame?"

"Better than you know," answered the man with many names.

"Then tell your tale," said the voice from the shadows, as thin as the wind rustling the autumn leaves. "Tell the tale which you have come to offer me, in payment for your meal."

*　*　*

"We who are privileged to be citizens of Raganza," began the story-teller, "are justly proud of our nation. It is the richest land in all the world in the fecundity of its fields, the intelligence of its people and the justice of its laws."

He paused for just an instant, hearing the sound of soft, strange laughter—but the woman who hid behind the curtains of tattered silk had no intention to interrupt him with her sad sardonic mirth, and so he continued.

"Because of this, alas, there are those among the gods who seem to nurture a special enmity towards Raganza, and are said to be avid to visit misfortune upon its people. Rumour says that it was the work of one such god which toppled the towers of Corama and earned it the name of the City of Death; legend argues that it is another of the same kind which sends his winged demons to fly among the flocks of birds which nest on the cliffs above Avillion.

"The wise man does not name such dire powers for fear of attracting their attention, but there are those among the Raganzan people, as there are among all peoples, who imperil their immortal souls by making names for the darker gods, and who are someimes driven by greed or fear or ambition or desperation to offer pleas and prayers to those they have dared to name. Even in this good and noble land, such dangerous prayers are all too often heard and vindictively answered."

Again, there was the sound of murmurous laughter, but the story-teller did not mind at all.

"Raganza is vast as well as rich," he went on, his smooth and practised voice settling readily into the careful and respectful tone of those who make up stories to flatter the rich and the vainglorious, "and it is inevitable that there should be poor people even in the richest and most righteous of nations. Far from the great and noble cities, far from the fertile river valleys, there are regions where the houses are crude and the soil is poor, even in Raganza.

"One such region lies on the north-west coast, equidistant from Corama and Avillion, where the shore is perennially chilled by the winds which blow from the Great Western Ocean. On the further edge of that region is a town called Miramor."

The laughter died, punctuated by an intake of breath—but there was less surprise in the gasp than there might have been, and the silence which followed was patient.

The story-teller smiled, as though he were very satisfied with the reaction of his listener.

"Miramor's men," he said, "draw their living from the old grey widowmaker, setting forth each day in their sailing-boats to chase the shoals of silver fish. That living is hard even at the best of times, and the poorest years always bring hardship in their wake. Few are the families which do not lose one in three of their children to disease and malnourishment, and many are those who must nurse bitter memories of hard decisions taken in the name of survival.

"From time to time the summer seas which send their boisterous waves to break upon Miramor's coast are afflicted by a strange red bloom which grows on their surface, infecting the fish with a sickness which turns their flesh to poison, and which kills all but a fortunate few. Though such blooms always die when autumn comes, they often do their work so well that the sea is nearly empty of unspoiled fish during all the long dark months of winter.

"The fisher-folk along this coast must trade with inland farmers for their bread and their meat, their apples and their sugar-beets; for they only keep tiny gardens of their own, where little but a few meagre turnips will grow. When the sea's harvest is good, the fisher-folk are a little richer than the farmers, and do not shirk to use this advantage in their bargaining; but when the red tides come, the fisher-folk become desperate, and the hardness of their bargains is returned to them in full measure. When the red bloom comes, all the fisher-folk know that some among their number will likely starve to death before the spring, when the fish increase their numbers once again."

The curtains stirred now, though it seemed that whatever held them together gripped them more tightly than before. Within the shadowed crack an eye could now be seen, inspecting the story-teller minutely. He stared back very steadily, and did not pause for an instant in the flow of his narration.

"When the red tide beats its mocking rhythm against the harbour-wall of Miramor," he said, "the fishing-boats must still go out, day after day, with their masters and their stronger sons avid to make what catches they can. In the meantime, their wives and younger children go scavenging along the shore, collecting seaweed and shellfish in their determination to keep hunger at bay. Sometimes a boat will go too far in search of a catch, and never return; sometimes, even the shellfish which the women find have been sickened by the red bloom, and have poison in their flesh instead of nourishment."

This time, she did interrupt him—and not with ironic laughter. "I know all this," she said, in her slight, strained voice, "and I do not believe that you are unaware of it. I know what tale you have come to tell, O man of many names. You need not lull me into drowsiness with such a long introduction. I am not afraid to hear the story of my life, even though I know full well that no man knows that story."

"I am glad that you understand," said the visitor. He spoke with a curiously tender warmth, despite what she implied about his nature. "And you have less cause to fear than you believe."

"I am not afraid," she told him. "Not even of the fires of Hell." But like her aged servant, she lied.

* * *

"In the year of the last red bloom but one," continued the story-teller, "there lived among the luckless fisher-folk of Miramor a man named Balthasar, who had a wife named Luca, two sons named Felix and Lo, and an infant daughter named Dione. Felix and Lo were old enough to take to the sea with their father, but Dione, who could barely walk, was too young even to go foraging along the shore.

"As that wretched autumn wore on, Balthasar and his sons took their boat further and further afield, and cast their nets deeper and deeper into the darkness beneath the bloom, but their efforts were mostly in vain and their catches very small.

"Luca was loud in her complaining, saying that they would surely fare worse than their neighbours because she had no one to help her search along the shore for shellfish, and had the additional burden of a useless girl-child to make things difficult. So, when the month of mists came, Felix and Lo were required to stay on shore, to join the women and the smaller children in the foraging. This was a deep humiliation for both of them, which they bitterly resented.

"Balthasar had no better luck alone than he had enjoyed when he had Felix and Lo to help him, and when the day of the winter solstice eventually came, the shore around Miramor had been picked so clean of weed and shellfish that there was precious little left to be gleaned from it.

"There came, in the miserable weeks which followed, a day when Luca said to Balthasar: 'If we go on as we are, we will certainly starve before spring. Four pairs of hands cannnot feed five mouths in times like these. You must take Dione with you tomorrow when you put out to sea, and cast her over the side to drown. She is not strong enough to live until the spring in any case—and she is, after all, only a useless girl-child for whom we must one day find a dowry, and not a boy whose strength would add to our resources.'

"Balthasar was very reluctant to do this, because he loved his daughter very dearly. He appealed to Felix and to Lo, hoping that they could not bear to see the murder done, but they sided with their mother.

"Felix said: 'My brother and I must scour the shore with the women while our mother tends to the little one's needs; Dione is a luxury which we cannot afford in such a season as this.'

"And Lo, in his turn, said: 'We love our sister as much as brothers should, but if you cannot do this deed, she will surely die a lingering death from hunger, and we will die with her. It is a kindness to save her from such misery as that.'

"Balthasar was saddened by the opinions which his sons expressed, but while he was not cunning enough to catch the fish which might keep all five of them alive he could not find sufficient reason to deny them their demand. He spent a sleepless and very troubled night, but in the morning he took Dione with him when he put out to sea, and took her far away from the shore.

"The sky was leaden that day, and the sea very sullen. A gentle drizzle soaked Balthasar's face, the tiny raindrops mingling with his anguished tears. For an hour and more he sat by the rudder of his vessel, cradling the crying infant in his arms, unable to act. But in the end, he closed his eyes against the horror of the sight and threw her over the side, crying out in his extremity that if it should be the will of any god that his daughter might live, that god must provide for her now. And in the extremity of his anguish, he named a god which never should have been named, and begged that god to preserve the daughter which all the better gods had failed to preserve from this evil fate.

"The waves must have swallowed her up immediately, for Dione was very small, and did not know how to swim or keep herself afloat.

"The next day, the luck of Miramor's fisher-folk turned, and new shoals of fish began to move into the waters which had briefly been lifeless. Balthasar was among the first to find these new shoals, and he was able at last to take home enough to eat, with a little extra to trade for bread and apples. After that, Felix and Lo were able to leave the denuded shore to resume their former station as boat-hands. All four of them had grown thin, but they soon began to put on weight again, and were returned to the full bloom of health even before the spring brought the land to life again.

"The bitter implications of this turn of events were all too plain to Balthasar, who could take no pleasure in the recovery of his good fortune. He knew full well that if he had only waited one more day before accepting the sentence of death which his wife and sons had passed upon his daughter, Dione would surely have been saved with the rest of them; they would have had enough to feed her too. But Luca never said a word about what she had told him to do, and neither Felix nor Lo ever expressed a word of regret about the way they had cast their votes.

"In the face of this refusal to mourn or regret the needless sacrifice of the little girl, Balthasar soothed his hatred by secretly praying to that god which he had implored for help when he threw Dione overboard—that god which he had named in forbidden fashion. He continued to pray aloud in Miramor's shrines, as he had always prayed, to those gods whose worship is licensed; but when he knelt down at night before going to his bed he offered more extravagant supplications. He said, in the privacy of his heart, that if any being at all had shown the tender mercy for which he had begged, then that god had his most ardent thanks. Furthermore, he asked that any god which might have been so kind as to take care of his beloved daughter should now send her home, so that the great wrong which he had done might be undone, and everything set to rights."

"To rights!" The words, spoken as though they were an echo from the shadows behind he curtains, concealed a strangled sob.

The story-teller paused, to see if his listener had aught else to add, but she said nothing more. He was about to begin again when there was a knock at the door, and the old manservant entered, carrying a lighted taper. The sun had set and the room was beginning to grow dark. The servant did not look at the story-teller until he had lit the candles mounted on a three-branched candelabrum, which stood on the table beside the bedhead.

"Thank you," said the story-teller.

"Will you stay the night?" asked the servant, querulously.

It was the invisible woman who answered. "He will stay," she said, "as long as he pleases."

* * *

When the old man had closed the door behind him, the woman spoke again. "Go on," she said. "I need to hear just a little more, before I can pick up the thread . . . only a little more."

"After a fortnight had passed," the traveller continued, "it seemed that the prayers which Balthasar had offered had gone unanswered; but then a marvellous thing occurred. A tiny child was discovered, alive and seemingly well, washed up on the beach to the south of the town. The foragers who found her recognised her immediately as Balthasar's Dione. The child was immediately brought back to Luca, amid rumours that a miracle had been accomplished.

"Although the women who brought Dione home said to Luca that she must have fallen in the sea while playing on the beach, no one was in any doubt as to what had really happened. There were others among the women of Miramor who had made such decisions in the past, and they understood why Luca had told her husband to do what he had done. But when the foragers brought her child back home, Luca could not help but feel that they condemned her with their curious stares and talk of miracles.

"Balthasar was filled with delight to have his daughter home again, and his wife and sons were anxious to pretend that they shared his pleasure. In truth, though, all three of them wished that it had not happened—for the child's salvation became a constant reminder of what they had ordered done.

"Dione had not the slightest memory of her mysterious sojourn in the sea, and no one ventured to tell her about it, but those who felt the guilt of it could not pretend to themselves that it had not happened. For this reason, the little girl grew up less loved than she might have been, without ever knowing why. Though Dione's brothers did not hurt her much more than brothers usually hurt their sisters, and she had full measure of her father's affection, still she was deprived of something which she sorely needed: her mother's love.

"Despite all her efforts, Luca was never again able to look at her youngest child without hearing accusing voices whispering in her heart, and the pressure of those accusations made her heart unyieldingly hard in spite of the fact that she might have wished it otherwise.

"Dione, though she grew up healthy and strong and beautiful, found herself a stranger in her own home. Her father's tenderness could not make up for the fact that she had not her mother's love to help in soothing the worst pains from her distressful life. The people of Miramor were soon able to put the evil season of the red tide out of their minds, but its legacy continued to affect all their lives—most especially the lives of Balthasar and his family."

"Enough!" cried the voice from behind the curtain, louder and stronger now. "I know the rest of the tale, and know it far too well. If you are Death, come to claim my soul for Hell, you need not tell me more."

Her visitor sat silently, waiting. He knew that the time had come when he must answer questions, even though he had given her the answers already.

After a while, she said: "Did my father really love me?"

He answered: "Yes."

Then, she said: "And was it really a dark and mischievous god who preserved me from death, and brought me back to the land?"

He answered: "It was a god, and men would deem him dark."

"And are you a messenger," she asked, finally, "sent by that curiously merciful god, to say that I might die at last, and pay what debts I owe?"

"I am a messenger," he said, knowing that she knew it, and had known it from the start. "And that is the message which I bring. But we need not hurry, my dearest Dione—we have time to talk, if you have aught to say."

* * *

"When I grew older," said the woman, dreamily, from the shadowy haven which she kept behhind her silken drapes, "I had no other ambition but to go with my father out to sea, but Felix and Lo could not stand to have me aboard the boat, and were loud in their protestation that a girl's allotted place was in the home. I could not understand why, but I see now that my father agreed with them because he knew that if I came with them on their many expeditions he would be constantly reminded of what he had done. So I stayed at home, racked by disappointment, with the mother who could not properly love or like me. I became more lonely with every year which passed.

"I became fond of walking on the beaches to either side of the harbour, for I liked the company of the sea, regardless of whether it wore its peaceful face of blue or its angry face of grey. My mother was always pleased to see me go, and sorry when I returned, and my days became utterly desolate.

"Despite that I was by no means uncomely, I had no suitors among the village boys. Although I had no particular desire to be married I was annoyed by this neglect, because I did not understand its cause. I see now that all the boys must have heard the whispered story of how I had been refused by the sea when I was sent for drowning, and were unanimous in considering me to be tainted."

"That is so, alas," the mesenger said. "Some argued that you must be a witch-girl, others merely that you would prove an unlucky partner, but in either case the result was the same. The fact that your own mother did not love you was seen as further support for the judgment."

He heard her swallow, as though something was stuck in her throat, and had o be cleared before she could continue.

"I could discover no sensible hope for an end to my loneliness when I grew to womanhood," she said, faintly. "More than once I thought, as I wandered along the shore, that I might as well cast myself into the sea and commit my fate to the merciless waves."

"Which were not so very merciless," the story-teller reminded her, "and would not have received you, while you still had work to do."

"I know now," she said, "that my father was a better man than I thought. Seeing my increasing unhappiness, he did what little he could to brighten up my life. He brought me gifts and told me tales, and hugged me whenever he could; but none of it could lighten my sadness for long. I sensed the unspoken shame which was entangled with his love and mistook it for insincerity—and besides, he was too often absent, drawing our living from the parsimonious waters of the ocean.

"One stormy day—during the month of mists, as chance would have it—I formed a firm resolution to cast myself down from a cliff into the wind-whipped waves. But when I tried to do it, I was seized by an terrible fear which made me hesitate and hold back, until I broke down and wept for her own weakness and frailty of spirit. I pleaded then for help, and prayed to a god I could not name, imploring him to come to me and lend me strength, to be a better mother than the unloving one I had, and a better father than the one whose love was shadowed and spoiled by mystery.

"I did not know then how certain it as that I would be heard—but I knew and understood that I was heard. I knew because as soon as I made a habit of offering such prayers, I began to dream very vividly. Do you know my dreams as well, messenger?"

"Oh yes," the traveller answered. "I know your dreams very well. Indeed, I know the dreams of mortal men far more intimately than I know their lives, for this form I wear is not my own. But you must tell me, if you would like to, how they seemed to you."

"They seemed most strange," Dione said. "I can understand now why they often began with a painful—and, as I thought, impossible—sequence in which my father took her out in his boat and threw me over the side to drown, but then it was an episode of nightmarish horror. In my dreams, though, the sea which claimed me was not the cold grey ocean at all, but a very different entity, which was neither wet nor grey nor salty—a sea of pure confusion, where lonely spirits swam. I guessed that it must be the sea of souls, where the gods were, and supposed therefore that some unnamable god must have heard my prayers, and had condescended to become the patient custodian of my soul.

"Because of that, I found some comfort in my dreams, though others might have deemed them nightmares, and the burden of my weary days was lightened a little.

"One night, I had a longer and more curious dream, in which I saw myself sitting naked upon a lonely strand, shedding a measure of my womanly blood into the sea. And then I saw myself walking away from Miramor to another place, where no one knew me, and where I could easily find the lovers who were denied to me in Miramor. I could not doubt that this dream was a god-sent revelation, and when the opportunity next came I took myself down to the beach, and sat naked in the sand while the waves lapped around me, and shed a little of my blood into the sea. Then I went home, collected my few possesions together, and went away, without pausing to say farewell to my uncaring mother. That was what my dreams bade me do, was it not?"

"It was," agreed the other.

"I walked for three days and three nights, without ever feeling tired, until I eventually came to an inland town named Valienne, where I was made very welcome. There I stayed for a while, taken in first by one man and then another.

"In the beginning, I was grateful for all the kind attention which I received, and played at being in love, but I could find no honest warmth in my own feelings, which remained as grey and cold as the Great Western Ocean. Soon, I began to play my games in a different spirit, becoming contemptuous of the delusions of those who courted me.

"Need I tell you every detail of my life in Valienne? It seems to me now a tawdry tale, and my waking life was never as much to me as my dreams? Or must we begin the sordid counting of my sins, in order to settle the punishments which are set aside for me in Hell?"

"No," said the man with many names, gently. "We need not count your sins."

"They are too many to need counting, anyhow," she said, her voice sinking again to the thnnest of whispers. "Two duels were fought in Valienne for my favours, which left one man dead and another crippled. One youth hanged himself, and one man's wife took poison. When the time came for me to leave—led by a summons which came to me in those lushly nightmarish dreams which she loved so dearly—I must have left behind a dire legacy of pain, confusion and bitterness. In spite of that, there were half a dozen men who begged me not to go, and proclaimed that their lives would be bleak and desolate without my presence to illuminate them.

"After that, I stayed for a while in Oremy . . . but then there was another town, and then another, all of them much the same. Even Escovalda itself, whose grandeur is said to be unequalled in the civilized world, was just another place to be . . . another sea of pallid faces, where I cast my nets for human prey . . . and landed it so easily.

"I suppose that I had by then acquired the manners and accomplishments of a bold and brazen courtesan. I leeched my wealth from old men prepared to pay the inflated cost of vanity, and used my leisure hours in extirpating the romantic illusions of younger men—so that they, in their turn, learned to devote their greatest energies to lewdness and lubriciousness. I moved in the very highest circles, but would not permit them to confine me. Do you know what I mean by that?"

"Certainly," he replied.

But she continued regardless. "Escovalda sits atop a labyrinthine Underworld," she said, bitterly. "A Hell on earth, where the hugest known army of the poor and desperate is sustained by the wastes and leavings of the rich and profligate. A Hell as vile, I think, as that one for which my wickedness has made me ripe. That Underworld offers . . . entertainments . . . of its own to those whose tastes are as broad and peculiar as mine increasingly became."

She laughed, dryly.

"But you know all that," she said, with a sigh "as well you might, if you are Death himself, and the emissary of those gods which hate the race of man. You know everything. Perhaps you even know the answer to the last question of all—the only question left to me to ask."

"Ask," he said.

"Why?" she asked—or tried to ask, though the word was half a sigh and half a sob. "For the love of whatever god my father named, why?"

* * *

"There are patient scholars who have tracked the story of mankind through hundreds of thousands of years," he answered, carefully. "What is written of the past is only the merest echo of what has been forgotten, but still these scholars have catalogued a thousand empires, and sifted through the ruins of a millon great cities. The one lesson which they have learned is this: that all empires fall into ruins, and that all great cities wither into huge great sores of dereliction—but before they fall and wither, the lawmakers and generals who might preserve them must lose their interest in law and strength, and devote themselves instead to a fierce pursuit of pleasure which knows no satiation. That they invariably do, because men cannot resist temptation. All aristocracies become rotten; all empires fall."

"And why must it be," she asked, tiredly, "that there are gods which feed men with temptations, to set that rot within their hearts and bring their empires down? Why are the gods so avid to populate those Hells which they have made for the men they hate?"

"You should not blame the gods," he told her, in an unreasonably quiet voice. "Men make their own gods to rule the whims of fate; it is the most magical power which they have. And the gods which they make cannot help but echo the quality of those who make them. The gods have many names, and are forever being named anew, but the gods cannot change while men cannot change, and while men are what they are, the gods must be what they are."

"Say you so?" she said, very tiredly. "But still there are gods, which play with human lives—and still, I think, there is a Hell for those who are their wicked instruments."

"No," he said. "There is no Hell. That is the message I have brought. There is no Hell, and no further need of fear."

"No Hell?" she echoed—but her voice had nothing in it of gratitude or hope renewed. "You little know what I have suffered here on earth, you who have come t tell me that there is no Hell."

"I know," he said. "But there is no punishment beyond the grave, Dione. The only Hells that exist are those which men devise, and visit on themselves with the power of their malevolent will. Many are the men and women whose lot it is to become instruments of that visitation, through no fault of their own. Many are those whose feelings are twisted and torn, so that they lose the power to love. It is the way of the world, and no one can tell whether there will ever come a day when things work differently, but it is only the way of the world."

"Is there justice in that?" she whispered.

"No," he answered, calmly. "No justice at all."

Dione was silent for a moment. Then, she sighed again, and said: "What became of my parents and my brothers?"

"In the days which followed your leaving," the traveller told her, "the red bloom came again to spoil the sea, killing all but a few of the fish and making them dangerous to eat. Luca your mother died from eating poisoned fish. Balthasar your father and both your brothers were weakened by starvation in the winter, and eventually perished of a very ordinary chill."

The hidden woman made no answer, but all of a sudden she reached out and drew the curtains aside, so that she might look at the person who had come to tell her the story of her life, and so that he might look at her.

She was old and grey and withered, but there was worse than that to see. Two horrible claws grew at the ends of her arms, where once there had been clutching hands, and two great scaly fins stood out from her shoulders like huge ugly wings, deforming her spine and her shoulders. Her wrinkled skin had a curious sheen upon it, as though it were turning to scales.

"Is there no justice in this?" she asked. "I think I might bear it better if there were."

"No justice," he told her, plainly. "No justice at all. But in the end, there is mercy. You have named me Death, and so I am, but I have many names and I am more than that. I took you once before to the world of dreams, and now I have come to bring you back, to your one true home. I came to tell you the story of your life, and that I have done—but I came also to bring you the news that when you next go to sleep, you need never wake again. Whenever you are ready, we may go together to the sea beyond the sea, where we may ride with the shoals of our master's silver sharks, and play with those handsome serpents which are the devourers of fishermen's souls. That solace which has long illuminated your sleep, allowing you to cherish the crystal chains of your bondage, is yours forever whenever you care to claim it."

"I am not bound for Hell," she said, as though she were still trting to believe it. "No matter what men say, and no matter what time has made of me, I am not bound for Hell?"

"No," he answered. "You have been in Hell, but now have had enough of it. No matter what men may think, and no matter what vile lies they tell one another, there is no punishment beyond the grave. There is no justice, you see, but only mercy—and the master whom we have served is far too wise a god ever to think that a girl-child was a useless thing."

Then the traveller reached out his hand, and used his fingers to snuff out the candles by the bedside, one by one.

Darkness fell.

THE STORY-TELLER'S TALE

The stars were shining brightly as the story-teller began his tale. His listeners formed a semicircle around him, close enough for him to see the starlight reflected in their round eyes; it was as if each and every gaze were intensely studious and informed by an altogether unnatural wisdom.

* * *

"I think there was a time," he said, "when I counted myself a reasonably fortunate man, but that was long before this tale began. Before I became involved in the escape from Kapan Kishk I had been a road-slave for six long years, and of all the men who broke their backs and hearts on the road from Dod Kadir, there was none who less deserved his fate than I, who never stole a coin or cut a throat, but only borrowed a rich man's youngest wife—and he with three more which he could by no means be said to have used up.

"You will think that I do not seem to be a strong man, and there is surely little meat on my bones, but not every road-slave is a ditchdigger or a breaker of stones; there is skill even in slavery and by day I was a mixer of concrete, which is made from broken stones, sand, lime and dross, and which binds our smooth Ancyran roads into highways fit for the hooves of horses and oxen and the wheels of carts. The overseers were pleased to give me such light work, because by night I still practised my old profession, and told tales to slaves and masters alike, lightening their burdensome lives with the labour of my tongue.

"The plan for our escape was hatched in the bold mind of Yash Aggarwal, who had not long been a slave and could not look forward to a long career, because he was hated by the overseers for having only one eye, and that an evil one. It was he, not I, who spread the tale that once the road to Kapan Kishk was finished we would all be thrown into the dungeons of that foul citadel—which as you know was never built by human hand—and there left to rot and die because it was not worth the empire's while to take us back to Dod Kadir and set us to work on another road. Yash Aggarwal it was who said that the midday sun had perforce been our guide for nine-and-ninety days, and that we should adopt it for our friendly star, making our own way southward beyond the empire's bounds, into the Withering Waste.

"We knew the reputation of the Waste well enough, but we had been living in a kind of hell for those nine-and-ninety days, and the black caves of Kapan Kishk were one more evil circle of that hell awaiting us. Yash Aggarwal soon gathered about himself a dozen men of strength and skill—mostly fighters and thieves, save for one Aor Gulamali who knew some healing magic. I was naturally included in his plans, for no group of a dozen men is complete without a story-teller to lift its spirits and dissolve its drear anxieties. And so, after the sun had set on the day when the dark gates of Kapan Kishk came in sight we rose against our violent masters, and went to the work of killing them with a keen appetite.

"Four of our own company were slain, and perhaps an equal number of those who were not included in our plan, but nine men survived to flee into the night, with three donkeys and their panniers of meal—and in the morning we had skirted the lonely mount on which Kapan Kishk was built, and had naught but the Withering Waste before us.

"None of us knew this land, and the stories in my stock which told of it were too dire by far to parade before my fellows, so I spoke instead of the lands believed to lie beyond the Waste, in the farther south—of golden cities and painted towers and seas of sapphire blue. That is the purpose of a story-teller, to give men heart when their minds are not resolute. It was not a lie, but a decoration. It would have been tactless to speak of the molochmen of the desert, or the plants which crawl and suck the blood of men and beasts, or those spiders which dress their webs with a poison to blight all kinds of flesh, though I had heard accounts of all of these things. Nor, of course, did I mention the lazarous demons, of whom the most horrible tales of all are told—and I even took care to keep *their* name from my own thoughts, as story-tellers have the skill to do.

"We travelled quickly that day, for we did not know whether they would send soldiers from Kapan Kishk to chase us. We had only killed a few overseers, who were little more than slaves themselves, but no one likes to leave an escaping slave unpunished lest it plant a seed in the minds of others and spark a greater rebellion. By the time we dared to stop we were sorely tired, and needed more than meal to soothe our aches before we slept, so I told the excellent story of the unlicensed moneylender of Zainul Zub and the ten temple whores, which they all loved, and which never failed to make them laugh—though Avan Goom and Kahin Chan, who had been on the road for three years and more, must have heard it half a hundred times before.

"The next day we found water, which seemed fresh enough and did the donkeys no harm, but even then we had come into a region the like of which we had never seen before, where no trees grew; where the grasses and grains were yellow and brown; and where great white toadstools reared their heads to the height of a mounted man. Poor Suleman Rham—who was ever a luckless thief, as could be judged by his lack of a right hand—strayed under one of these growths while it was spilling a cloud of spores from its underside, and having breathed in a great quantity went mad with delirium, and turned quite black in the face before he died. We made masks out of rags and the sleeves of our shirts to protect us, and made our way circumspectly after that.

"The misfortunes of that day were not ended, for one of the donkeys was bitten by a serpent, and though it did not seem likely to die its foot was so swollen that it could not go on. We paused to kill and butcher it, and some of its blood was drunk by one of our number named Anakali, who was from the western lands where they sup the blood of beasts to give them strength. Alas, the serpent's poison must still have been in the blood, and far more edally to a man than to the beast. Anakali was racked with dreadful pains all night, and in the morning was vomiting up his own blood with the donkey's. By noon he was stinking most evilly, rotting while he lived. Yash Aggarwal cut his throat out of kindness before we left him.

"We dared not eat that donkey's flesh, and so killed another, but even then were reluctant to eat it, even though our supply of meal was near run out. In the end Alaric Lod, a northerner who had been a mercenary before he was condemned for treason against his hirer, agreed to try the meat, and it seemed to do him no harm. We feasted well on the animal that night, and carried smoked meat away with us, in good heart despite our losses.

"Only one more night was to pass, however, before another of our company died. This was Arb ab Abassi, who slept a little distance away from the rest of us, and far too soundly for his own good. When we woke in the morning we found that three of the loathsome plants which crawl had come to him, and were sending their thirsty roots deep into the flesh of his left leg.

"Arb ab Abassi begged Yash Aggarwal to cut out the plant, for he knew that it would leave him naught but a stem-entwined skeleton if left to its own devices, and knew that he would feel no pain because the roots kill the feeling of the flesh which they invade. Good Yash Aggarwal did his very best, and there never was a man more clever with a slitting-knife, but it was all to no avail, for the tendrils of those plants grow horridly fast, and Arb ab Abassi had bled to death before the last of the rootlets could be cut away. His death was a little eased, however, by the fact that I distracted his mind by telling him once again his favourite of all my tales, of how the daughter of Kartar Var fared in the harem of the King of the Ghouls.

"The next day we dined well on the meat of the last-but-one donkey, but our water supply was running perilously low. We knew that it would take many days to cross the Withering Waste, and that water would be the most important factor limiting our chances of survival. When Kahin Chan climbed to the top of an outcrop of bare rock, and told us that he could see green foliage in the east amid the yellow dunes and parched brown grass we unhesitatingly altered out course. We might have guessed, of course, that where there was water in a barren land we would likely find other drinkers, but it could not have deterred us. If we had to fight for our water, still we must have it, and fight we would.

"When we came close to the oasis we smelled fire on the lazy wind, and approached most stealthily. There were a dozen molochmen camped by the water-hole, with seven misshapen mounts of a vile reptilian character. Because they were twelve and we were but six we had to wait for dead of night before attacking their tents, but before then we had noted that four were females, and that only three of the males were armed with iron. One of these was sent forth as sentry, but he did not expect such enemies as us, and it was easy for Yash Aggarwal to slit his throat. The other males we killed with little fuss as they woke in surprise from their slumbers. Alaric Lod slew no less than five, and it was easy to see that he had not forgotten the way of a warrior while he was unluckily enslaved.

"One female had to be killed, because she attacked Avan Goom with a fury which would brook no other interruption but a blade in the throat, but the remainder we saved. I do not really care for molochite women, because their skins are always leathery and their slits uncommon slimy, and they have faces like leering apes—but a man cannot be too fussy when he is a roadslave, and we had all learned to be less than particular in seeking companions for our beds. The one which I shared with Aor Gulamali was perhaps the ugliest of the lot, with a scarred face as rough as sharkskin, but she served her purpose.

"In the morning we killed them all—they had not the promise of giving us sufficient pleasure to make it worth our while to feed and water them, and had we fallen into their hands instead of they into ours they would have done far worse. I have heard that the favourite sport of molochmen is to cut a man's belly, take away his intestines most carefully, and fill the empty cavity with small rough stones and excrement, and then to stitch him up again.

"We took the molochites' beasts of burden, their weapons and their supplies, and had an easy time of it for two whole days, but then Kahin Chan and Alaric Lod rode their beasts through a thicket, not knowing that it was infested with the spiderwebs which blight, and in a matter of hours the flesh of animals and men alike had begun to soften and turn milk-white. They lay all night unsleeping, terribly feverish but unable to drink because every time we brought water they foamed at the mouth and screamed in panic. They begged us to cut their throats, and Yash Aggarwal had no option but to do it, though the loss of Alaric Lod was most unwelcome, given that he was by far the best warrior in our party."

* * *

The story-teller paused. His mouth had run dry, and he wondered whether he dared to ask for a drink, but when he looked into those eyes which gleamed with starlight—so inscrutable, so expectant—he felt that he must at all costs continue, lest he lose the pitch of dramatic tension which he was struggling to maintain.

* * *

"On the next day," he continued, "we were pursued by another band of molochmen. Whether they had found their slaughtered kin and followed our trail from the oasis, or whether they had heard the screams of Alaric Lod and Kahin Chan echoing in the desert night we could not tell; we simply fled from them on our stolen animals, leaving behind the last of our donkeys. The molochites were fifteen or sixteen strong, all mounted, whereas we were four, and though our blades were made of stronger stuff than theirs we would have had no chance at all in a stand-up fight.

"The beasts we rode were identical to their own, and they must have caught us up had they continued the chase through the day, but when Avan Goom was thrown after his mount stumbled they stopped to seize him, and let the rest of us go. Perhaps they only wanted a toy to play with, and thought that they could amuse themselves sufficiently with one hardy lad who might live for days under subtle torture, but for myself I think they were afraid of us, and glad of the excuse to settle for one instead of risking injury to capture all four.

"Yash Aggarwal was in a foul mood that night, saying that had he taken his choice of the nine who set out he would have kept any one of the others before the two who now remained to guard him. Aor Gulamali's healing magic had not so far served to save a single man from ignominious death, and I had not told a single story which he had not heard already. But the old hedge-wizard bound a festering wound which he had on his arm, and put some ointment on it which soothed it well, and I told him the story of merchant Hamadeh who persuaded a nephew he did not like to recover a treasure from a well, and how the curse that was on the treasure caught up with him nevertheless. It is not one of my finest stories, but it was one which Yash Aggarwal had never heard before, and he was pleased enough to listen to it.

"The next day and the next after that we continued southwards, into a region even more frightful than the ones through which we had already passed, where even the bronzed and ochreous grasses no longer grew, and the grey ground itself seemed cankerous. There were coloured lichens on the rocks, and leopard-spotted slugs, and great lumps of amoeboid slime which shone by night with their own internal light, but there was no creature we dared to kill and eat save for the beasts we had with us, and on the second night we slaughtered one, knowing that one of us would have to walk on the next day.

"Aor Gulamali dared not quarrel with Yash Aggarwal, and I had not the courage to take him on alone, so it was left to Aggarwal to decide who would ride and when. On the next day we had little water left, and Yash Aggarwal kept it entirely to himself, and one of the animals died so that we had only one to ride. We had no doubt that Yash Aggarwal would keep it for his own use, and we guessed that he would soon desert us, thinking that he could go further and faster without us, and that we were not skilled enough as fighters to make it worth his while to stay with him. There was nothing to do but kill him, and so we did—I slit his throat as he had slit so many others in his time. It was no crime to do it, but merely a matter of sour necessity.

"I took care to share what little water was left with Aor Gulamali, and to take fair turns in riding our sole remaining beast—not because I valued his prowess as a fighter, or even as a healer, but because I did not want to be left alone in that dire and awful place. I cared for him as much as I could, but he was an old man, and his healing magic had ever been too feeble to preserve his youth and strength past their natural span. He fell sick, and I had to leave him while I searched for water, and though I returned to him when I had found it he was already half-devoured by scavengers. He was yet alive, but all sense and intelligence had fled from him, and when I cut his throat the blood that flowed from the wound was a meagre trickle.

"Although I was now alone, and very frightened, I was determined to go on as far as I could, and I instructed myself most sternly that if there was a southern limit to the Withering Waste which a man might reach, then I would be the man who reached it. I did not fear the molochites, who were less than men; I did not fear the plants which crawled; and I did not fear the spiderwebs which blighted; for I had seen all of these at work, and knew them well enough. I did not think at all of the lazarous demons, which I had resolved to put out of my mind, and had done so—I am a teller of tales, and I have the skill to banish from my thoughts that which it is not to my advantage to contemplate."

* * *

As he spoke these words, uneasily—remembering that he was repeating himself—the story-teller looked around once again, trying desperately to measure the opinion of his audience. He could not do it; their eyes were like mirrors, and told them nothing of their dark and horrid thoughts.

* * *

"That is the whole of my tale," he said, haltingly, "as far as I can yet tell it. What end it will have is entirely up to you—but I would urge you very sincerely not to decide too quickly what you will make of me, for as I have advised you and you can surely see for yourself, there is very little meat on my bones.

"I judge from the patience which you have already shown me that I have the ability to amuse you, and if this poor tale of my own sorry adventure can capture your attention I have no doubt at all that you would love the story of the unlicensed moneylender Zainul Zub and the ten temple whores, and would certainly find much to interest you in a well-crafted account of how the daughter of Kartar Var fared in the harem of the King of the Ghouls.

"After all, there is surely no intelligence in all this great wide world, however monstrous, which does not love a well-told tale—and though I must confess that I have never before had the ambition to live among the lazarous demons, I really do believe that I could get used to it . . . if you will only give me the chance . . . "

THE UNLUCKIEST THIEF

In Capracola, which is on the northern rim of the Maundering Marshes, the land lies low and the climate is warm and moist. The region is a perfect home for fevers of every kind, and the people who live there recognise two gods opposed in every way: one who is handsome and honest, and who brings good health to those who please him; and one who is ugly and deceitful, who curses those he hates with vile disease. The dutiful and orthodox majority of men worship the former god, and pray hopefully for his protection, but they shelter in their midst a heretic few who see the world differently. Fevers, as everyone knows, can excite as well as kill, and wherever there are fevers there are men who are avid to live more vivid lives, reckless of destruction; such men are readily turned to the fearsome carnivals which are the clandestine rites of the Lord of All Fevers. So it is that in Capracola there are men who think themselves men of quality, but who turn nevertheless to the worship of that unclean demon of ague and hot excitement.

During one long, hot summer when Capracola was seared by more than the usual number of epidemics, there was built in a secret glade of one of the region's most noisome swamps a gaudy temple to the ugliest among the gods. A master mason was inspired to hew from glossy soapstone an image of his patron, which rivalled in misshapeliness the worst of all the gargoyles on the gaudy temples of the distant capital. In order to provide a worthy image of the bloated cyclopean eye of the Emperor of Decay the legendary jeweller Chiravar—the greatest goldsmith and gewgaw-polisher in the nation—was seduced into the secret cult, and fully half the wealth of its members was given to purchase a massive piece of amber, which Chiravar carved and smoothed to the limit of his artistry.

Chiravar was ever a boastful man, who dearly loved to see his work displayed, and once the eye was in place he became very ardent in the cause of seeking converts to his odious god, in order that the greatest feat of his artistry could be more widely appreciated. Alas, rumours of the wondrous nature of the Amber Eye were so profligately put about by its maker that they soon attracted the attention of a clever jewel-thief and devout lover of beautiful things, who went by the name of Umbalila. It immediately became Umbalila's dearest ambition to steal the gargantuan gem from the secret temple, and sell it for a handsome price in some far-distant city.

Umbalila knew full well that this robbery would be the most dangerous he had ever planned, but he reckoned that the ruination of a monstrous idol would surely be deemed a very virtuous act by the god who was worshipped by the majority of his fellows. Were he successful, he reasoned, he would not only be rich for the remainder of this life, but might legitimately hope to be forgiven the many petty sins which a man of his profession was unfortunately compelled to commit. He knew that the victims of his crime would pursue him vengefully to the very limit of their abilities, but he also knew that a company devoted to illicit worship could hardly go crying to a magistrate to complain about the desecration of their idol, and thus he calculated that the risk was tolerable.

Emboldened by these arguments, Umbalila set out to make his way along the treacherous trails which led to the secret temple, following silently in the footsteps of an unwary idolater. Once arrived there, he hid himself away until darkness fell. By that time, the edifice was quite deserted. He crept furtively from his hiding-place, and went expeditiously to work with his chisel, and a solvent which would loosen the glue which fixed the huge amber eye in place.

The work was not easy, for the eye had been cleverly set in the stone face, but Umbalila was both patient and efficient in his labour. With great skill he disfigured the image of the god of disfigurement, and mutilated the cunningly-carved face of the emperor of all mutilation.

Within an hour the mighty gem was in his leather bag, and the rough-hewn face of the Visitor of Maladies was even more scarred and scratched and blemished than it had been before.

The delighted Umbalila rushed northwards into the night, intending to cross the foetid swamp before first light and reach the mouth of the pass which would take him through the mountains to the great cities of the fertile plain.

Before he had gone a mile along his chosen path, however, there became audible to Umbalila a soft but oddly alarming noise, which was like the sound of bubbling laughter. It came from no particular direction, but no matter how he accelerated his pace, he could not leave it behind.

Umbalila told himself that the noise was only marsh-gas gurgling in the stagnant pools, but no sooner had he come to that conclusion than the sound began to grow in volume. It was quickly amplified into a hoggish chuckling, which no one but a noodle could have mistaken for the rustling of wind in the treetops, or the chittering of insects in the grass. Umbalila, who was no noodle, realised that the god of corruption himself had witnessed the desecration of his idol, and had taken leave to be interested in the fate of its yellow eye.

Umbalila's heart was pounding in his chest, and his breath became difficult to draw, but he ran on and on, as fast as he possibly could. He splashed through muddy pools until he was smudged and daubed with slime and grime from the hair on his head to the space between his toes. Invigorated by sheer terror, he ran like a maniac or a man set on fire; but the laughter which chased him only grew, first into a guffaw, then into a bellow, and finally into a helpless howling which informed him that the god's scabby sides must be about to split and spill his festering guts upon the ground—if there were any ground in that mysterious world beside the world where the gods dwelt.

Umbalila's panting turned by degrees to sobbing, and when he stumbled into a patch of soft and clinging mire, which caught his booted feet and held them very stickily, he made no immediate shift to stir himself again. He decided that he had no alternative but to beg for mercy where he was, and he prayed for the eventual cessation of that ludicrous laughter.

By degrees, the laughter ebbed away, until the voice which had blasted his ears with it was capable of ordinary speech.

"Oh, Umbalila!" said the invisible god of pestilence and plague. "Thou art a sad and sorry sneak, who hast chosen a very peculiar way to worship me."

It had been no part of the thief's intention ever to worship the god whose temple he had raided, but Umbalila was not about to confess this fact to the deity himself, if that deity were pleased to think otherwise. He had some suspicion of how sensitive the gods might be about such matters as the homage they desired.

"I have served thee far better than that ridiculous poseur Chiravar," answered Umbalila, cunningly, "for he, in his vanity, sought to give thine idol an unnaturally beautiful eye, while I have given it instead a ghastly blindness, which surely does more justice to the representation of a god of debility and imperfection."

"Why else would I laugh?" asked the hoarse and wheezing voice. "I am a merry god, unlike my stern counterpart. I have always loved a macabre jest, and there is only one thing which could amuse me more than to see my idol blinded by a cocksure thief."

"And what is that?" asked Umbalila, who disliked to be offered riddles, even by a god.

"To see the thief entrapped by his hurry to escape, of course," replied the god. "To see the silly fellow's feet securely gripped by a slimy bog, so that he may be drawn most glutinously down into its depths, until he drowns very soggily in wet black filth."

While this answer echoed in his ears, the unlucky thief began to struggle agitatedly, regretting that he had not thought better of pausing in his flight at this particular place. But the god's words had captured the truth of the situation. He had by now sunk knee-deep into the mire, and was sinking still. The more of him was beneath the surface for the mire to grip the more eagerly it clutched him, and he was sinking faster by the second.

"Thou must save me," cried Umbalila to the invisible presence, "or else thy gorgeous eye will be lost forever, never to be seen again by the worshipful eyes of men."

"But thou hast told me how horrid its loveliness must seem to my own jaundiced eye," replied the voice of the god, "and thou little knowest how right thou art in that matter. In any case, I count the swamp my faithful friend, for it is host to countless splendid fevers, and I could not be so mean as to deprive it of its hapless prey—for I am a god of generosity, as well as jests."

"It seems to me," replied Umbalila, who was by now submerged to the level of his waist, "that thy jests are lacking in authentic humour—and I have seen no evidence at all of thy so-called generosity."

"I am sorely wounded by thy bitterness," answered the voice, with an odd thrill of delight. "Thou cuttest me to the quick, indeed thou dost! And in return, I shall be very pleased indeed to grant thee one last boon before thou chokest on clammy mud. Canst thou guess what it will be?"

"I wish I could," said Umbalila, whose head and shoulders only were now above the surface of the cold and viscous pool. "But I fear that I have not the time to receive it, let alone to guess it."

"Do not be dismayed," said the voice, "for I am a god, and have it in my power to make a single second last for an apparent eternity. I will do that if thou wilt only beg me to, so that you may have all the time you need to think and feel and say whatever is in your mind."

Umbalila saw that the time which remained to him was short indeed, for the bog was very hungry to devour him, and so he did not hesitate at all before crying out: "That will be boon enough for me, if thou wouldst be good enough to oblige me in it—but I bid thee to hurry up, for I am sorely in need of some delay."

No sooner had Umbalila spoken than he ceased to sink, with his head still safely above the noisome surface of the glutinous mire. It did not take him long, however, to realise that this was not the most desirable position in which to spend eternity.

"Perhaps," he ventured, "thou wouldst grant me a further boon?" He was not entirely certain that the suggestion would be kindly received, for he had heard rumours of the impatience of gods whose generosity had been tested too far. But it seemed that the Lord of All Fevers was indeed a good-humoured sort, for the laugh which answered him was by no means derisory.

"Fear not, little thief," chuckled the god. "The boon I had planned to grant thee is but half-delivered, and the stopping of time is only the first and lesser part of the whole. I permitted the interruption of thy destiny merely in order to enable thee more fully to enjoy a far greater gift—for what, in my infinite generosity, I have decided to do for my worshipful thief is to let him look upon my real and actual eye, so that he may see how poor a thing he stole."

And then, displayed before the helpless Umbalila—who now discovered that the freezing of time would no longer let him speak, or turn his head, or close his eyes—there appeared the actual countenance of the loathsome god whose idol he had spoiled. He saw that the ugliness of the real face was a million times as horrid as any image which might be carved by an earthly sculptor, and realised that he was doomed to look into that dreadful cyclopean eye until the Emperor of Decay consented to let time and nature take their murderous course.

It would make no sense to say that the interval lasted for a thousand years, or a million. No time at all elapsed—and yet, for Umbalila, it was an eternity.

Even the most ardent and feverish worshipper of the Visitor of Maladies would have found the experience unbearable, but Umbalila had ever been a devout lover of beautiful things, and he knew better than any man alive what an antithesis of beauty was paraded before him.

And whether the experience was unbearable or not, Umbalila had no alternative but to bear it.

There was opportunity enough, when the Lord of All Fevers allowed the stream of time to flow again, for Umbalila to utter a single scream of terror and madness, which echoed very eerily in the humid wilderness of Capracola. There was opportunity too for the god of plague and pestilence to let loose a gale of lusty laughter, whose echoes filled the desolation of his own eternal world. Both of which circumstances go to prove how very dearly the ugliest of all the gods loves his little jests.

It merely remains to add that of all those who have heard this story, none has ever doubted that it is competently titled. Umbalila was certainly the unluckiest thief who ever lived . . . and, eventually, died.

THE LIGHT OF ACHERNAR

As the Earth neared its end and the sun grew weary, the baleful light of stars more virile and virulent shone ever more brightly upon the southern continent of Zothique. Among these fiery potentates, which no longer waited for sunset before displaying themselves in the purple sky, none blazed more keenly than vile Achernar, whose flagitious rays visited plague after plague upon beleaguered Zothique. The Silver Death, which devastated the mighty cities of Tasuun and Yoros and slew the torturers who followed their vocation in Uccastrog, was neither the least nor the last of these.

The astrologers who had foreseen the advent of the Silver Death and mapped its devastation had anticipated that the contagion would, in time, be removed by the etheric winds to other worlds. No sooner had their prophecies been vindicated, however, than they became busy with further divinations, eager to know what malefice would next be visited upon Zothique by the uncanny radiance of Achernar. None laboured harder in this regard than Giraiazal, who had been fortunate enough to be exiled to the isle of Cyntrom a year before the Silver Death laid waste to Yoros.

Cyntrom had long paid tribute to the kings of Yoros, and was regarded by them as a useful place of exile for nobles and magicians whose presence had become inconvenient. Its convenience in this regard was partly determined by its relative remoteness and small population—which numbered less than twenty thousand—and partly by the violent tendencies of the native families, who could always be trusted to make sure that any exiles who threatened to make further trouble in Yoros would wind up dead in alleyways, on payment of a very reasonable fee.

As a scholarly man who counted Fate his one and only mistress, Giraiazal would not have been inclined to make trouble for his former masters even if they had survived. He was quite content to be installed in a lonely turret in the largest edifice in Cyntrom Port, from which he could make his observations of the changing constellations and calculate their influence on the fortunes of his consultants. The edifice in question was still known as the palace, although a thousand years had passed since the last king of Cyntrom had been deposed and replaced by a baron who lorded it over the islanders in the name of Yoros. Giraiazal was not among those who hailed the destruction of Yoros by the Silver Death as a blessing, but when the heads of the oldest and most prolific families of Cyntrom, Orlu and Viragan, consulted him as to whether the time was ripe for them to obtain control of their own political destiny he was glad to confirm that the baron had outlived the favour of the stars as well as his utility.

There was much that Giraiazal might have said which might have tempered the revolutionary zeal of his clients, but he had learned enough from his condemnation to exile to be convinced that a popular prophet ought to be generous in his disposition of the good news and miserly in hoarding the bad. He had also taken note of the mischance which had deflected the ship carrying Fulbra, the young king of Yoros, to Uccastrog instead of Cyntrom, and was prepared to hope that his might be a sign that the light of Achernar was better disposed towards Cyntrom than towards Yoros. Had the fleeing Fulbra arrived at his intended destination, he would have brought the Silver Death with him, but he had instead been washed ashore on the Isle of the Torturers, thus ensuring that one plague would exterminate another.

The combined forces of the former rivals Orlu and Viragan had little difficulty in slaughtering the defenders of the palace. The baron was beheaded in the plaza which extended from the palace gate to the principal quays of the harbour. In order to reduce the likelihood of a schism in their newly consolidated ranks, the two conquerors decided that they would be content to be reckoned merchant princes of equal rank, and that they would establish as king whoever proved to be the proper heir to the crown that had been abolished a thousand years before—provided always that the person in question would be prepared to follow the good advice of his councillors.

Having consulted the mouldering records stored in a corner of the palace's empty wine-cellar, Giraiazal concluded that the true heir to

Cyntrom's throne was the elder of two brothers resident in a decaying manse on a headland named Lamri, on the southern shore of the island. Orlu and Viragan were glad to find that the heir in question, Lysariel, was a handsome but conspicuously innocent and somewhat unsteady youth of nineteen. He seemed to them to be the ideal puppet, and they immediately established him in the palace, along with his younger brother, the seventeen year old Manazzoryn. Manazzoryn was not as handsome as his brother,and was only marginally his superior in cunning and enterprise.

King Lysariel was as tractable as his discoverers had hoped, issuing any and all decrees requested by his two guardian princes. The new aristocrats found that the habits formed in the days when they were reckoned notorious pirates were by no means out of keeping with the etiquette appropriate to the conduct of merchant princes, and their wealth increased by leaps and bounds. Orlu and Viragan were careful to make sure that the king and his brother received a commission sufficient to feed their own appetites for grandeur and glory, but Lysariel and Manazzoryn were not exceptionally greedy; as boys on the threshold of manhood they were easily distracted from mere avarice by the other rewards of royal status. For the first year of Lysariel's kingship the brothers hurled themselves into a career of dissipation, exhausting themselves daily with meat and sweetmeats, wine and opium, and the delights of love.

Although the two merchant princes kept fast to their agreement that neither would make any attempt to seize power on his own behalf, lest the ensuing conflict destroy them both, they were perfectly prepared to indulge in subtler competition for lesser advantages. Giraiazal was persuaded to advise the king and his brother that they ought to marry, in order to secure their dynasty, and that the best brides in Cyntrom were to be founded in the houses of their loyal merchant princes: Calia, the daughter of Orlu, and Zintrah, the daughter of Viragan.

Calia was undoubtedly the more beautiful of these two, but she had a certain hardness about her, while Zintrah was more sensitive and more seductive. It was not clear which of the two might be the most desirable—nor was it clear which of the brothers might be the better husband, if the obvious advantage of Lysariel's crown were set aside. After a period of confusion, when it seemed that either youth might wed either maid, the issue was finally resolved according to what seemed to Orlu and Giraiazal, if not to Viragan, to be the most reasonable configuration. Lysariel was engaged to be married to Calia, and Manazzoryn to Zintrah.

It so happened that Giraiazal's patient researches began to bear their most abundant fruit while the double wedding was in the planning. The astrologer was able to see, therefore, when he cast the horoscopes of the two royal couples, that the starshadow of Achernar lay very blackly across their future. Giraiazal was deeply disconcerted by this revelation, all the more so because he knew full well that the prospective husbands and fathers-in-law would react badly to the news of any supernatural impediment to the impending unions. Given that anyone who had disturbed the plans of Orlu and Viragan had always tended to suffer a fatal accident, even in the days when they had been mere shipmasters with a happy knack of picking up jetsam unwittingly or unwillingly abandoned by less fortunate captains, he thought that it might be best to keep his discoveries to himself.

"Who am I, after all, to speak out against the whim of my mistress Fate," Giraiazal murmured. "It would be silly to prove my astrological skill if the cost of that proof was my own imperilment. Better to make what preparations I can for my own protection."

Mercifully, the horoscopes in question were not without an element of hope. Although the nefandous fires of Achernar seemed avid to consume the founding members of the new royal house, one by one, the tale told by Fate was that the short and misfortunate reign of King Lysariel—whose latter phases were destined to be overlaid by the brief Regency of Manazzoryn—would be followed by the far longer reign of Lysariel's son, whose authority would not only outlast that of many self-appointed merchant princes but would also survive the blight which was destined to descend on Cyntrom in belated compensation for the negligence of the Silver Death.

Although the star-chart made no specific provision for Giraiazal the Astrologer, its humble reader knew perfectly well that the authority of a child-king could not endure without the sound advice of a prophetically-gifted vizier.

Giraiazal was not a man without heart, and he immediately began to search for magical devices which might help the royal brothers and their brides to mount some defence against the various evils that threatened them. He knew that what has once been written in the Book of Vergama cannot, in essence, be defied—but he knew, too, that a man who knows what Destiny has in store can employ palliatives against its worst effects and draw profit from its most piquant revelations.

For Calia, whose lovely flesh was destined to be afflicted with agues and lesions of an unusually drastic character, Giraiazal decided to provide a silver amulet. The stone set in its face was a crystal formed at the juncture of overlapping dimensions in which time flowed to very different rates, which had thus become a rich repository of endurance.

For Lysariel, whose worst trials would be afflicted upon him by debilitating delusions, Giraiazal settled upon a magnum of wine bottled in ancient Yethlyreom. The sealed bottle had survived the fall and ruination of Cincor's capital and its contents still had power to infuse their drinker with a kind of pride and zest that had long since vanished from the decrepit world.

For Manazzoryn, whose eventual penalty would be exacted in revenge for a reckless and horrible act, Giraiazal manufactured a girdle from hemp-plants which grew in the impact-crater of a meteorite strayed into the skies of Earth from some long-disintegrated galaxy. This had the power to dull moral sensation in its wearers, and to still the guilt which might otherwise feast on a sinner's heart.

For Zintrah, who would suffer the deaths of her husband, sister-in-law and brother-in-law before eventually giving up her own ghost, Giraiazal collected pollen from a rare species of mandrake. This ultrafine dust had the property, when breathed, of numbing pain and fostering dour courage in the face of disaster.

None of these wedding-gifts was easily come by, including the ones for which Giraiazal was solely responsible, but a magician fortunate enough to have skilled tradesmen at his beck and call is better placed to provision his science than most. Orlu was happy to lend the astrologer an expert agent to assist in negotiating the purchase of the amulet, while Viragan was equally glad to locate the magnum of wine on Giraiazal's behalf and assist in its acquisition.

When the astrologer presented his gifts to those he was commissioned to advise, he was discreet in summarising their properties. The accounts he gave of their power were deliberately vague, but to each recipient in turn he said: "This will be infinitely precious when the need arises; keep it safe until then, but be prepared to use it when I tell you that the time is ripe."

* * *

Following their marriage, Lysariel and Calia were deliriously happy for forty days and forty nights. For the first time, the young man became fully conscious of the fact that he was a king, entitled to do what only kings could do-and for this awareness, he had Calia to thank. He decided that he would have an image made of her extraordinary loveliness. He asked all his courtiers to nominate the greatest artist in Cyntrom, and after some discussion a consensus of sorts was reached, the laurel falling to a sculptor named Urbishek.

Lysariel immediately summoned the sculptor. "I want you to make a full-sized likeness of my wife," he said. "It must be no ordinary likeness, no common-or-garden statue. It must be made in the finest and most unusual material we can obtain, so that there will not be an image like it in the whole world."

Urbishek was delighted with this commission, and with the opportunity to make a statue that might become the stuff of legend, but he was not sure that he could find any material suitable for sculpture which had not already been put to use by the artists of past eras. It transpired, however, that Lysariel had his own ideas about this.

"When Manazzoryn and I were children," the king told the sculptor, "my beloved father told us of a peculiar coral which grows in a grotto etched into the southern shore of the isle, not far from our home in Lamri. It is uniquely prolific and very solid, but nevertheless pliable."

"Coral is not a good medium for sculpture," Urbishek replied, dubiously. "It may be carved into tiny effigies, but no one has ever made a full-sized human figure out of coral."

"That is why it is perfect for our purpose," Lysariel told him. "Perhaps it will require unparalleled ingenuity—but so much the better."

Urbishek remained reluctant. "I have heard rumour of this grotto," he said. "The coral is said to be uncommonly difficult to gather. The cave is deep and it has a bad reputation. Furthermore, it is thoroughly infested with vicious giant eels. No diver will venture into it."

"The divers will be well-paid for their trouble," Lysariel said. "Provided that the statue pleases me, you may name your own price, over and above the glory that will inevitably be attached to your name if you can make the most of your opportunity."

This was a temptation no artist could resist, and Urbishek agreed to make the statue. Lysariel gave the sculptor money to hire twelve best divers in Cyntrom; they were not entirely delighted by the opportunity to serve their lovely queen, but they did their work with such heroic determination that only six were killed and eaten by the monstrous eels before they had accumulated a mass of coral the colour of brass which Urbishek deemed sufficient.

On the very first day that she posed for the sculptor, however, Calia happened to take up a bunch of luscious grapes which her father Orlu had obtained by way of taxation from a ship which had strayed too close of Cyntrom while en route from Kalasperanza to Aztyrka. When she held the grapes above her head, opening her mouth to welcome the most pendulous, two hairy spiders fell from the bunch. One fell into her open mouth while the other landed on her left breast. Astonished, she swatted the one with her free hand while trying to spit out the other.

Neither attempt was successful. The spider at the queen's breast responded to the ill-treatment by biting her; the other refused to be expelled, and scrambled so deeply into her throat that she had no alternative but to swallow it. The shock caused her to faint and she was carried to her bed.

By the time Urbishek had summoned Lysariel and Lysariel had sent for Giraiazal, Calia was feverish and the breast which had been bitten had turned hard and brittle; the superficial flesh was already beginning to crack under pressure from within, and pus was leaking through the cracks. Giraiazal managed to wake her and force her to swallow a liberal dose of an emetic, but nothing showed within her vomit that might have been all or part of a spider.

"I fear, your majesty," said Giraiazal, "that those grapes were a curious vintage, and that their apparent succulence was a lure. You must bring the amulet I gave to your bride from her jewel-box and place it around her neck. Do not look for a rapid cure, I beg of you, for this poison will not be expelled in a day; it will take forty days at least. Pray that the amulet will give her the strength, in the meantime, to endure all that the poison will inflict."

Lysariel brought the amulet, and placed it around his wife's neck, laying the jewel between her breasts.

The queen's fever grew steadily worse through the evening and the night. She could not sleep because her body was constantly racked by violent paroxysms, and she had to be given copious draughts of water to compensate for the perspiration which poured from her skin.

The abscess in Calia's left breast continued to grow, and the cracks in her flesh continued to leak, but when the hardened tegument would not give way the soft tissues beneath the tumour were rent, and the pus was expelled into her gullet, from which it was expelled by a long serious of coughing-fits. The bowls in which her retchings were collected were inspected very carefully, but there was no sign therein of anything resembling the whole or any part of a spider.

By the time the next day dawned, Lysariel was convinced that his wife would die, and his unsteadiness of character immediately became apparent as he threw himself down, weeping and wailing prodigiously. Orlu came to see his daughter, and was equally distressed by her appearance, but he was made of sterner stuff than the king.

"How can I help to save her?" Orlu demanded of Giraiazal.

"If you could find the ship from which you extorted the tax," the astrologer replied, "and obtain the name of the cultivator of the grapes, you might be able to go Kalasperanza and seize him. If you were to tell him that you would destroy his lands, his crops and his entire family unless he could provide an effective remedy for the evil his produce has wrought, he might be able to produce an antidote. Pray, in the meantime, that Calia can endure until you can deliver some such remedy."

This was the kind of instruction that Orlu was well equipped to understand and follow. All of his ships set sail on the afternoon tide, and a dozen other vessels with them, lent by his fellows to assist him in his quest.

Lysariel soon recovered from his panic, but not from his despair. Twisted and tormented by grief and anguish, he summoned Urbishek—who had, of course, abandoned his work when the queen fell ill. "You must redouble your efforts," Lysariel told the sculptor. "You must complete the image lest this horrible sickness should obliterate her beauty, whether she survives it or not."

Urbishek did as he was told. Fortunately, the horrors which afflicted Calia's body did not immediately spread to her lovely face—but the abscess within her stony breast swelled again, and the infection spread by its first explosion caused secondary tumours to form in her belly and her right breast. The flesh overlaying her abdominal cavity hardened exactly as her breasts had hardened, but it remained sufficiently flexible not to crack in the same manner. The result of this failure was that the abscesses did not leak and came much faster to the point of bursting, which they did inwardly.

The resultant pus was expelled from both apertures of the queen's churning gut, but not so copiously as to leave no residues. These residues caused the surrounding tissues to suffer a necrosis whose blue-black colour was clearly visible through the queen's increasingly-translucent outer flesh, and the multitudinous worms which bred in the necrotic organs could also be seen wriggling beneath the skin as they migrated into her limbs. When they reached the limits of their exodus, in her hands and feet, their movements grew more urgent, as if they were seething in frustration.

Giraiazal had no alternative but to slice the palms of Calia's hands and the soles of her feet with razors, so that the worms might escape from her flesh. Like the pus which still spurted from her mouth and anus the worms were collected in bowls by servants, then killed by plunging them into boiling sulphur. Giraiazal had compresses made from cream and mustard, which were applied to Calia's glassy skin in the hope of easing its continuing transition, and they did indeed bring some relief to the beleaguered queen. On the fifth night of her illness she was able to take a little food, and even to obtain a little sleep.

"She is getting better!" the ever-excitable Lysariel cried, exultantly.

"The effect arises purely from relief of the symptoms, I fear," Giraiazal told him. "I have no cure for the underlying malady, and will not, unless and until brave Orlu returns successful from his quest. If he does not come soon, our only hope is that the queen can endure until the disease has run its full course."

From that moment on, however, Calia's fight for life was more evenly balanced. The abscesses and worms continued to grow and multiply, but the rate at which they were expelled came into balance with the rate of their formation, and the queen was able to take sufficient nourishment to fuel their reproduction without further depletion of her own inner being. That inner being had been so extensively ravaged as to bring her to the brink of extinction, but with the amulet's help she remained suspended there, barely alive but not yet dead, as five days extended to ten, and ten to twenty.

* * *

In the meantime, Urbishek continued to work on his statue. The coral Lysariel had chosen as his material was, as the king had promised, uncommonly lumpen and relatively easy to shape. Although he had to form each piece into a relatively small part of his statue, Urbishek fitted them together so cunningly that the seams were invisible.

The likeness slowly took shape: first the head, then the torso, then the arms, then the abdomen, and finally the legs.

It was as well that the sculptor had chosen this order of procedure, because Calia's own legs retained their form reasonably well, while her face eventually began to show the strain of her agony. Although her features never hardened as her breasts had done, never erupted in boils or blisters, and were never blurred by the writhing of multitudinous worms, they were rewrought nevertheless by the intensity of her torment.

By the dawn of the twenty-first day of her illness, Calia was no longer one of the most beautiful women in Cyntrom, and it seemed doubtful that she would ever recover the full bloom of her youth, even if she were to win her struggle for life.

When Urbishek's statue was complete, on the twenty-fifth day of Calia's distress, Lysariel thanked him, paid him and sent him away. The king immediately retired to one of the remotest apartments of the palace and took up residence here, placing the beautiful image in his new bedchamber.

He never came to his wife's bedside again.

Giraiazal continued to labour night and day to keep the queen alive, although he wondered more than once why he bothered, given that the day of her death was clearly marked in her horoscope. "It is my responsibility," he told himself, whenever his dedication weakened momentarily. "She is my queen. In any case, if I am to hope for favourable treatment by my own adamantine mistress, then I must prove myself to be her loyal servant. Given that I have been enlightened as to the destined day of sweet Calia's death, it is my evident duty to make certain that she survives until that day. Were I to neglect my work, she might die tomorrow, and the wrath of my mistress would be immeasurable."

In spite of all his skills, and notwithstanding the power of the amulet, Giraiazal might not have won the battle to bring the queen through the phases of her sickness had it not been for the further assistance of Zintrah and her husband Manazzoryn. When Lysariel returned to his distant apartment, seemingly content with a mere likeness of his wife, Zintrah was afraid for what might happen if ever she too were to fall ill, and she demanded reassurances from Manazzoryn that he would never treat her thus. Manazzoryn, being desperate to prove that he was a better man than the brother in whose shadow he had always lived, immediately began to criticise Lysariel as a weak man and a weak king. The younger brother stepped into the breach that the elder had vacated, and laboured alongside Giraiazal to provide the relief that his sister-in-law required. Whenever Manazzoryn retired from this labour to rest, Zintrah invariably took his place. By so doing, the two of them won the admiration of the entire court.

Gradually, these collective efforts were rewarded. No new abscesses formed in the queen's flesh, and those already established ceased to renew themselves. Calia's vomitings became less hectic, and she began to eat and drink more heartily. The cracked skin on her breasts began to fuse again, and she began to sleep for several hours at a time. Her sleep was racked by awful nightmares for a further ten days, but in the hour before daybreak on the thirty-eighth day of her illness, she opened her mouth to cry out in her sleep and a living spider emerged therefrom, huge, bloated and seemingly intoxicated.

Giraiazal brushed the creature to the stone-flagged floor and crushed it beneath his heel. After that, the queen slept and breathed more easily, and the lines etched by agony upon her face began to ease.

Manazzoryn and Zintrah were overcome with joy—they, unlike Giraiazal, did not know what still lay in store—but when they sent news to Lysariel he would not come. He sent word back that his wife had been quite well for a full thirteen days, and that he and she were exceedingly happy in their new apartment.

When the queen finally recovered full consciousness of herself, she was quick to ask where her husband and father were, Zintrah told her that they had both gone forth in search of remedies for her condition. It was not a lie which could be long maintained, but Giraiazal did not complain, thinking that that Calia might as well be allowed to maintain her illusions until Fate delivered her *coup de grace.*

On the afternoon of the fortieth day that had elapsed since she had suffered the spider-bite, Calia was found dead on the terrace beneath her bedroom window, having fallen therefrom and cracked her skull.

Even though the unlucky Calia had recovered all but a modest fraction of her former beauty, Lysariel had refused to return from his seclusion to see her. He was equally firm in his refusal to look at her corpse or even to acknowledge that Calia was dead. His beloved wife, he assured Giraiazal and Viragan, was with him still, as lovely as ever and beyond the reach of any conceivable corruption.

Those who wept longest and loudest at Calia's funeral, therefore, were

Zintrah and Manazzoryn—although Giraiazal condescended to shed a few fugitive tears. It was whispered among the common people that it was perhaps as well that Orlu had not returned from Kalasperanza, given that he was the kind of man who was wont to give expression to grief and wrath in a rather violent manner.

Three days after Calia's interment, however, Giraiazal was summoned to the king's new bedchamber. He found the king somewhat distraught and immediately asked him why, but Lysariel would not speak to him in the room where the coral statue stood and drew the astrologer out on to a balcony overlooking the plaza and the harbour. Although the sun had not yet set a dozen stars shone ominously bright in the evening sky, and Achernar was the most vivid of them all.

"Faithful Giraiazal," the king said, in a hoarse whisper, "I am in dire need of magical assistance. I want you to procure a love potion, for I fear that my wife no longer loves me as she should."

"What makes you think so, your majesty?" Giraiazal inquired, as solicitously as he could.

"There is a new hardness in her gaze, Giraiazal," the king replied. "For three days now she has looked at me as if I had disappointed or neglected her. I swear that it is not so, and I have begged her to explain, but she continues to show me the same expression. Her passion is fading, Giraiazal, and I need to reignite it. I need an aphrodisiac, and you are the only man who can obtain it. Help me, I beg of you."

"I fear that your wife might not condescend to drink such a potion were I able to devise one," Giraiazal replied. "Happily, there is another way to approach the problem. You must send down to the cellars for the wine of Yethlyreom that was my wedding-present to you. You need only take a sip to be restored in the sight of your beloved to glorious manhood. If ever she should look askance at you again, merely take another sip, and the accusation will vanish from her eye."

Lysariel seemed unsure as to whether this advice was credible, but Giraiazal persuaded him that there could be no harm in trying, and he sent for the wine of ancient Yethlyreom. He removed the cork, poured the merest drop into a goblet and raised it to his lips.

No sooner had the liquor touched his tongue than the king was filled with a remarkable self-confidence. He whirled around to face the likeness of his dead wife, and was immediately wreathed in smiles.

"How could I have doubted you, good Giraiazal!" he said, warmly.

"There is no greater magician in all Zothique! You have the gratitude of a great king—and I do not need to tell you how precious a gift that is."

"Indeed not, sire," murmured Giraiazal, as he made his exit. He returned immediately to his lofty attic, where he set about examining the sky. His suspicions were not unfounded; there was a new comet in the constellation of the scorpion, and a nebula which had never been visible before had begun to shroud the red star Apollyon. New possibilities had arisen which must be figured into the charts that would some day be bound into the Book of Vergama. Nothing that he had already divined could be altered, but new and disturbing detail could now be discerned within the pattern.

The next day, Manazzoryn came to see the astrologer, in company with his father-in-law Viragan. "The king is irredeemably mad, Giraiazal," said Manazzoryn, although there was something in his voice which suggested that the words had been suggested to him by another. "He is no longer fit to reign, and needs to be put away for his own good. Viragan has offered to give him asylum in his own house, and I am ready to assume the duties of regent."

"Your concern does you credit, sire," the astrologer assured him, "but it is possible that the king will soon recover from this unhinged state of mind into which he has been cast by grief. In any case, it might be unwise to take such a decision in the absence of one of the nation's two merchant princes. Perhaps we should allow forty days to pass before taking precipitate action, in order to give the king every chance to come to his senses and to allow Orlu time to return from his errand of mercy."

Manazzoryn hesitated for a moment, then nodded his head. He was too young to have learned patience, but was under the erroneous impression that he had forty years and more still to live, and thought that forty days was a trivial sacrifice.

Viragan was quick to agree with his son-in-law, but he had a rider of his own to add to the agreement. "It seems to me," he said, "that our good and noble king must have been the victim of vile sorcery. If, indeed, it becomes necessary to strip him of his crown, it would be as well if we could find and punish the guilty party, so that the minds of the people might be set at rest. Otherwise, there would probably be loose talk, and perhaps some anxious disagreement as to the wisdom and justice of the action."

"That is an astute observation," Giraiazal admitted. "Do you have any theory as to who might have visited this atrocious curse upon our beloved ruler?"

"Is it not obvious?" said Viragan. "Who else but Urbishek, the forger of that foul homunculus which lured Lysariel from the sickbed of his dear wife?"

"It must be true," agreed Manazzoryn. "Why else would my brother, who had formerly been the most devoted of husbands, have deserted his wife in her hour of greatest need, refusing even to attend her funeral?"

"You had better leave it to me to make inquiries," Giraiazal told them. "If Urbishek is as powerful and ingenious a sorcerer as you suppose, it would be direly dangerous for anyone unaccomplished in magic to investigate his nefarious activities."

* * *

Giraiazal did indeed make careful inquiries regarding the sculptor Urbishek and the mysterious grotto which had supplied the coral from which the likeness of Calia had been made. Of Urbishek he heard nothing but good, even from rival artists who considered him their superior. Everyone who knew him well agreed that he had no ambitions beyond the aesthetic, but that he would venture anything for art's sake.

What was said of the grotto, however, was rather more interesting. Had Giraiazal been born in Cyntrom he would doubtless have heard the tales before, but he had arrived only a year before the fall of Yoros and had not taken the trouble to acquaint himself with local folklore. Now, he began to regret the fact that he had taken no steps to repair that omission when Lysariel had first entered into negotiations with Urbishek.

The divers who had survived the process of extracting the coral on Urbishek's behalf waxed very eloquent on the subject of the bad reputation which the reluctant sculptor had mentioned. They were unanimous in declaring that the grotto was no natural sea-cave; in their expert opinion, it gave every indication of having been hollowed out with considerable deliberation, and not by human hands.

The divers' spokesman told Giraiazal that the deep trenches which lay some way off the southern shore of Cyntrom were well-known to be the habitat of monstrous burrowing creatures which had come from outside the Earth. Perhaps, he suggested, many such species were making such expeditionary forays, intending to await the extinction of humankind, the further diminution of the sun and the final darkening of the sky before claiming the ice-roofed empire of the oceans for their exclusive property.

At any rate, the unusual coral was probably the unnatural excrescence of parasites which had travelled with these patient monsters from their own place.

"It is my belief," the diver concluded, "that while Lysariel and Manazzoryn were living in seclusion on the wild southern shore, they fell under the influence of the diabolical intelligence innate within the coral. The king was probably commanded to give it a form in which it might walk the land, thus enjoying a measure of freedom while the opportunity still remained."

When Giraiazal suggested that this opinion might sound a trifle treasonous to a less educated ear than his own, all the divers were quick to assure him that they intended no criticism of the king. "Besides," their spokesman said, "there is no proof that the coral is actively evil, even though the grotto in which it was formed provides harbour to some of the largest and most aggressive eels it has ever been my misfortune to encounter."

With these speculations in mind, Giraiazal went to see the king again, intending to take advantage of Lysariel's infallibly good mood to make a closer inspection of the statue.

At first the astrologer could see no clear evidence that the statue was anything but what it seemed to be, but the longer he looked at it the more convinced he became that there was an exceptional hardness in its opaque gaze, and he was possessed by the strangest feeling that he had somehow failed in his responsbility to the person whose image was represented there. By this time, seventeen of the forty days which Giraiazal had requested of Manazzoryn had elapsed, and the magnum from Yethlyreom was half-empty.

After further consultation of the patterns emergent within the ominous sky, the astrologer returned to Viragan and informed him that he had bound the sorcerer Urbishek with powerful spells, and that it was perfectly safe for Viragan to seize and imprison him. "While I am safe and well," he told the merchant prince, "you have nothing to fear from my rivals in magic. You may torture Urbishek as extensively as you may desire, and if the whim takes you while so amusing yourself to obtain a confession of his foul crimes, by all means do so—but I implore you to hold it confidential while I make further enquiries as to the possibility of lifting the curse that has been put upon the king."

Viragan agreed to this, and had the sculptor seized. While the merchant prince was engaged in the leisurely business of shaping the sorcerer's confession, the astrologer busied himself with the next phase of the plan which his mistress had revealed to him in the horoscopes he had cast before the royal weddings.

Giraiazal went secretly to Zintrah, and pleaded for her assistance in winning Lysariel back from his sinister captor. "Had I only known earlier what kind of material this coral is," he told her, plaintively, "I might even have saved Calia. So distressed was I by her illness that I paid no attention to anything else. Had her husband been by her side when she emerged from her ordeal, he would surely have kept close enough watch over her to prevent her from falling from the balcony. It is all my fault, and if Manazzoryn finds out he will probably have me beheaded. You are the only one who might be able to help me, and the only one who might be able to help poor Lysariel."

"What can I possibly do?" she asked.

"He must, at all costs, be distracted from his obsession. I would not ask it of you if I were not desperate, but I am perfectly certain that there is no one else with sufficient natural charm combined with with such abundant intelligence. If there is any merely human being equal to the task, you are the one—but it will require considerable patience and great courage, for our adversary is more than human, and also worse."

"No one else with sufficient charm and intelligence?" Zintrah echoed, pensively.

"No one," Giraiazal assured her. "This is the supreme test of human strength of character, and the woman who can do it deserves to be celebrated in history and legend."

"Calia was always my dearest friend," Zintrah declared, bravely. "We were sisters in spirit even before we married brothers. I owe it to her to try. But I shall not tell Manazzoryn, in case I should fail. He would blame me then, for being too weak to save his beloved brother."

"That is very wise," said Giraiazal. "This shall be our quest and our secret. Together, we shall prevail."

From that day forward, Zintrah visited her brother-in-law every day, sometimes in the company of Giraiazal and sometimes alone. At first, Lysariel did not seem pleased to see either of them, but Giraiazal took him aside and told him that he ought to make an effort for the sake of his wife, whose closest friend Zintrah had been since infancy. After that, the king took a sip of the wine of Yethlyreom every time Zintrah appeared, and seemed to draw therefrom the strength to be moderately merry and full of life.

While Zintrah distracted the king, Giraiazal paid close attention to the statue, studying its contours with the utmost care. He soon became convinced that the seams which Urbishek had concealed so cleverly were, in fact, no longer there at all, and that the coral was now fused into a single mass whose colour made it seem like a casting in brass.

He noticed, too, that the statue had changed its position by minuscule degrees since it had first been assembled, having raised its arms a little and moved its legs apart as if to initiate a walking movement. Its features had softened slightly—all except the eyes, which were as hard as adamant and feverish with some emotion whose measure Giraiazal could not quite identify.

* * *

When the forty days agreed upon had passed, Manazzoryn and Viragan came to Giraiazal again. "I fear the worst," said Manazzoryn. "My wife assures me that my brother has begun to show some improvement, but I cannot see it. Moreover, we now have firm proof of his enchantment. My father-in-law has secured a confession which testifies to an astonishing depth and breadth of depravity on the part of the sorcerer Urbishek. We should not cease our attempts to save my brother's sanity, but for his own sake he must be separated from that terrible statue. Viragan has kindly renewed his offer of safe asylum, and I am still ready to do my duty as my brother's regent."

"Will you not give me a little more time?" Giraiazal asked, knowing full well what the answer would be. "I admit that progress has been slow but I think I might still succeed, if only I can be granted sufficient time. Orlu may return from Kalasperanza any day now."

"We are exceedingly grateful for your efforts," Viragan told the astrologer, "but the time has come to act. As for poor Orlu, I fear that his ships must have gone into dangerous waters in search of a remedy for his daughter's distress and suffered some catastrophe. If they do not return it will be a terrible loss to Cyntrom, but the possibility makes it all the more imperative that we offer firm proof to the world that Cyntrom remains strong, and has a ruler with his wits about him."

"I bow to your better judgment," Giraiazal said, graciously. "Take Lysariel away, if you must—but do so gently, I beg of you, for his sister-in-law is with him. Loyal Zintrah has given as much time and care to the king these last twenty days as you, faithful Manazzoryn, gave to the queen in her darkest hours."

"I will be gentle, for my daughter's sake," Viragan promised—and would doubtless have kept his promise, had he not arrived as Lysariel lifted the magnum to his lips for the final time, hoping to find a last drop which simply was not there.

Denied that comfort, the king lashed out in rage and pain at those whose sought to help him, proclaiming wildly that he would not be separated from his beloved, and that no prison had been built which could keep him apart from the most beautiful and most desirable woman in all the world. He had to be dragged screaming from the apartment and from the palace, disconcerting everyone who saw him. The unease caused by this unwelcome spectacle was, however, considerably quieted when the notorious sorcerer Urbishek was burned alive in the plaza that very same night, with half the population of the port looking on and applauding.

It was not until the following day that Viragan sent his men back to Lysariel's apartment with orders to smash the coral statue and throw the pieces into the sea. It had not occurred to the prince that there was any considerable hurry, and he felt that it would have been a pity to deny his most loyal servants the chance to enjoy the public execution. He had cause to regret his complacency when the men returned to his house in some distress with the news that the statue had disappeared.

Viragan immediately summoned Giraiazal and demanded to know what had become of the statue, but Giraiazal confessed that he was none the wiser. The two of them went together to Manazzoryn, but he had no more idea than they what might have become of the likeness of Calia.

"It must have been stolen by thieves," Viragan suggested. "When I find them, I'll give them cause to regret their temerity."

"I am not so sure," said Manazzoryn. "My wife Zintrah was frightened when I told her that the statue had gone. It appears that she has visited my brother more than once in the hope of redeeming his distress, and she formed the impression that the image had lately acquired the power of independent movement. Is that possible, Giraiazal?"

"Perhaps it is," Giraiazal conceded. "I have the greatest respect for Zintrah's intelligence and judgment and the divers who harvested the coral on Urbishek's behalf have being telling anyone who will listen that it is animated by an alien intelligence that was always intent on finding a road to freedom. If the statue was merely tired of serving as an object of adoration for a besotted madman, then its animation would be no cause for alarm. If, on the other hand, it still relished its role, that would be a different matter. Poor Lysariel is well enough guarded against any ordinary attempt to release him or to do him harm, but who can tell what a living statue might be able to accomplish?"

Viragan frowned when he heard this, but his expression cleared again soon enough. Knowing as he did the traditions and tendencies of his countrymen, he still believed that the statue had been stolen.

Manazzoryn was by no means so sure. "Who can tell what mission an animated image might have in mind?" he mused. "If it has absorbed the spirit of poor dead Calia, a reunion with its mad lover might not be the first object in its regretful mind."

As he spoke, the king's brother plucked nervously at his chemise, and it fell open at the front. Giraiazal observed that the girdle Manazzoryn had received as a wedding-present was tightly wound about his waist, disposed in such a manner that it would usually be invisible beneath his clothing.

How long, the astrologer wondered, had Manazzoryn been wearing the girdle? What action had put it in the young man's mind that he might need its protection?

"Whatever the situation is," Giraiazal said, by way of conclusion, "it is obvious that we ought to locate the statue if we can. If thieves have stolen it, we must recover it, but if it has indeed contrived to animate itself, we must be circumspect. Although it might eventually become necessary to publicize the object's loss and offer a reward for its return, it might be prudent in the shorter term to commission trusted men to make discreet enquiries."

"I will do that," said Viragan. "My men are very discreet, for they know that they might lose their tongues if they were not."

Viragan was presumably correct in his estimation of the integrity of his servants, but enquiries inevitably generate a momentum of their own. Within five days the news was all around the island that the statue of Calia forged out of ensorcelled coral by the black magician Urbishek had come to life and gone to ground, with the undoubted intention of planning mischief. By the time that Manazzoryn issued a royal proclamation to the effect that the statue had been stolen and that a lavish reward was offered for information leading to its recovery, the move was widely seen as a belated attempt to cover up the truth.

Giraiazal apologised profusely for his error, and was forgiven; Manazzoryn and Viragan were both intelligent enough to know that if only the statue had been found during those five days the problem would never have developed. In any case, it did not seem that the rumours could do them any harm, and Viragan knew how valuable it was to a newly-ensconced regent to have the taverns and marketplaces preoccupied by harmless gossip of matters supernatural rather than the discussion of practical politics.

As time went by the rumours regarding the statue grew more fanciful, as rumours invariably do. The idea that immediately occurred to Manazzoryn, that the force animating the missing likeness might be the unquiet spirit of dead Calia, was reproduced again and again. The notion that the queen had been recalled from beyond the grave by the power of her husband's love had an intrinsic melodramatic appeal, as did the fancy that the separation of the two lovers had driven the entrapped spirit to such distraction that it had contrived to vivify the coral. The supposition that the ensouled work of art was now wandering the island's interior in search of her lost love exerted such an influence on the popular imagination that sightings of the statue were soon reported in some profusion from the farmlands inland of the port, each alleged witness asserting that the statue seemed to be searching for something, weeping as it went.

On the thirtieth day of his regency Manazzoryn summoned Giraiazal to ask him again whether it was possible that these speculations were true, and that the spirit Calia really had returned from the afterlife.

"I have certainly heard tell of statues rendered ambulatory by such questing spirits," Giraiazal admitted, "and love is, in essence, a supernatural force—all the more so when it is allied with conspicuous insanity. Unless and until I can communicate with the entity in question, however, I am unable to determine whether some kind of larva has taken possession of it-and, if so, exactly what kind it might be."

"Can the spirit be dispossessed?" Manazzoryn asked. As he spoke, his right hand slipped unthinkingly inside his chemise, the fingers reaching out as if to touch the girdle that he secretly wore beneath.

"Almost certainly," said Giraiazal, "but not, I fear, until it has been conclusively identified and squarely confronted. The wisdom of lore and legend instructs us that an exorcist must know the name of the spirit he seeks to banish and must do his work at close quarters. While the image remains in hiding, all that we can sensibly do is to keep searching for it."

On the following day, Manazzoryn doubled the reward offered for information leading to the recovery of the statue.

On the day after that, Zintrah announced that she was with child.

This latter news was cause for considerable celebration throughout Cyntrom. Although Manazzoryn was only a regent he was the king's brother, so his first-born son would be heir presumptive to the throne. Because it seemed highly unlikely that the widowed Lysariel would ever be able to sire an heir apparent, Zintrah's child would one day be king, provided only that it was a boy.

"Will my child be a son?" Zintrah asked Giraiazal, anxiously, when he had confirmed her pregnancy and made an estimate of the child's most likely day of birth.

"He will indeed," replied the astrologer, who had already compiled a hypothetical horoscope based on the most likely day of the child's delivery.

"Will he be as handsome as his father?" Zintrah demanded. "Will he be king of Cyntrom? Will he be one of those rare and lucky men who live long and prosper?"

"All the signs that presently bear upon the question assure me that he will be all of that and more," Giraiazal told her, "but I shall be able to make a more accurate and far more detailed calculation when I know the precise hour of his birth."

* * *

Viragan immediately made plans to host a lavish feast in celebration of his daughter's good fortune, and set them in train. For thirty days his ships were active as never before, sailing in every direction in pursuit of rich cargoes—including a few that were eventually bought with honest coin, out of the necessity for haste.

For his part, Manazzoryn gave his father-in-law free use of the palace, its apartments and its servants, so that the magnificence of the occasion would not be constrained by the narrower confines of Viragan's own house. The ceilings were bleached, the marble floors repaired and polished and the wall-hangings renewed with fine and elaborate fabrics. Jugglers and fire-eaters were hired, dwarfs and dancers recruited, and every musician on the island was ordered to tune his instrument to the best of his ability. A huge supply of giant lobsters was laid in, and birds of gaudy plumage collected for the roasting.

These elaborate preparations were not in vain. The feast was undoubtedly the most fabulous ever celebrated in Cyntrom, and was declared to be a great success by everyone—except, presumably, the two men-at-arms who drew black chips in the lottery held to determine who would stand guard on Lysariel's cell. When the rest of Viragan's servants returned home shortly after dawn they found these two unfortunates lying dead, their necks cleanly broken. One man's half-pike was missing and the other had not a trace of blood upon its blade. The lock on the door had been shattered, and Lysariel had vanished.

The island's rumour-mongers, whose narrative skills had been honed to perfection by their recent practice, went to work with a will. The tale was told all over the island within a matter of hours that Calia had returned to reclaim her lost lover, and had borne him triumphantly away. For seven days different accounts competed for the privilege of specifying where the coral bride might have taken her groom, but when no sight or sign of the couple was found the prevailing opinion took hold that she had carried him first to lonely Lamri, and then into the tempestuous sea, so that they might set up home as merfolk in the eel-infested grotto from whose walls the queen's new body had been hewn.

This tale might have attained sufficient authority to become the stuff of legend had it not been for the fact that Lysariel returned to his palace forty days after his disappearance, quite alone.

No one tried to stop the king as he walked through the streets of the port, partly because the gleam in his eye put all who encountered him in mind of the wicked glare of Achernar and partly because there was a half-pike with a razor-sharp blade clutched tightly in his two hands. He said not a word until he was within the palace gate, the guards posted there having stood aside to let him through on the grounds that he was, after all, the king. Once he had gained admittance to the newly-decorated corridors, however, he began to run in the direction of the throne-room, crying out at the top of his voice.

The word he cried was: "Murderer!"

It happened that the regent was meeting with his councillors at the time, and it was not at all clear when Lysariel burst into the throne-room exactly who the target of his accusation might be. Although the majority of the councillors appointed by the new merchant princes had almost contrived to forget that they had ever been anything else, the sight of a madman wielding a half-pike was exactly the kind of trigger required to remind them that there was not one among their company whose hands were entirely clean. So far as the one-time pirates knew, the only men in the room who had never done anything that might be regarded, if only technically, as murder, were Manazzoryn and Giraiazal.

It was doubtless for this reason that Cyntrom's ministers scattered in every possible direction when Lysariel made his dramatic entrance, leaving a clear path between the mad king and the throne on which his younger brother sat. This, at least, was the explanation they eventually offered for their negligence. The men-at-arms stationed behind the throne offered the equally-plausible excuse that the confused councillors had blocked their way.

It turned out, alas, that the throne was Lysariel's appointed destination and Manazzoryn his intended victim. The transfixed regent stared at his lunatic sibling with utter horror, unable to move a muscle as the vengeful blade was directed at his heart. Even Giraiazal, who had seen a sketchy record of this atrocity written in the stars, was struck dumb with astonishment as the elder brother charged full tilt upon the younger and drove the blade of the half-pike into his sternum with such force that the bone was sheared in two, the heart behind sliced lop-sidedly and the stomach beneath it burst asunder.

Blood and chyme leapt from the wound in a great gout, and Manazzoryn expired, the air rushing from his lungs in a strange whistling gasp that might have been an aborted attempt to scream.

Lysariel was seized by a dozen hands as soon as he became quiet and disarmed himself—which he did immediately after the fatal blow had been struck. When he released the haft of the firmly-embedded weapon, however, he promptly fell into a swoon and the men who took hold of him had to bear him up again. He was carried away unconscious, and was taken back to Viragan's house, where he was placed in the same room as before. The lock on the door had been repaired and reinforced, and Viragan gave orders that four guards were to remain on duty outside the door at all times.

The fact that the king had been very obviously mad did not prevent speculation as to the possibility that there had been method—or motive, at least—in his madness. Cyntrom's rumour-mongers had now become so confident in the exercise of their dubious art that it required no more than a minute for them to work out that if Manazzoryn *had* been a murderer, and

Lysariel a duty-bound avenger, then Calia's fatal fall could not have been an accident. Either Manazzoryn must actually have cast her down, or she must have tumbled while trying to avoid his illicit amorous advances.

This, it was now said, if only in discreet whispers, was why Calia had returned from the grave to possess her likeness. She had come to demand the settlement of a score and the punishment of her would-be rapist. Now, presumably, she would be able to rest in peace. The statue must already be dispirited, and would likewise rest in the quiet of its grotto.

The bold diver who had appointed himself the spokesman of the team assembled by Urbishek had been so affected by his recent celebrity that he volunteered to test this hypothesis by venturing into the grotto to see if the statue was actually there, but nothing returned to the surface but a faint trail of blood, which was taken as testimony that he had been torn apart and eaten by voracious eels.

In the meantime, Viragan assumed the regency. He could not have done so before because Manazzoryn, although very young, had been the king's brother, but now that the sole inheritor of the true royal blood was Zintrah's unborn son—who was also Viragan's grandson—it seemed entirely appropriate that he should do so.

Zintrah was, of course, utterly devastated by the tragedy, but she bravely accepted the burden of her new responsibilities. She took what comfort she could from the wise counsel of Giraiazal, although she was a trifle resentful about the apparent failure of his earlier assurances.

"You told me that I might save the sanity of the king," she reminded the astrologer, having called him to a conference in the apartment she had shared with Manazzoryn. "You assured me that I alone in all the world had charm enough to win his affections away from the coral courtesan—but what were your flatteries worth, in the end? My beloved husband is dead and Lysariel's madness is responsible for his murder."

"You did not fail in what was asked of you, your highness," Giraiazal informed her. "What I told you, if you remember, was that you alone had charm enough to *distract* Lysariel from his fetish. That you most certainly did—and it was neither your fault nor mine that I had not time to complete the penetration of the statue's secret."

"It seems that he was faithful to his statuesque hussy in the end," Zintrah complained. "She released him from his prison, it seems, and sent him forth to commit fratricide. For her sake, he killed his own brother."

"If you will forgive my saying so," the astrologer said, very meekly, "that is merely the allegation of popular gossip. We cannot be certain that the statue was ever fully animated, either by the spirit of Calia or some demon. The possibility remains that it was merely stolen. There is no proof that anyone assisted Lysariel in his escape, but if assistance was lent, it is perfectly possible that it came from a merely human being. As to what he might have been told, or otherwise came to believe, about his brother, we can as yet only speculate."

"He called him murderer," Zintrah pointed out. "It cannot have been true, of course—but Lysariel must have believed it."

"Unless," said Giraiazal, speaking very softly, "he had some other reason to wish his brother dead."

"You may be a magician and a man of unparalleled cleverness," Zintrah replied, sharply, "but that remark is suggestive of disloyalty. Will you tell me what other reason he could possibly have had?"

Giraiazal bowed his head, reverently accepting the implied rebuke. "Your highness is undoubtedly right," he conceded. "I have always been a scholarly man, preoccupied by my study of the ever-evolving firmament. It is the penalty of those who strive too hard to decypher mysteries that they sometimes give too much thought to the unlikely, and not enough to the obvious. I admit that I failed to protect Manazzoryn from the madness of Lysariel, just as I failed to protect Calia from the petty malice of Fate, but I beg you not to doubt my loyalty or my sincerity. You know better than anyone else how long I laboured to snatch Calia from the jaws of death, and how deftly I attempted to pluck Lysariel from the clutches of obsession."

"I do," Zintrah conceded, "and you may be assured that I shall continue to treasure your friendship. Surely all will be well now, will it not? You have already promised that my son will live long and prosper. Am I similarly armoured against disaster?"

"No human hand will ever do you harm, your highness," Giraiazal said, with a disarming smile. "The violence that will soon erupt in Cyntrom will not reach this inner sanctum. You may await the birth of your son without fear of injury."

"What violence?" Zintrah demanded. "Have you warned my father that rebellion is in the air?"

"Your father knows everything that he needs to know," said Giraiazal—who had, indeed, warned Viragan that very morning of the inevitability that there would be trouble when Orlu's ships belatedly made their way home. Viragan had replied, rather churlishly, that it did not require an astrologer to foresee that eventuality and that one of his captains had already brought news of the fact that the remnant of Orlu's fleet had made landfall in Psidium in order to repair the damage inflicted by the last in a series of storms which had tormented them ever since they had left Cyntrom.

* * *

In anticipation of the bad temper his fellow merchant prince would be in when he finally made port—and the even worse mood that would overtake Orlu when he heard news of recent events—Viragan sent a few of his own ships to harass Orlu's, in order to further weaken his fleet by patient attrition, instructing their commanders that they must on no account show their true colours. This was a necessary precaution, for Viragan did not doubt that Orlu himself would eventually succeed in returning home. He had Giraiazal's assurance of this, but hardly needed it; he knew what manner of man his former rival was, because he knew his own likeness when he saw it.

When Orlu finally brought his remaining ships to shore, a hundred days after the murder of Manazzoryn, he disembarked his men at Lamri rather than bringing them to the port, and then marched overland before making camp some several miles inland of the city. Then he sent careful messengers to summon Giraiazal from his turret, begging the astrologer to keep the assignation secret.

When Giraiazal was brought to Orlu's camp in Cyntrom's interior, the former pirate thanked him profusely for his trouble. "I have it on good authority that you succeeded in spite of my failure," he said. "I am deeply ashamed that I could not find a cure for my daughter, but I know that you nursed her through her illness regardless, and for that I thank you with all my heart. I beg you to tell me now what went wrong thereafter. They say that my daughter was foully murdered—is it really true?"

"The circumstances of her death remain shrouded in mystery," Giraiazal told him. "It seemed to be an accident at the time, but we may have taken that inference too readily. I have tried to use my powers to solve the puzzle, but astrology is more useful for looking into the future than uncovering the secrets of the past. I cannot say for sure—but I certainly do not believe that Lysariel's final cry can be taken as firm proof that

Manazzoryn was guilty of her murder. Indeed, I believe that the younger brother loved your daughter almost as much as the elder."

"I remember," said Orlu. "It was the merest whim of chance which determined that Calia captured Lysariel and Manazzoryn had to be content with Zintrah. Viragan was disappointed, I know—but it seems that he has come out ahead in the end. He is regent now, is he not? The king went mad, I understand, almost as soon as I had left Cyntrom on my expedition."

"Alas, yes," Giraiazal confirmed.

"And the two people who then stood between Viragan and the regency died soon afterwards, did they not?—one slain by an unknown hand and the other by a madman who had been in Viragan's custody until he was mysteriously set free."

"You are very well informed, for someone who has been away so long," admitted Giraiazal. "The servants you left behind have evidently been vigilant on your behalf.

"How I wish that I could have returned earlier!" Orlu lamented. "You would not believe the trouble I have had. The ship I sought seemed to have vanished into thin air, as if it had changed its name and destination as soon as I had collected the tax it was due to pay. False trails were laid to lead me astray, and into danger. Storm after storm assailed me, as if set to pursue me—and the ships I sent in other directions suffered similar misfortunes. Then, when I gathered my fleet together again and tried to make repairs, I was harassed by pirates. Imagine that! I had always thought that Cyntrom's first families exercised a collective monopoly on piracy in these far-flung waters."

"You seem to have had a devilishly bad time of it," admitted the astrologer.

"You can see where this chain of absurd circumstance is leading, can you not, Giraiazal?" Orlu went on, darkly and coldly. "One setback could be counted as mere misfortune, two as unhappy coincidence, but three, four and five seem to me to be clear evidence of active malice. And who has benefited from all this? Viragan is regent, ruling in the name of the unborn son of Manazzoryn."

"The unborn son of Zintrah," Giraiazal countered, in a tone which suggested correction rather than amplification.

For a few moments, Orlu merely looked perplexed—but then the implication of what Giraiazal had said sank in. "Only Zintrah's?" he said, incredulously. "Are you saying that the child is not Manazzoryn's?"

"I wish I knew," Giraiazal answered. "Alas, as I have said already, astrology is a far better guide to the future than the past. The only thing of which we an be certain is that the child is Zintrah's—the grandson, therefore, of Viragan."

"Is that why Calia was killed?" Orlu demanded, his voice as frigid as polar ice. "Is that why Manazzoryn was murdered?"

"Who can tell?" said Giraiazal, disingenuously. "Rumour has it that Lysariel was released from Viragan's custody by a coral statue animated by the spirit of Calia, whose maker confessed himself a sorcerer after suffering for days at the hands of Viragan's torturers, but I do not know who started the rumour. The statue, it is said, has since returned to the bosom of the sea—but all that I can say for sure is that there has been no reliable sighting of it since the day that Viragan's men first seized Lysariel and carried him off to his prison. I wish that I could be of more help to you, but I cannot. What my art *has* told me, however, is that Cyntrom will soon be subject to a time of troubles: that the island will be racked by fighting, hunger, and disease."

"That I can believe," said Orlu, grimly. "And what will follow this time of troubles, Master Prophet?"

"A time of peace," said Giraiazal. "Unlike Yoros and Tasuun, Cyntrom will survive for several lifetimes yet to come, and Zintrah's son will maintain firm authority for many years, presumably with the support of strong and prescient advisers. Of this I am certain, for these are matters on which the judgment of astrology can be trusted."

"If that is the promise of Fate," aid Orlu, "it only remains to mere men to make certain that the young king is properly advised—by good and honourable men, and not by villains."

"Indeed it does," said Giraiazal, piously looking up into a dark and drear sky, where the only visible star peeping through a narrow gap in the thick and lowering cloud was irresistible Achernar.

It was so late by the time that Giraiazal returned to the palace that he slept much later than usual, and eventually had to be awakened so that he might hear the terrible news. An hour before dawn, while bloated Achernar still lay bright upon the cushion of cloud which still dressed the western horizon, two hundred men led by Orlu had attacked Viragan's house, killing dozens of the regent's servants. It was only by a freak of chance that Viragan had made good his own escape before the house was put to the torch.

Orlu had seized Lysariel before withdrawing into the shadows.

Giraiazal refused to hurry the everyday business of dressing himself, and was therefore late in arriving at the plaza, where Viragan—who was not in a mood to wait for advice—had already issued a proclamation from the palace gate, declaring that Orlu was a traitor and an outlaw, who must be hunted down with all expedition and put to death.

In order to accomplish this, every man in Cyntrom who had been charged with the responsibility of maintaining arms and armour had to put on the royal colours and report for duty to his appointed commander. Had every man supposedly subject to this charge obeyed the order and rallied to Viragan's standard the matter would have been easily settled, for Cyntrom was too small an island for an outlaw band to hide. Even as the regent was speaking, however, the rumour had been flying through the streets that Orlu had made a new pledge of allegiance to King Lysariel, who was mad no longer.

The ordinary grief occasioned by the king's loss of his beloved Calia had, it was said, been exacerbated and perverted, first by the malignity of a seductive statue and then by the effects of a magnum of wine. The latter had been given to Lysariel as a wedding-present by the astrologer Giraiazal, who had been under the mistaken impression that it had come from ancient Yethlyreom. In fact, rumour alleged, another wine had been substituted for the intended gift by the agent entrusted with the purchase: Viragan's agent. The intoxicating effect of the addictive liquor had been further amplified by the consequence of its withdrawal, which had plunged the king into such abyssal depths of confusion and anguish that he had slain his own brother. In time, however, the king had recovered his former equilibrium, and now understood exactly what had been done to him and *by whom*.

That was the extent of the rumour which circulated on the first day of Cyntrom's civil war, but Giraiazal suspected that Orlu was too sharp a player to lay out all his cards at once, and that there would be more and worse to come. It turned out that this first propagandistic salvo was more than sufficient to instil doubt into the minds of many of the yeomen who were bound to answer a summons to the defence of the realm. Many of those who put on the royal colours were not at all sure whether they should go to the palace to receive orders from the regent's men, or whether they should go inland in search of King Lysariel and his general Orlu. Some did, in fact, take the latter course, while a far greater number hesitated, keeping their options open while awaiting further developments.

The next day brought a new raft of rumours, all of them so carefully crafted that even Giraiazal was lost in admiration of their craftiness. Now it was said that the great artist Urbishek had not been a sorcerer at all, but had been deluded into thinking the eel-guarded coral would be the ideal fabric for a statue, as had the unfortunate Lysariel. It was now suggested that the mischievous spirit which had possessed the statue had actually been imported into it by the man who had condemned Urbishek as a magician and had extracted a false confession from him by torture: Viragan.

As for the murder of Calia, if it had indeed been a murder at all—Giraiazal was deeply impressed by the cunning modesty of the claim—rumour now said that no one could possibly take seriously the claim that Manazzoryn had been responsible. Only one person had gained by the tragic death of Cyntrom's queen, and that had been the man who now ruled as regent in the name of his unborn grandson: Viragan.

This second broadside of hearsay sent more men-at-arms to gather about Lysariel's standard, but it had an even greater effect on those who had already reported for duty to Viragan's commanders, who began to desert in considerable numbers, thinking that the impending war now seemed far too finely balanced for their liking.

Viragan saw that if he were to act he must act immediately, before his incompletely-gathered forces suffered any further depletion, and he marched out of the port with a force of nine hundred men, intending to meet Orlu on the nearest convenient battlefield.

Orlu, having only seven hundred men as yet at his disposal, chose to retreat, and for three days he kept his little army on the move, requiring Viragan's army to pursue him. Wherever Orlu went he requisitioned the food his followers required from the local landholders, then burned all the remaining supplies—with the result that Viragan's men, bound by necessity to follow in his wake, became hungry and frustrated.

In the meantime, a third round of rumours took wing, which said that the child whose emergence from Zintrah's womb was now imminent was not Manazzoryn's at all but Lysariel's.

* * *

If there had not been confusion enough in the minds of Cyntrom's liege-men, the supposed revelation that Manazzoryn's wife had betrayed him with Lysariel brought in a prodigal harvest of uncertainty. By the time Orlu and Viragan actually met, their battle was little more than a skirmish and the men not related by blood to either general had little stomach for fighting. By the tacit consent of those involved the field was kept clear for Orlu and Viragan to engage one another directly, and once their blades had clashed even their closest henchmen paused to await the outcome.

For fully half an hour the two merchant princes, who had worked so well together when they had collaborated in the re-establishment of Cyntrom's monarchy, traded blow for blow. The onlookers were almost convinced that the conflict would end with both men falling exhausted to the ground when Orlu slipped in a pool of his own fresh-leaked blood and Viragan contrived to run him through.

Because it was a belly-wound, Orlu had time enough to curse his slayer very loudly and with some elaboration before Viragan was able to haul the blade upwards sufficiently to split his victim's diaphragm.

Orlu's former followers immediately threw down their weapons and proclaimed their loyalty to Viragan and Zintrah's unborn child, but it was obvious even as they gave the oath that they were troubled by the necessity. Although near to collapse himself, Viragan had voice enough to welcome them, and wisdom enough to order no immediate reprisal for their temporary dereliction of duty. He did, however, command that Lysariel be found and brought to him immediately.

This proved to be impractical. Although Lysariel had been seen in Orlu's close company when the battle began, he had evidently left the field some time before the end. There was no sign of him—and while he remained at large, the rumours that Orlu had put into circulation and enforced with his dying curses could not be conclusively laid to rest.

After pausing for a few hours in order to allow his men to fill their bellies Viragan marched them back to the port. He left behind a legacy of bitter resentment which extended throughout the farmlands of Cyntrom's interior. Although the campaign had been brief, there was hardly a single farmer whose barns had not been robbed and fired, or a single husbandman whose herds and flocks had not been decimated and distressed. Although much of the pillage had been conducted by Orlu's men, Orlu's men were now Viragan's men again, and Viragan's victory had established him as the only person from which recompense might be sought. In the wake of the returning army, therefore, there followed a host of the partially-dispossessed in search of compensation that was not soon forthcoming.

As civil wars went, Cyntrom's had been a trivial affair, but it left a bitter legacy nevertheless. There were shortages in the marketplaces, which further inflamed the bad moods of men who had become resentful, suspicious and secretive. The death of Orlu had put an end to overt conflict but not to covert confusion—and mysteries still remained. Where was Lysariel? Was he sane or insane? Would he ever return—and what would he do if he did return?

All of these questions were, of course, put to the astrologer Giraiazal by Viragan and Zintrah.

"The dictatorship of Fate will ensure that you will both see him again," Giraiazal told them, "but only once, and briefly. The thread of his life is near to breaking."

"Have we anything to fear from his brief reappearance?" Viragan wanted to know.

"He will do no bodily harm to either of you," Giraiazal promised, "nor will it be profitable for you to raise a hand against him."

Such comfort as Viragan and Zintrah took from this news was moderate, for Giraiazal had already warned them that their time of troubles was not yet concluded. The shortages in the marketplace grew worse as the ravaged fields of Cyntrom produced their poorest yields in many years. The depleted herds and flocks grew thin for want of fodder, and a murrain spread among them. Worse still, the fishing fleets which had long been the island's principal bulwark against famine found that its neighbouring waters had become suddenly and unaccountably barren.

The gloom induced by this slow crisis was, however, somewhat alleviated by the approach of the day when Zintrah's son was due to be born. News of Giraiazal's guarantee that the child's reign would be far longer than Lysariel's had been generously spread, and the islanders were virtually unanimous in considering the advent to be a happy occasion. Although the celebrations would inevitably be muted by the dearth of provender, preparations were made in a brave and generous spirit.

Zintrah did not have the easiest of births, and there was more than one occasion during her arduous labour when she begged for the phial of mandrake pollen which Giraiazal had given her as a wedding-present—but he assured her that she would come through the ordeal well enough, and that the precious pollen might be better saved for another day.

Giraiazal's promise was fulfilled, and Zintrah completed her task with a little of her natural fortitude still in hand. She remained confined to her bed for the next seven days, but the infant suckled well and she recovered her strength while supplying his. Viragan and Giraiazal came frequently to her room in order that they might share in her joy and continue to reassure her that all was as well as could be expected beyond the walls of her confinement.

The child was named Hatarus.

On the seventh night after the birth, and despite the fact that baleful Achernar was brighter and more livid in the sky than ever, the whole palace slept content—including, it seemed, the guards set to watch the gate and the sentries on the corridors. How else could it have been that Zintrah, awakened by a sound and a premonition, could open her eyes to find Lysariel standing over the crib that lay alongside her bed?

For a moment or two the mother of the new-born king dared not breathe. She studied the face of the former monarch with great concentration and greater anxiety, searching for signs of madness. She remembered what Giraiazal had said concerning this last encounter, and trusted the astrologer's judgment that there would be no profit in raising her hand against Lysariel, so she made no movement.

Lysariel, for his part, was content to look down at the child—which he continued to do for seven or eight minutes before he turned to Zintrah, meeting her anxious gaze without the least hint of surprise or embarrassment.

"Is he mine?" he asked, softly. "Is he truly mine?"

Zintrah hesitated for a moment, but eventually said: "Yes, he is yours. I was a little too successful in distracting you from your coral bride, was I not?"

"It was the one moment of real comfort I had during my madness," Lysariel replied. "Had it not been for the wine of Yethlyreom, I think I would have died, but had it not been for your kindness, I think it might have been better if I had."

Zintrah would have said more, but the door of her room opened then, so that the light of the lamps in the corridor startled her. Silhouetted in the frame were Giraiazal and Viragan.

"So," said Viragan to his companion, "you were right." He said it in the grudging tone of a man who did not like to trust the word of an astrologer.

"Steady, sire," said the astrologer, gently. "There is nothing here to warrant alarm. Lysariel has no intention of hurting anyone."

"It is true," Lysariel was quick to say. "I have no quarrel with you, Viragan. You were right to restrain me while I was mad—I only wish you had done so more efficiently. My first release was no liberation; all that was set loose was devilry and dolour. My second only brought me misery and woe. I will go now, and you will never see me again—but I had to see my son before I went. Will you tell me his name?"

"His name is Hatarus," said Zintrah.

"Not so fast, sire," said Viragan, silkily. "There are questions you must answer first. Who broke the lock when you were first released from captivity? Who told you that Manazzoryn was a murderer? Who took you away from the field where I slew Orlu? Who has given you shelter since that evil day?"

Lysariel smiled wanly. "Easily answered, old friend," he said. "Calia, Calia, Calia and Calia."

"Calia is dead," said Viragan. "If she were not, how could Manazzoryn be a murderer?"

"If Manazzoryn had not tried to take her by force, so causing her to fall," Lysariel replied, "she could not now be so angrily and so enviously alive. It is because she was murdered that she will outlive us all."

"Calia is dead, Lysariel," said Giraiazal, softly. "You would not believe it at the time, but you were mad then. Now you are sane again, I beg you to accept my word. When the living become the restless dead, their natures are much changed. Whatever the coral woman is, Lysariel, she is not your wife, let alone your beloved. Whatever demon it is that inhabits the statue is a pretender and a liar; it has no claim on you."

Lysariel shrugged his shoulders. "I am too unsteady in the head to debate definitions with a philosopher," he said. "Perhaps, after all, my wife is dead—but that does not make her demands less clamorous, nor her wrath less furious. I must go to her now, and meet that wrath, whatever its consequence might be. Perhaps I was foolish to come, but a man has his pride, and must show a certain zeal in its demonstration even when he is unremittingly sober. The child is my son, after all."

"It is because he is your son," said Giraiazal, his voice weighed down by sadness and sympathy, "that you must go away now, and never return."

"I know that," said Lysariel. "You will not see me again, I promise you." So saying, he went towards the door. Giraiazal and Viragan drew apart in order to let him pass, and although Viragan's right hand clenched reflexively into a fist, the former king was allowed to depart as quietly as he had come.

"Well," said Viragan, "that is over and out of the way. We can forget about Lysariel and look to our own welfare. This time of troubles is not over yet."

"He is no longer mad," whispered Zintrah, addressing herself to Giraiazal. "He knows what he is doing now—and what he has done."

Giraiazal met her eyes, and was surprised to see a glimmer there that might have been understanding, but he quickly concluded that it was merely sympathy. "You are right, highness," Giraiazal replied. "He is no longer mad. That cannot work to his advantage, but we must pray that it works to ours."

Two days later, the body of Lysariel, still recognisable in spite of the hideous mutilations to which it had been subjected, was washed up on the southern shore of Cyntrom, midway between his birthplace and the grotto from which divers had harvested coral for the manufacture of Urbishek's statue.

* * *

When the dead king had been safely buried in the grounds of the house in which he had been raised, Giraiazal retired to his turret in order to busy himself with new observations of the movement of the stars and new calculations as to their significance. He discovered no less than three new nebulae that had previously been invisible and two new comets, and cursed the heavens for their inconstancy. How could Fate be other than a fickle mistress when the writing she inscribed on the walls of the universe was so soon scribbled over by graffiti? His new calculations confirmed everything that he already knew, but when he attempted to draw more precise and detailed accounts of the future of Cyntrom, his equations filled up with intractable unknowns, and threatened more than once to lead his reasoning into mocking paradox.

As the comets' tails began to unfurl like those of displaying doves in the days that followed, contagion crept out of the sewers of the port into the narrow streets, and plague extended its dread hand upon the old and the young.

Giraiazal knew that of everything he had foreseen before Lysariel was crowned, one crisis alone remained to come and go. The astrologer had been patient before, because his sights had always been set on the next step in a continuing sequence, but now the sequence was approaching the terminus of its revelation he grew anxious. His inability to penetrate the mirk of unsettled possibility that lay beyond that final ominous declaration distressed and bothered him. He was obliged to take the view, familiar to ordinary folk, that time alone would tell him what part he would have to play in the long reign of Hatarus—and he soon became impatient with the slowness and secrecy of the steadfast hours. By the time news of the final act was brought to him the astrologer was more fretful and less self-controlled than he had ever been in the sixty years and three that he had lived in Cyntrom.

So irritable was his state that Giraiazal had not the capacity for relief when he was summoned from his refuge by a panic-stricken messenger sent by Viragan. "Come down!" the messenger said. "You must come down, Sir Magician, for the old king's coral widow is coming along the shore, and will be here within the quarter-hour!"

"Has no one tried to bar her way?" Giraiazal asked.

"Oh yes," the messenger said, while they hurried down the stair. "They have put up barricades, some set afire; they have showered her with spears and arrows; they have even taken sledgehammers to her brazen limbs—but she is neither soft nor brittle. Some say that she has killed seven, others four or five times as many, but what is certain is that no man now will dare to step into her path before she reaches the palace gate—and even then, the guards will not find it easy to deny her access. Whether magic can stop her no one knows, but no one believes that anything less than magic will do."

Zintrah and her father were waiting in the throne-room, Zintrah with Hatarus in her arms and Viragan clutching a double-headed axe. Four servants of the royal household and six men-at-arms stood with them, twice that number having already fled.

"Why has it come to this?" Viragan demanded of the astrologer. "Why have you not exorcised this demon? You have had a full year to do it?"

"One cannot exorcise a demon if one does not know its name," Giraiazal retorted, unashamedly, "and even if one knows its name, still it must be confronted at close quarters."

"Well," said Viragan, "it seems that we must confront it now. We can only hope that we can hold it at close quarters long enough for you to ply it with impertinent questions, and pray for time to act upon the answers." He sounded sceptical, and Giraiazal could hardly blame him.

"I shall do what I can," the astrologer said, knowing full well—as he had known for a year and more—that any opportunity for the coral bride's interrogation would have to be bought with blood.

It was obvious to everyone present that Viragan was terrified, but equally obvious that he stubbornly intended to stand his ground against the enspirited statue. He had time a-plenty to choose his position and his stance, for the commotion at the gate was clearly audible by now, and the cries of the onlookers in the plaza provided an eloquent commentary on the monster's progress.

Giraiazal subsequently found out that the guardsmen had not fallen back as they had before Lysariel when he came to kill Manazzoryn, but their resolution did no good at all. They were thrown aside and the gate breached, and within a minute of the door being broken the image of Queen Calia appeared at the threshold of the throne-room.

Viragan ordered the creature to halt, but it did not pause.

The regent had only time for a single glance at Giraiazal before conceding that the first attempt to thwart the demon must be his. "Demon!" Viragan shouted raising the axe above his head and bounding forward. "Regicide! May all the good gods come to my aid in this hour of need!"

That was a strange prayer to come from the lips of a man who had never before admitted that any gods might be good, and must have been too late a repentance if it were not entirely futile. As the axe fell from above the statue raised high its hands, caught the double blade beneath its palms, and wrenched it sideways. Then, as Viragan stumbled, it wrested the weapon from his grip, spun it around and launched a horizontal sweep which struck the regent's head clean off his shoulders.

The statue bathed in the fountain of blood which gushed from the neck of the headless man, and its brazen form was extravagantly spattered with red. It looked around from side to side, but no other blade was aimed at it now. All six of the men-at-arms were in full flight, and the four servants with them.

Zintrah, on the other hand, had moved towards the throne so that she might set Hatarus down upon it. Now she positioned herself squarely in front of her son, so that the demon could not see the boy.

"You shall not have him," Zintrah said to the bloody statue.

"I would not harm a hair of his head," the brazen creature replied, in a voice that no human throat could ever have produced. "He is the child of my beloved, Lysariel, and should have been mine. It is you that I have come to kill, traitress." As it spoke, however, the statue dropped the axe which it had used to kill Viragan, and stretched out its arms as if to welcome Zintrah into a fond embrace.

Zintrah remained where she was, but she turned her head so that her eyes might search for help or inspiration.

"Giraiazal?" she aid, anxiously. "Where are you, Giraiazal?"

"I am here," the astrologer said, stepping forward—but he was very careful not to interpose himself between Zintrah and the image of her former friend. "I will do what I can."

The statue turned its own head to follow the direction of Zintrah's gaze. "What can you do, Giraiazal?" asked the unhuman voice. "What have you ever done, save watch and wait and capitulate with the instructions of your vile mistress? What use are you in defying the dictates of Fate?"

"Only tell me your name, and I will show you exactly what a magician may do," Giraiazal replied. His irritation was gone now, having withered away. Still he felt no relief, but he considered himself to be calm and moderately well-collected.

"You know my name," the statue said. "I am Calia, and have been since the day my other self was killed, although it took me far longer than was convenient to recover my power of movement."

"Then you can have no grievance against me," Giraiazal said, "for you know how hard I laboured to save your life when you were bitten by the spider. Nor can you have any real grievance against Zintrah, who laboured alongside me with the best will in the world. She never set out to seduce Lysariel, who was in any case a widower so far as she could know, any more than the Calia of flesh and blood set out to seduce Manazzoryn. I ask you, therefore, to let this matter rest. Go—not to your grotto full of hungry eels, but to the grave, your resting-place. Go now!"

"You know my name," the beautiful statue replied, "but not my nature." So saying, she took a stride forward, and then another, reaching out all the while as if to take Zintrah in her arms.

"I forbid it!" Giraiazal called out, in the most authoritative voice he could contrive. "Go! By the power of the light of Achernar, I command you to go!" He astonished himself by so doing, for it was not what he had planned or expected to say, and he knew as he pronounced the words that it was a reckless thing to do.

"Oh well!" the unhuman voice replied. "Since you put it that way, I suppose I must. Farewell, dear sister! Farewell, astrologer accursed!"

Still reaching forwards, the statue was suddenly struck rigid. Its momentum caused it to teeter, and then to tumble. It fell very slowly, but as soon as it hit the marble floor it shattered into a thousand tiny pieces, showering Zintrah and Giraiazal with stinging flakes and unmetallic shards.

"I did not think you could do it," Zintrah said, as she wiped a tiny trail of blood from her cheek.

"Neither did I," said Giraiazal faintly, full of foreboding that he had done an exceedingly unwise thing.

* * *

On the next morning, neither Zintrah nor Giraiazal was able to get out of bed. They were both in the grip of a high fever, which racked them with terrible spasms. Their skin grew hard over the entire extent of their bodies, and their flesh became vitreous. They were in agony, but neither had a voice with which to scream, although their eyes stood out from their heads as they strove to give vent to their anguish.

When her servants told Zintrah that Giraiazal could not come to her because he was similarly stricken, she begged them to fetch the phial of mandrake pollen which the astrologer had given her for a wedding present. As soon as it was given to her she opened it and breathed its contents in. The pain immediately abated, and she felt strong again.

So powerful was the dusty draught that Zintrah did not suffer a moment's distress until she died, which she did three days thereafter.

When his own servants told Giraiazal that Zintrah had used the gift that he had provided, and what benefit she had gained therefrom, he laughed, and he continued laughing while the disease made free with his flesh.

The astrologer's skin erupted in boils and his belly swelled up with cysts, and he wept black blood, but he did not die. He wished that he had laid in a second supply of the mandrake pollen, and cursed himself for his failure, He wished, too, that in the absence of any such relief, he might simply let loose his hold on life and pass away, but he could not do it—and he cursed himself for that failure too. His body became a battleground, tattered and torn, then seared and scorched, but the battle was too evenly balanced to be won, and its forces were dispirited as if by bitter doubt born of malicious rumour. He wished that he had sufficient power of fantasy to escape into delirium, but he had ever been a scholarly man, excessively determined to know and live within the truth. He remained conscious of his suffering and conscious of its source, and he cursed himself again and again for his choice of mistress.

When the fever finally abated, Giraiazal was able to take nourishment enough to restore his strength, but the broth on which he was fed had to be spooned into his mouth through the bars of an iron cage, for he had become violently mad, and could not be trusted not to injure those who toiled to help him.

Giraiazal lived in that cage within his turret for forty more years, as carefully tended as circumstances would permit.

The astrologer was neither banished nor forgotten, because his madness caused him to babble incessantly about the cruel ways of implacable Fate, the betrayals of wayward chance and the dubious enlightenment conveyed to sensitive souls by the evil radiance of Achernar—and within this babble, if only one listened patiently and carefully enough, there was a measure of prophetic truth to be found.

So successful was this oracle, in spite of all the difficulties attendant upon its consultation, that its cunning use enabled the boy king Hatarus to come unscathed through all the conspiracies and plots which surrounded his throne while various upstart merchant princes vied for the privilege of filling Viragan's bloodstained shoes.

When Hatarus was no longer content to be called the boy king— preferring to style himself, vaingloriously, Hatarus the Great, Emperor of Cyntrom—the babbling of Giraiazal the Oracle faded to a mere whisper, and its potency as a wellspring of prophecy was altogether lost. Hatarus continued to keep and maintain him anyway, on the grounds that no emperor could sensibly count himself great who had no magician at his beck and call, while none who had such an ancient and talented adviser need reckon himself utterly trivial.

Had he only had possession of his senses, Giraiazal would surely have laughed at the thought of a king, however long-lived and secure in his authority, who counted himself great even though he had naught to rule but a small, desolate and plague-ridden isle whose population was numbered in the hundreds, and no ambition to pass to his descendants but the hope that they might somehow cling to ownership of the merest fraction of a world already lost and damned. Instead, it was his dainty mistress Fate who laughed, while Vergama turned yet another page in the book whose title is *Futility*.

THE MANDRAKE GARDEN

The root of the mandragora often divides itself in two, and presents a rude appearance of a man. In ancient times figures were often cut out of the root, and wonderful virtues ascribed to them . . . Some mandrakes cannot be pulled from the earth without fatal effects, so a cord used to be fixed to the root and round a dog's neck, and the dog being chased drew out the mandrake and died . . . the Emperor Julian, in his epistles, tells Calixenes that he drank its juice nightly as a love-potion.

E. Cobham Brewer, *The Dictionary of Phrase and Fable*, rev. ed. 1894

* * *

The most effective mandrake-roots are those which cannot be pulled from the earth without fatal effect, and this has always posed a problem for its cultivators. When the great mandrake garden at Philippi supplied the Cleopatra who beguiled Mark Antony the task was given to slaves who had become too old to work, many of whom were glad of the appointment, but the art was in its heyday then. When I worked in the garden west of the Thracian town of Xanthi that had been the life's work of my father Labros, all mandrake-growers—and there were few enough of us remaining—had been reduced to the use of dogs.

The creature we employed to unearth the root that we drew on the day before the catastrophe—it was in the first week of July—was an old hunting-dog which in his prime had harassed bears and brought down stags, but was now so feeble that he barely had strength to respond to the whip. I did not want to beat the poor beast more fiercely than was necessary, but a well-developed root clings hard to its bed.

"Lay on, Pachytos!" cried my father, thumping his staff upon the ground. "Let the lazy cur know who's master here!"

Labros was unquestionably the master, for all that he now had trouble walking without his staff for support. He had never been afraid to "lay on" when teaching me the way of the world, but when I was beaten I never wore a cord around my neck that might choke me if I pulled too hard without effect.

"Come on, old man!" I commanded, as persuasively as I could. "One last effort, and home to Elysium! Fail, and you'll howl eternity away in Tartarus." It was, of course, absurd to make promises and threats of those kinds to a dog, which had no knowledge of Latin and no faith in any kind of afterlife, but it helped to focus my attention. I was obliged to speak of Elysium and Tartarus instead of Heaven and Hell, not so much out of loyalty to our glorious emperor as because my father could hear me. My father had a lower opinion of Christian beliefs than Christian believers had of him, if any such abysmal depth could be imagined.

The mandrake we were pulling was the cream of the crop, intended as a tribute for Julian himself. We had received news three days before that he had crossed the Tigris and was searching for the Persian king, whose punishment could not be long delayed. He had taken abundant supplies from our garden with him, but the ever-dutiful Labros could not bear to consider the awful possibility that he might run out before his noble work was done.

The old dog strained so hard that his tired eyes bulged within his hairy head, and his paws fought for purchase in the soft earth. For a full half-minute it was touch and go as to whether the root would yield or the cur would choke and die with the job undone.

"Lay on, fool!" my father cried. "What's your right arm for, you useless wretch?"

Stubborn as always, I let the trailing end of the whip fall limply upon the ground. "Once more, son of Arctophonos!" I urged the animal on—and although he could not possibly have understood the compliment which linked him to Orion's faithful hound, he hauled with all his might and ripped the root from the ground.

The mandrake shrieked in bloodcurdling fashion, as the finest roots always do.

I had seen men swoon on hearing such a cry, but there was no one nearby on that awful afternoon who had not heard such screams a hundred times before. The dog, by contrast, dropped dead without uttering so much as a whimper.

It was the soundlessness as much as the instantaneousness of such deaths that had led my ancestors to believe that dying while uprooting a mandrake was a good death—a great mercy, devoutly to be desired by those to whom life had become a burden. I had never been sure of it myself. Mandrakes are, after all, as perverse as they are powerful; I had always wondered whether the agonised screams which they emitted might be stolen from the poor wretches commissioned to uproot them, whose deaths were thus redoubled in their ignominy.

My father hobbled along the narrow pathway between the double row of plants to inspect his new produce. Even he was tempted to grunt with satisfaction when he saw it.

The root was neatly divided, and as near perfect in its configuration as any I had ever seen. Before mandrakes were first brought under calculated cultivation in the days of Alexander the gatherers who searched the forests of Arcadia for wild specimens were glad if the whole root held the least impression of human form, but twenty-seven generations of my family had succeeded in selecting specimens for breeding with such craft and guile that our own were rarely less than exquisite. The mandrakes grown in our garden always had figures in each half of the root, usually so easily distinguishable that it was immediately possible to tell which was the male and which the female. These two were so precisely-carved and so obviously virile—the male a veritable Hercules and the female a very passable Venus—that it would have been a crime to split them. Fortunately, the emperor had commanded that none of the roots supplied to him should ever be broken.

Most noble users of mandrakes, even in those days, were only interested in figures of their own sex, valuing them for the most elementary kinds of erotic assistance, but Julian was a connoisseur of sensation. His enemies—especially the Christians whose teachings he had banned—were fond of likening him to Nero and Caligula on that account, but he was far their superior as a general, a writer and a man of vision.

"Get it cleaned," my father instructed, brusquely. "Then go down to the tavern and rouse that swine Barbatio. In my young days, we had real runners, not scum who work sitting down."

That was a grotesque exaggeration. No emperor had made significant use of runners for a hundred years. Everyone knew well enough that in a one-to-one race a strong man could outrun a single horse over fifty miles by virtue of superior stamina, but they also knew that a rider who changed horses at sufficiently regular intervals could cover the ground in a quarter of the time. The western reaches of the divided empire had been so sorely afflicted by the barbarians that it was well-nigh impossible to maintain the stations closest to the borders, but this was the civilized east which still had its strength, thanks to Julian.

I set about cleaning the root under the watchful eye of my impatient parent. "Get on with it!" he barked, as soon as I paused for rest. "A root like that will give the emperor the strength to crush the Persian rebels utterly. Do you want to be the man responsible for its late arrival?"

It was understandable that my father had such an inflated opinion of the kinds of virility which mandrakes enhanced, and I would not have dreamed of correcting his overestimation. Nor would it have been diplomatic to point out that given the time it took news to travel from the heart of Persia to mid-Thrace, whether by courier or by ship, Julian must have found the Persian army four or five days ago, and would likely be embarked on his homeward journey before a messenger could get the root into his hands. It might allow him to enjoy the tenderest fruits of his triumph a little more, but it could do nothing for the cause of the war.

I did take note, however, that my father had referred to me as "the *man responsible*," which was a greater concession to my age and capability than he was accustomed to make.

* * *

As soon as I had the root wrapped and pouched I set off towards the town. It was a good two hours walk and I wanted to be there before nightfall. The roads were supposed to be safe, but a young man in possession of a powerful instrument of magic never knows when he might run into a brigand or a lamia.

The early evening was warm and breathless; the setting sun hung in the hazy sky behind me like an overripe orange while the first delicate shades of darkness crept upon the horizon ahead. I had gone more than two miles before I saw a man hurrying in the other direction. Even at a hundred paces I recognised Cyllo, who had been one of my companions during such schooling as I had had, and was the nearest thing to a friend I had in Xanthi nowadays. In my early youth, it had been a pleasant town where everyone minded his own business, but in the last five years evangelists had turned half its citizens into petty moral tyrants and made resentful curmudgeons of most of the remainder.

"Pachytos!" Cyllo shouted, as soon as he caught sight of me. "Wait there! Thank the gods I found you!"

I did not pause in my stride. "I have no time," I called back. "I have an important parcel for Barbatio."

He was clearly out of breath but he roused himself regardless to reply. "You have less time than you think—especially if that parcel is what I think it is."

By this time, we were close enough to be able to stop shouting. Poor Cyllo had over-exerted himself, and he stopped before I drew level with him. When I came to his side he reached out an arm and placed his right hand on my shoulder, as much for support as to implore me to halt.

"Why, what is it, man?" I asked. "Are the barbarians sweeping southwards?"

"Worse!" he said. "A ship docked at Iasmos this morning carrying terrible news. The Persians took Julian's army in the rear. The attackers were beaten back three times, but our soldiers were direly short of water. Julian was mortally wounded by an arrow and Jovian is proclaimed emperor in his stead."

"That is a tragedy," I admitted, "but you did not have to race along the road to tell me. I would have heard the news the moment I set foot in Xanthi."

"And you'd have been lucky to survive the telling! Labros has kept you far too closely confined to that miserable tract, else you'd know what this means. Jovian is a Christian, or is said to be, and the Christians are rejoicing that the man they call spawn of the devil has been slain by their jealous god. They have borne their recent suppression very ill, and all their frustrations have burst forth in a rush of violence. They have been busy all day smashing idols and burning the goods of every declared supporter of Julian. Labros has been the loudest of all such proclaimers, and he supplies the emperor with mandrakes! The mob will march on your garden as soon as it has had its fill of common looting—by then it will be a hundred strong, and every one roaring drunk!"

I was sincerely astonished by this speech. I had known, of course, that ever since Constantius had died the Christians had suffered terrible anguish, supposing that all their hard-won gains had been conclusively lost. Every follower of that niggardly faith in the crumbling empire must immediately have set about praying for some such disaster as this. Had Julian's death been delayed another ten years, they might have had no emotions left but relief and gratitude, but after a mere two their wrath was still seething. There was no one in the region who took more pride in the old gods and the old ways than Labros, who was never reluctant to inform Christian passers-by that his precious garden was the true source of the emperor's strength. If the Christians of Xanthi had had their way, mandrake-growing would have been outlawed twenty years before; if the looters still had strength to march once they'd supped enough stolen wine, they would certainly march westwards.

"We must flee," Cyllo told me. "I shall set off for Kavala tomorrow morning, and you should come with me—Labros too, if you can persuade him. I have an uncle there, and Jupiter still commands due respect in the streets—but you and I must first make sure that we are safe for the night."

He was taking the wisest course, and I knew it. No Christian himself, he doubtless had his own reasons for leaving town so hurriedly, and he probably needed a friend as badly as I did, but it was good of him nevertheless to bring me warning. Unfortunately, I could not see that the warning would do me any good.

"Labros will never leave the garden," I said. "No force on earth could move him."

I knew exactly what my father would say in response to Cyllo's news: *I tended this garden before that imbecile Constantine embraced the religion of his slaves, and I tended it for thirty years while cowards and curs flocked from the old temples to the new. I did not care then that they despised me, and I do not care now. This is a sacred trust, which I will hold until I die.*

"We must make him see sense," Cyllo insisted. "And if he will not, you must leave him to his fate."

"It is impossible," I judged. "Labros has never seen sense in his life, and his blindness is invincible"—but I turned around regardless and hastened back along the road, because I knew that I was honour bound to try.

I had anticipated the old man's response almost to the letter, although—according to my usual fashion—I had not quite foreseen the extent to which he would turn his wrath upon me.

"You craven fool!" he raged. "You hear a whisper of disapproval and you are ready to run! Why did you not go on into the town to rally the true men to our cause? Have you no brain at all?"

"Father," I said, "there is not a single man left in Xanthi who would take up arms to defend a mandrake garden. The aristocrats will buy our figures, and the citizens will buy our powder, but they avert their eyes when they do it. If the evangelists have taught them nothing else, they have certainly taught them the meaning of shame. Julian has been proud to accept your gifts, but everyone who has paid your prices these last thirty years has done so with gritted teeth."

He only cursed me for a fool, heaped insults upon the memory of my poor mother—including, of course, the suggestion that I must be another man's son—and thumped his staff upon the floor with force enough to break half a dozen tiles. There was not the slightest chance of changing his mind.

"Why are you not sharpening your spear, making ready for the defence of your inheritance?" he demanded, when I tried to usher him to his chair. "Bring me my sword, that I may teach these angry cowards how to turn the other cheek!"

Cyllo attempted to describe the awful scenes he had witnessed in the town, and did his level best to assure the old man that when the first flush of violent triumph had died down it might be safe to return to the house, but Labros would have none of it. If Jupiter himself had appeared and said "Labros, get thee gone!" he would only have offered him the gift of the mandrake-root that Julian could no longer accept, with leering promises as to its potency, and asked for the price of a thunderbolt with which to smite his enemies.

In the end, Cyllo dragged me away from the confrontation and said: "You must come with me now. If they catch you here with him, all the tolerance and forbearance you have shown to them in the past will count for nothing. You have protected him while you could; now you must leave him."

"I cannot," I said.

"Why not?" he cried. "What has he ever done for you but use you and beat you and tell you how worthless you are? What has he ever taught you but the care and cultivation of magical monsters? Great Pan is dead, Pachytos, and the old ways are dying in his wake; even Julian could not turn back time. You cannot imagine that the mob will leave you a crop to tend, even if they spare your life. We must go."

"What will they do?" I asked him, bitterly. "Will they tear every plant up by the root and make a pyre for them? Count them, Cyllo! I make it twenty-four full ripe and forty still green. The younger ones might not raise more than a murmur when drawn, but even they can hurt a man. Or will they bring a pack of dogs and rope for harness? Of all the gardens in Thrace, this is the only one that has never been troubled by thieves or vandals. How much courage do your drunken ascetics have?"

"I don't know," Cyllo said, in a strained tone. "But I know that this is the worst day of all to put the matter to the test."

I did not doubt him. Although I had not seen what he had seen I had no reason at all to question his judgment—nor, for that matter, his opinion of my father. But I could not go with him. To do so would have been to confirm my father's opinion of me, and that I would not do.

"Keep going westwards," I said to him. "You know well enough which houses are safe. Someone will give you shelter for the night. I won't tell them that you've been here. Go to your uncle in Kavala, if you think that best, or find some nearer refuge and return to Xanthi when the fury has died down. I'll do what I can here."

"You can do nothing," he assured me.

"So I have always been told," I replied.

As soon as Cyllo had gone I went to the pens and released the dogs. I did not want them hurt, or used. They would not run away at first, being fearful of the darkness and anxious to stay where they were regularly fed, but I took my whip to them and forced them out into the night, heedless of their plaintive howls.

I had time thereafter to bury our meagre hoard of gold and silver, and the few other items of value we possessed, but I did not take the trouble. Nor did I take the trouble to sharpen my spear; I knew that it would be no more use than a hoe. I did not even offer up a prayer, not so much because I had not the least idea to which god it might be profitably offered as because I had no faith left in the efficacy of any kind of pleading. I knew that the dream of empire would die with Julian, and that all the mandrakes in the world could not have preserved its virility.

* * *

By the time the mob arrived the sky was pockmarked with stars and the full moon was as bright as a lantern, but there was still a haze in the air which hid the fainter stars and turned the livid face of the moon a sickly yellow. Although they had light enough to see their way, the crowd brought half a dozen torches anyway, so that they could take care where they were treading and would not be short of a brand if the mood took them to set a house or a haystack afire.

I had done everything I could to persuade my father to stay in the house while I talked to the Christians, but to no avail. I do not suppose for an instant that I could have made them turn back—tired as they were after their long walk, they would hardly have relished the thought of retracing their steps without having achieved their purpose—but I might perhaps have prevented the night's events from taking the particular shape they did.

As it was, it was Labros who met the mob, not on the path which led to the house but at the edge of the garden, with the eight parallel rows of mandrakes at his back.

He did not have his sword, which had proved too heavy to be effectively lifted, but that did not improve his temper at all. He cursed the invaders roundly, in the names of Jupiter, Pluto and Julian.

They cursed him back, in the name of Jesus.

Labros told them that he was a great magician, heir to twenty-seven generations of cunning mandrake-men, who could and would blight their crops, cause their livestock to sicken and strike their children down.

They assured him that they were well-protected from all the devil's charms, and that he had no power at all to hurt *them*.

Labros boasted that he could trace his royal warrant back to Alexander the Great, and that his forefathers had supplied all the Caesars with the finest potions.

They informed him that Alexander and all the Caesars had been heathens, condemned to Hell by their use of magics and their sacrifices to demonic idols, and that all the former holders of his royal warrant would burn throughout eternity.

Labros threatened that if they took one more step towards his crop he would smite them with his staff—and that I, his son, would cut the legs from under them with my spear.

They pointed out that if he were to raise his staff he would very probably fall over, and that his son was not actually carrying a spear.

It was, I suppose, the last observation which drove him mad and provoked him to turn his wrath upon a safer object. He cursed me, in all the names which he could think of—except, of course, Jesus—and called my

147

dead mother a worthless whore.

This caused the crowd to laugh, and one who thought himself a wit called attention to the fact that here was a magician so great that he could not even command his own child.

It is always good when one's enemies begin laughing, no matter what moves them to mirth. That seemed to me to be the perfect moment to step forward and say: "You are right. My father is quite harmless, as am I. We are no threat to anyone. You can safely leave us to our own devices."

It was no use, alas. "*Diabolical* devices!" another voice cried out.

"A crop in dire need of blight!" opined another.

I came to stand beside my father, and gripped his right arm as powerfully as I could.

"In that case," I said, "we shall stand aside while you do what you have to do. We shall offer no resistance."

They *might* have condescended to let us stand aside, if the old fool had to take it into his head to yell at them again: "Yes! Come forward one and all! Pull up my plants with your bare hands, and see what the protection of your crucified carpenter is worth!"

After that, there was no chance of our being left out of it. They rushed forward to seize the pair of us.

One of them, who knew our methods, had already gone to look at the pen where we kept the dogs. If any of the animals had sneaked back in search of familiar shelter they had taken flight again when they heard raised voices and sniffed the smoke of the torches. The mob's next move was perfectly predictable, and I took my courage in both hands, hoping that my father might have been right all along about the merciful release of those condemned to draw mandrakes from their beds.

"Take me," I said, when I saw the rope brought forth. "Let my father go."

If my plea had any effect at all, it made them all the more eager to harness Labros and force me to watch. They dragged me away from him, and seized him avidly.

"Fools!" he yelled in their faces, as they struggled to hold him still while the rope was tied about his shoulders. "Do you think that the mandrakes will kill *me*? Do you imagine that they do not know me? They will gladly add their strength to mine, so that I may avenge the insult given to them by this blasphemy!"

The Christians did not like to hear their actions called blasphemy, that being a word they had long sought to monopolise. They secured the other end of their makeshift harness to the base of the nearest mandrake stem and they fell back, save for one who had a whip identical to the one that I habitually used, in my father's stead, to urge our dogs to their final effort and sacrifice.

They let him keep his staff, because they were not sure whether he could stand unaided—but they would have used the whip, if he had been stubborn.

He *was* stubborn, but not in the way they expected. As soon as they stepped back he pressed forward, planting his staff before him and using it as a lever, straining with all his might to rip the mandrake from the ground. He must have taken note, as I had, of the fact that it was an unripe plant, too green to be lethal in its effect, but that was not why he did it. He believed what he had said to them. He believed that the mandrake would suffer itself to be uprooted, and would donate its strength to him, so that he might become a Hercules and scatter the rabble that had come to destroy the garden.

The root came free without so much as a murmur—but Labros gasped with the effort, and very nearly collapsed. He did not die, or even fall unconscious, but he did not grow stronger either and was forced to lean upon his staff for support.

The greater number of the Christians, knowing little more of mandrakes than their fearful reputation, were astonished that he did not drop dead, but two who ran forward to look at the dislodged root were quick to cry out that it was ill-formed and unready for the harvest, with barely a suggestion of human form in either branch. The rest immediately seized the inference that it was only the state of the plant that had prevented their subtle execution, and two of the ringleaders made haste to find one whose foliage identified it as a mature specimen.

Inexpert though they were, they quickly identified the plant which was now the best in the garden, only a little less luxuriant than the one we had excavated that afternoon as a belated gift for an emperor six or seven days dead.

That was when I concluded that I had no recourse left but violence. I had surrendered so meekly to the two men who held me, and had kept so still since they dragged me away from my father, that their grip was loose and easily broken. They were so astonished by my sudden reversal of policy that they were fatally slow to react. I brought a knee up into one man's groin and stuck a thumb into the other's eye. Neither had much immediate opportunity for reprisal and I was able to snatch a torch from one of the nearer bystanders, which I swung back and forth in front of me as I leapt to my father's side, forcing the men who held his arms to retreat in some disorder. The other end of the rope that was secured about his shoulders still dangled free.

"Run!" I said, not caring how ridiculous the instruction was.

He did not run. Instead, he used his staff as a lever again, thrusting himself forward to take up a position beside the plant identified by his persecutors—and then he dropped the wooden pole in order that he could take a mature mandrake in each hand.

I was afraid that he would fall, sprawling ignominiously in the dirt, but he was balanced on feet that were half a stride apart and he steadied himself. When he began to pull both plants at the same time, his ancient muscles tightened in a fashion I would never have thought possible.

Where he found the strength I could not tell, but find it he did. If the mandrakes offered their usual resistance, there was no sign of it. Both roots came smoothly free from the glutinous ground, and Labros lifted them both aloft.

They screamed.

Perhaps there were only two magical voices howling their magical agony at the stars in that first horrid moment, and perhaps there were three; I dare not offer a judgment. I can say with certainty, however, that as the terrible chorus extended from one instant to the next *other voices* began to join in.

The evening had been perfectly still while I ran back with Cyllo, and the night had been undisturbed by the lightest breeze until that moment, but the air was suddenly ripped by a terrible wind: a storm more violent than any I had ever seen.

The force of the wind toppled the Christians like skittles, extinguishing all their torches, including the one I had stolen—and the moon grew suddenly dark as a circular shadow seemed to draw across its jaundiced face. The stars trembled in the sky—and that terrible scream grew in volume and in feeling, until all the agony in the world seemed enwrapped within it.

It was a scream that had less pain in it than anguish and remorse. It was the kind of scream that Prometheus might have sounded when the eagle came to tear out his lights. It was the kind of scream that an empire might sound on receiving the news that its favourite son and last hope had been cruelly slain.

I think I was the last man standing, but I might be wrong. If what eventually struck me down was a club wielded by a human hand, I suppose that I must be wrong—but I lost consciousness so abruptly that I had not the slightest idea what it was that felled me, and have not to this day. I only know that when I woke the sun had risen in the east, and I was alone. I was bruised and I ached in very limb, and when I took stock of my injuries I concluded that I had been kicked and trampled by many angry feet, but somehow I had not been seriously hurt.

My father's body lay where it had fallen, with a mandrake stem still clutched in each hand—but the roots attached to both stems were crushed and mangled. If they had ever borne the least resemblance to human form, they did not now. They had been smashed by clubs, slashed by knives and crushed beneath well-shod heels.

The Christians had solved the problem of destroying the remaining mandrakes easily enough. They had not drawn them from their beds, but had attacked them in the ground. They had cut the foliage of every plant to ribbons, and then had thrust downwards into the soil whatever implements came to hand: hoes, spades, axes, spears and pointed stakes. Where each one had been set, in careful array, there was a crater full of debris. No remaining part of any root bore any more resemblance to a homunculus than the ones my father held. Had the remnants been powered they might still have had some commercial value, but I could not believe that the powder would have any real virtue.

When I looked at the wreckage of the garden I saw the wreckage of the empire, and the ruination of civilization. Mandrakes are not hardy perennials, nor can they be grown from cuttings. Their flowers are fragile and evanescent, and their only pollinators are bees which make a honey so fine that sweet-toothed men and beasts have driven them almost to extinction. Mandrake-growing is a very delicate art, which cannot stand much disaster. I looked at the craters left by the murderous barbarians, and I saw a battlefield blasted by the ire of a petty god, who would not be as parsimonious as those who had gone before him in supplying thunderbolts to his faithful followers.

* * *

I buried my father among the ruined mandrakes. I hoped, but could not believe, that a small miracle might allow one or two of them to find new life in feeding on his flesh. Then I left, travelling westwards. I had some vague notion of going to Kavala and searching for Cyllo, but in the event I kept on going, and have been a wanderer ever since. I have been a seaman and a fighting-man, a merchant and a thief, but I have never tended any sort of garden. I have been happy, in my fashion.

I still have the *other* root: the one intended as an offering to the emperor Julian, who is nowadays called Julian the Apostate by the faithful followers of the Galilean. I still treasure it, as I believe he would have done, as a testament to the virility of my will and the potency of my thought.

One day, I dare say, some vagabond will murder me in order that he might grind the root into a powder that he can trade in secret as a powerful love-potion—but I have every faith in the fact that the passion it will induce will bring no joy to anyone else. Like a faithful dog, the mandrake knows who its real master is.

CHANTERELLE

There was once a music-loving carpenter named Alastor, who fell in love with Catriona, the daughter of a foundryman who lived in a Highland village near to the town of his birth. Catriona was known in the village as the Nightingale, because she had a beautiful singing voice. Alastor loved to play for her, and it was while she sang to his accompaniment that she fell in love with him.

When Alastor and Catriona were married they left the Highlands for the Lowlands, taking up residence in the nation's capital city, where Alastor was determined to make a living as a maker of musical instruments. Their first child, a son, was born on the first Monday after New Year's Day, which is known throughout Christendom as Handsel Monday.

A handsel is a gift made to celebrate a new beginning, as a coin might be placed in the pocket of a freshly-tailored coat. Alastor knew that his son might be seen as exactly such a gift, bestowed upon his marriage, and he was determined to make the most of him.

"Should we call him Handsel, do you think?" Alastor asked Catriona.

"It is a good name," she said.

Every choice that is made narrows the range of further choices, and when the couple's second child was due Alastor said to Catriona: "If our second-born is a girl, we must not call her Gretel. There is a tale in which two children so-named are abandoned in the wild forest by their father, a poor woodcutter, at the behest of their step-mother. The tale ends happily enough for the children, but we should not take chances."

"You are not a woodcutter, my love," Catriona replied, "and we live in the city. We left the wild forest behind us when we left the Highlands, and I am not sure that we should carry its legacy of stories and superstitions with us."

"I think we should," said Alastor. "There is a deal of wisdom in that legacy. We may be far away from the haunts of the fairy-folk, but we are Highlanders still. There have been those in both our families who have had the second sight, and we have no guarantee that our children will be spared its curse. We should be careful in naming them, and we must take care that they hear all the stories we know, for whatever their guidance might be worth."

"Here in the city," said Catriona, "it is said that children must make their way in the real world, and that stories will only fill their heads with unreasonable expectations."

"They say that," admitted Alastor, "but the city-dwellers have merely devised a new armoury of stories, which seem more appropriate to the order and discipline of city life. I would rather our children heard what *we* had to tell—for they are, after all, *our* children."

"What name did you have in mind?" Catriona asked him.

"I hope that our son might choose to follow me in working with his hands," Alastor said. "I would like him to master the grain of the wood, in order that he might make pipes, harps, fiddles and lutes. I hope that our daughter might complement his achievements with a singing voice the equal of your own. Let us give her a name which would suit a songstress."

"Ever since I was a girl," said Catriona, "I have been nicknamed Nightingale—but if you mean what you say about the wisdom of stories we should not wish *that* name upon our daughter. No sooner had it been bestowed upon me than I was forced to listen to the tale of the little girl who fell into the care of a wicked man who knew the secret of training nightingales to sing by day. Even today, I shudder when I think of it."

"She was imprisoned in a cage by a prince, was she not?" said Alastor. "She was set to sing in the depths of the wild forest, but suffered misfortune enough to break her heart, and she refused to sing again, until she fell into the clutches of her former master, who . . . "

"Please don't," begged Catriona.

"Well," said Alastor, "we must certainly avoid the name that was given to *that* girl—which was Luscignole, if I remember rightly. I wonder if we might call our daughter—if indeed the child you are carrying should turn out to be a daughter—Chanterelle, after the highest string of a musical instrument? "

"Chanterelle is an excellent choice," said Catriona, "I never heard a story about a girl named Chanterelle. But what if the baby is a boy?"

There is no need to record the rest of the conversation, for the child *was* a girl, and she was named Chanterelle.

* * *

When Handsel and Chanterelle were old enough to hear stories, Catriona was careful to tell them the tales which were popular in the city as well as those she remembered from her own childhood in the Highlands, but it was the Highland tales that they liked better. Although there was not the faintest trace of the fairy-folk to be found in the city it was the fairy-folk of whom the children loved to hear tell.

Handsel, as might be expected, was particularly fond of the tale of Handsel and Gretel. Chanterelle, on the other hand, preferred to hear the tale of the foundryman who was lured away from his family by a fairy, until he was called back by the tolling of a church bell he had made, which had fallen into a lake. Catriona told that story to help her children understand the kind of work her father did, although she assured them that he was not at all the kind of man to be seduced by a fairy, but it was Alastor who told them the story of the little girl whose wicked guardian knew the secret of making nightingales sing by day. Catriona could not tell that story without shuddering, and she did not altogether approve when her husband told the fascinated children that she had once been nicknamed Nightingale, even though she had always been able to sing by day.

"In actual fact," Catriona told her children—using a phrase she had picked up in the city—"nightingales are not very good singers at all. It is the mere fact of their singing by night that is remarkable, not the quality of their performance."

"Why can we not hear them?" Handsel asked. "I have never heard *any* bird sing by night."

"There are no nightingales in the city," she told them. "They are rare even in the forests above the village where I was born."

"As rare as the fairy-folk?" asked Chanterelle.

"Even rarer, alas," said Catriona. "Had more of my neighbours heard one, they might have been content with my given name, which comes from *katharos*, or purity."

As Alastor had hoped, Handsel soon showed an aptitude for woodwork, and he eventually joined his father in the workshop. He showed an aptitude for music too, and was soon able to produce a tune of sorts out of any instrument he came across. Chanterelle was no disappointment either; she proved to have a lovely voice. She sang by day and she sang by night, and on Sundays she sang in the choir at the church which Alastor and Catriona now attended.

All was well—until the plague came.

"It is not so terrible a plague as some," Alastor said to Catriona, when Handsel was the first of them to fall ill. "It is not as rapacious as the one in the story of the great black spider—the one which terrified and blighted a Highland village, infecting the inhabitants with fevers that sucked the blood and the life from every last one. This is a disease which the strong and the lucky may resist, if only fortune favours them."

"We must do what we can to help fortune," Catriona said. "We must pray, and we must nurse the child as best we can. He *is* strong."

The instrument-maker and his wife prayed, and they nursed poor Handsel as best they could—but within a week, Chanterelle had caught the fever too.

Alastor and Catriona redoubled their efforts, praying and nursing, fighting with every fibre of flesh and conviction of spirit for the lives of their children. Fortune favoured them, at least to the extent of granting their most fervent wishes. Handsel recovered from the fever, and so did Chanterelle—but Catriona fell ill too, and so did Alastor.

The roles were now reversed; it was the turn of Handsel and Chanterelle to play nurse. They tended the fire, boiled the water, picked the vegetables and cooked the meat. They ran hither and yon in search of bread and blankets, candles and cough-mixture, and they prayed with all the fervour of their little hearts and high voices.

Catriona recovered in due course, but Alastor died.

"I was not strong enough," Handsel lamented. "My hands were not clever enough to do what needed to be done."

"My voice was not sweet enough," mourned Chanterelle. "My prayers were not lovely enough for Heaven to hear."

"You must not think that," Catriona said to them. "Neither of you is at fault."

They assured her that they understood—and it seemed that Handsel, perhaps because he was the elder, really did understand. But from that day forward, Chanterelle refused to sing.

156

Catriona did everything she could to coax her out of her silence, even steeling herself to tell the tale of Luscignole and the guardian who knew the secret of making nightingales sing by day—but if anything, the tale made matters worse.

"I could not believe when my father told me the tale," the little girl told her mother, "that the wicked old man would ever have done to the lovely child what he had earlier done to the nightingales—but I believe it now. The world is a cruel place."

Catriona realised that she had made a mistake, and wondered how she had ever thought that such a story might help, given that it did not have the happy ending that stories ought to have. She realised, belatedly, that she had told it because Alastor had told it, making an echo to sound in his absence.

"I believe Luscignole began to sing again because she wanted to recover the joy of it," Catriona said to her daughter. "I don't think it had anything to do with the wicked old man."

Perhaps Chanterelle knew that for a lie, or perhaps she simply despaired of recovering the joy of song. In any case, she would not rejoin the choir at the church, nor would she sing at home, by day or by night, no matter how hard Handsel tried to seduce her voice with his tunes.

* * *

Catriona and Handsel tried to complete the instruments that Alastor had left unfinished. They even tried to begin more—but Handsel's hands were only half-grown and his skills less than half-trained, and Catriona's full-grown hands had no wood-working skill at all. In the end, Catriona and her children had no alternative but to sell the shop and their home with it. They had no place to go but the Highland village where Catriona's parents lived.

The journey to the Highlands was long and by no means easy, but their arrival in the village brought no relief. The plague had left the highest parts of the Highlands untouched, for no fever likes to visit places that are too high on a hill, but it had insinuated itself into the valleys, descended on the villages with unusual ferocity. When the exhausted Catriona and her children finally presented themselves at the foundry they found it closed, and the house beside it was dark and deserted.

Neighbours told Catriona that her mother had died, and her mother's sister, and her father's brother, and her father's brother's wife, and both their sons, her only cousins.

The catalogue of catastrophe was so extended that Catriona did not notice, at first, that her father's name was not included in it—but when she did, the flicker of hope that burst forth in her frightened mind was quenched within a minute.

"Your father," the neighbours said, "was driven mad by loss and grief. He fled into the wild forest, determined to live like a bear or a wolf—for only bears and wolves, he said, know the true joy of unselfconsciousness. Before he went he cast the bell that he had made for our church into the tarn, declaring that the spirits of the lake were welcome to roll it back and forth, so that its echoes would toll within his heart like the knell of doom. He had heard a story, it seems, about another founder of bells who went to dwell in the wild forest, among the fairy-folk."

"He told me the story half a hundred times, when I was a child," Catriona admitted. "But that was a tale of vaulting ambition, about a man who sought unprecedented glory in the mountain heights because he was seduced by a fairy. If what you say is true, my father has been stolen rather than seduced, by demons and not by fairies."

"We are good Christians," the neighbours said, piously. "We know that there is no difference between demons and fairies, no matter what those with the second sight may say. The house is yours now, by right of inheritance, and the foundry too—you are welcome to make what use of them you will." Perhaps that was honest generosity, or perhaps the villagers thought that the foundry and house were both accursed by virtue of the death and madness to which they had played host. In either case, the donation was useless; if Catriona and Handsel could not run a workshop in the city they certainly could not run an iron-foundry in a Highland village.

"There is only one thing to be done," Catriona told the children. "I must go into the wild forest to search for my father. If only I can find him, I might make him see sense. At least I can show him that he is not alone. Pray that the idea of meeting his grandchildren for the first time will persuade him that it is better to live as a human than run wild as a bear or a wolf."

"Will he not be a werewolf, if he has been away too long?" Handsel asked. "There is a story, is there not . . . ?"

"You are thinking of the tale in which an abandoned boy became king of the bears," Catriona told him, firmly, although she knew that he was thinking of another blood-curdling tale of Alastor's. "He called upon their aid to reclaim his inheritance, if you remember, and they obliged. What I must do is help my father to reclaim *his* heritage."

"But what shall we do," Chanterelle asked, in the whisper that was now her voice, "if you are lost, and cannot return? What shall we do if the fairy-folk take you away, or if the werewolves eat you? What will become of us then?"

"I *will* return," said Catriona, even more firmly than before. "Neither fairy nor werewolf shall prevent me." She knew even as she spoke, however, that there were too many stories in which such promises were made and never kept—and so did Chanterelle.

Handsel had sense enough to hold his tongue, and wish his mother well, but Chanterelle was too frightened to do anything but beg her not to go. Handsel had enough of the city in him to know that stories were not always to be taken literally, but Chanterelle—perhaps because she was younger—did not. Catriona could not comfort her, no matter how hard she tried.

Catriona realised that when *she* had been a child she had known the reality of the wild woods as well as the stories that were told about them, while Chanterelle knew only what she had heard in stories. Alastor had overlooked that point of difference when he had insisted that the children must be told the stories that he had known when he was a boy.

"Please don't be afraid, Chanterelle," Catriona said, when she finally set out. "The fairy-folk never harmed me before."

"But they will not remember you," said Chanterelle. "You're a stranger now—and we are stranger still. Don't go."

"I must," said Catriona. "What earthly use is an iron-foundry without an iron-master?"

* * *

The two children found that the charity of their new neighbours lasted a full week. At first they were able to go from door to door, saying: "We are the grandchildren of the village iron-master and our mother has gone to search for him in the wild forest. Could you spare us a loaf of bread and a little cheese, or perhaps an egg or two, until our mother returns?"

As the days went by, however, the women who came to the door when they knocked began to say: "We have fed you once; it is someone else's turn"—and when the children pointed out that everyone in the village who was willing had taken a turn, the women said: "We have no guarantee that your mother will ever return, and even if she does she has no means to repay us. The parish has its own poor; you are strangers. We have done all that we must, and all that we can."

When ten days had gone by without any sign of their mother, Handsel and Chanterelle went to the village church, and said to the priest: "Advise us, please, as to what we should do? We have prayed long and hard, but our prayers have not been answered."

"I am not surprised, alas," said the priest. "Your grandfather was a good man once, but in casting the bell intended for our church into the dark waters of the tarn he committed an act of sacrilege as well as an act of folly. There is a story, you see, about an iron-master who was seduced away from faith and family when a church-bell he had founded was lost in a lake. Your grandfather was knowingly putting himself in that man's place, asking for damnation. It is good of you to pray for his return, but if he does not ask forgiveness for himself one can hardly expect Heaven to grant it, and even then . . . "

"Yes," said Handsel, "we understand all that. But what shall we *do*?"

"There is no living for you here, alas," said the priest, with a sigh, "You must go into the forest in search of your mother, and pray with all the might of your little hearts that *she* can still be found. It is possible, after all, that she is still alive. The forest is full of food, for those bold enough to risk its hazards. It is the season for hazel-nuts, and bramble-berries, and there are always mushrooms. It is time to commit yourself to the charity of Heaven, my little darlings. I know that Heaven will not let you down, if you have virtue enough to match your courage. There is a story about a boy named Handsel, as I recall, and his little sister, which ended happily enough—not that I, a priest, can approve of the pagan taint which such stories invariably have. In the final analysis, there is only one *true* story, and it is the story of the world."

"That isn't so, sir," said Chanterelle. "There are hundreds of true stories—perhaps thousands. I only know a few, but my grandfather must be old enough to know far more."

"You are only a child," the priest said, tolerantly. "When you are older, you will know what I mean. If your grandfather can recover his lost wits, he will be wise to forget all the stories he ever knew, except for the one which holds the promise of our salvation. I wish you all the luck in the world, little Gretel, and I am sure that if you deserve it, Heaven will serve you well."

"My name is Chanterelle, not Gretel," Chanterelle corrected him.

"Of course," said the priest serenely, "and can you sing like a nightingale, Chanterelle, as your mother could when she was young and lovely?"

"My mother is lovely still," Chanterelle replied, with unusual dignity in one so young, "and she can still sing—but I have never heard a nightingale, so I don't know which of them is better."

"When we say that a human sings like a nightingale," the priest said, with a slightly impatient smile, "we do not mean it *literally*. That is to say, we do not mean it *exactly*."

"Thank you," said Handsel, taking his sister's hand. "We shall take your excellent advice." Even Chanterelle could tell by the way he said "excellent" that he did not mean it *exactly*—but the advice was taken nevertheless. On the morning of the next day, Handsel and Chanterelle set off into the wild forest to search for their mother. Their new neighbours waved goodbye to them as they went.

* * *

The priest had told them the truth, at least about the season. There were indeed hazel-nuts on the hazel-trees and ripe bramble-berries on the brambles. The only problems were that hazel-trees were not easy to find among all the other trees, none of which bore any edible nuts, and that brambles were equipped with ferocious thorns that snagged their clothing and left bloody trails on their hands and arms.

There were mushrooms too, but at first the two children were afraid to touch them.

"Some mushrooms are poisonous," Handsel told his sister. "There are death-caps and destroying angels, and I do not know how to tell them apart from the ones which are safe to eat. I heard a story once which said that fairies love to squat on the heads of mushrooms, and that although those which the good fairies use remain perfectly safe to eat, those which are favoured by naughty fairies become coated with an invisible poisonous slime."

Even Chanterelle did not suppose that this story was entirely trustworthy, but she agreed with Handsel that they ought to avoid eating mushrooms, at least until the two of them became desperate with hunger.

By the end of the first day they were certainly hungry, but by no means desperate, and it was not until they had been searching for a second day that desperation and its cousin despair began to set in. On their first night they had slept long and deep but even though they were exhausted they found it more difficult to sleep on the second night. When they finally did go to sleep they slept fitfully, and they woke up as tired as they had been when they settled down.

Unfortunately, the wild forest was not consistent in its nature. Although the lower slopes were host to hazel-trees and brambles such plants became increasingly scarce as the two children went higher and higher. Their third day of searching brought them into a region where all the trees seemed to be dressed in dark, needle-like leaves and there was nothing at all to eat except for mushrooms. They had not yet found the slightest sign of their mother, their grandfather or any other human soul, even though Handsel had shouted himself hoarse calling out to them.

"Well," said Handsel, as they settled down to spend a third night in the forest, bedded down on a mattress of leaf-litter, "I suppose Heaven must be on our side, else we'd have been eaten by wolves or bears before now. If we're to eat at all tonight we must trust our luck to guide us to the most nourishing mushrooms and keep us safe from the worst."

"I suppose so," said Chanterelle, who had been keeping watch on all the mushrooms they had passed, hoping to catch a glimpse of a fairy at rest. She had seen none as yet, but that did not make her any happier while they made their first meal of mushrooms, washed down with water from a spring. They found it difficult to sleep again, and tried to comfort one another by telling stories—but they found the stories comfortless and they slept badly.

They made another meal of white mushrooms, which settled their hunger after a fashion and caused their stomachs no considerable upset. As the day's journey went higher and deeper into the forest, however, they found fewer and fewer of that kind.

Handsel continued to shout occasionally, but his throat was raw and his voice echoed mockingly back at him, as if the trees were taunting him with the uselessness of his attempts to be heard. Chanterelle helped as best she could, but her voice had never been as strong as it was sweet, even when she sang with the choir, and it seemed much feebler now.

When darkness began to fall yet again, and the two of them were badly in need of a meal, Handsel proposed that they ought to try the red mushrooms with white patches, which were much commoner in this region than the white ones they had gathered on the lower slopes. Chanterelle did not like the look of them at all, and said that she would rather go hungry.

"Look at this," said Handsel, showing her a specimen which had already been half-consumed. "They must be safe for animals to eat, else the creature which ate half this one would be lying dead beside it."

Chanterelle still refused to believe that the red mushrooms were edible.

"Oh well," said Handsel, "I suppose the sensible thing to do would be for *one* of us to try them, so that their safety can be put to the proof." Having reached this conclusion, he made a meal of a handful of the red mushrooms while Chanterelle ate the last of the white ones that Handsel had prudently hoarded inside his shirt.

Again they found it difficult to go to sleep, but they decided to suffer in silence rather than tell discomfiting stories. The forest, of course, refused to respect their silence by falling silent itself; the wind stirred the branches of the trees restlessly—but tonight, for the first time, they heard another sound.

"Is that a nightingale?" Chanterelle asked her brother.

"I suppose so," Handsel replied. "I never heard of any other other bird that sings at night—but it's not as sweet a singer as the birds that were kept in cages by people in the city. They had at least a hint of melody about their songs."

"It may not have much melody," said Chanterelle, "but I never heard a song so plaintive."

"If it *is* a nightingale," said Handsel, "I can't begin to understand why the old man in the story thought the secret of making them sing by day so very precious."

"I can," whispered Chanterelle.

When she finally fell asleep, Chanterelle dreamed that an old man was chasing her through the forest, determined to make her sing again even if he had to do to her what the old man in the story had done—first to the nightingales, and in the end to Luscignole. Usually, such nightmares continued until she woke in alarm, but this one was different. In this one, just as the old man was about to catch her, a she-wolf jumped on his back and knocked him down—and then set about devouring him while Chanterelle looked on, her anxious heart slowing all the while as her terror ebbed away.

When the wolf had finished with the bloody mess that had been the old man she looked at Chanterelle, and said: "You were right about the mushrooms. They'd been spoiled by fairies of the worst kind. You'll have a hard job rescuing your brother, but it *might* be done, if only you have the heart and the voice."

"Mother?" said Chanterelle, fearfully. "Have you become a werewolf, then? Is grandfather a werewolf too?"

"It's not so bad," said the she-wolf, "but grandfather was wrong to think he'd find the solace of unselfconsciousness in the world of bears and wolves. Remember, Chanterelle—*don't eat the mushrooms.*"

Having said that, the she-wolf ran away into the forest—and Chanterelle awoke.

* * *

Handsel was already up and about, and he had gathered more mushrooms ready for them to eat. He seemed much fitter than he had been the previous day, and he was much more cheerful than before, but he seemed to have lost his voice entirely. When he spoke to Chanterelle it was in a hoarse and grating whisper.

"You must eat *something*, Chanterelle," he told her. "We must keep our strength up. The red-capped mushrooms are perfectly safe, as you can see. I've suffered no harm."

Had Chanterelle not had the dream she might have believed him, after some hesitation, but the dream made her determined to let the red-capped mushrooms alone.

"Did you dream last night?" Chanterelle asked her brother.

"Yes I did," he croaked, "and rather frightening dreams they were—but they turned out all right in the end."

"Was there a wolf in your dream?"

"No. There were other monsters, but no wolves."

"I can't eat the mushrooms," Chanterelle told him. "I just can't."

"You will," he said, his voice hardly more than a gasp "when you're hungry enough. You'll need all your strength, I fear, because I can't shout any more. I must have overdone it yesterday, and now I can't raise my voice at all. It's up to you now. You have to sing out loud and clear."

"I can't do that either," said Chanterelle, her voice falling to a whisper almost as sepulchral as his. She was afraid that he would become angry, but he didn't. He was still her brother, even if he had eaten mushrooms enslimed by naughty fairies.

"In that case," he said, "we'll have to hunt for mother without calling out."

That was what they did, all morning and all afternoon. The forest was so gloomy now that even the noonday hours hardly seemed daylit at all. The dark-clad branches of the pines and spruces were so dense and so extensive that it was difficult to catch the merest glimpse of blue sky—and where the sun's rays did creep through the canopy they were reduced to slender shafts, more silver than golden.

Chanterelle grew hungrier and hungrier, and she hunted everywhere for mushrooms of the kind she had already eaten safely, but there were none to be found hereabouts. In the meantime, Handsel continued to pick and eat the other kind, growing bolder and happier all the while. If his voice had recovered its strength he might have made more effort to persuade Chanterelle to eat, but without the power to argue he had to be content with his earlier judgment that she would eat when she was hungry enough.

For four days they had wandered without catching sight of any predator more dangerous than a wildcat, although they had seen a number of roe deer and plenty of mice. That afternoon, however, they were confronted by a bear.

It was not a huge bear, and its thinning coat was showing distinct traces of mange, but it was a great deal bigger than they were and its ill-health only made it more anxious to make a meal of them. No sooner had it caught sight of them than it loped towards them, snuffling and snarling with excitement and showing all of its yellow teeth.

Handsel and Chanterelle ran away, as fast as they could go—but Chanterelle was smaller than Handsel, and much weaker. Before they had gone a hundred yards she was too tired to run any further, and her legs simply gave way. She fell, and shut her eyes tight, waiting for the snuffling, snarling bear to put an end to her with its rotten teeth. She felt its foetid breath upon her back as it reached her and paused—but then it yelped, and yelped again, and the force of its breath was abruptly relieved.

When Chanterelle opened her eyes she saw that Handsel had stopped running. He was snatching up cones that had fallen from the trees, and stones that had lodged in the crevices of their spreading roots. He was throwing these missiles as quickly as he could, hurling them into the face of the astonished bear—and the bear was retreating before the assault!

In fact, the bear was running away. It had conceded defeat.

"He wasn't hungry enough," Handsel whispered, gratingly, when the bear had gone. "Are *you* hungry enough yet, Chanterelle?"

"No," said Chanterelle, and tried to get up—but she had twisted her ankle, and couldn't walk on it.

"It'll be all right soon," she said, faintly. "Tomorrow, we can go on."

"If the bear doesn't come back," Handsel said, very hoarsely indeed. "When it's hungry enough, it might. If we can't search any longer, you really ought to sing. A song might be heard where shouting wouldn't."

"I can't sing," said Chanterelle—and wondered, as her brother looked down at her, whether he was thinking about the way in which the old man in the story had forced Luscignole to sing again, as if she were a nightingale.

Handsel said no more. Instead, he went to gather red-capped mushrooms. When he came back, his shirt was bulging under the burden of a full two dozen—but all he had in his hands was a tiny wooden pipe.

"I found this," he murmured. "It couldn't have been hollowed out without a proper tool, and the finger-holes are very neat. Mother had nothing like it, but I suppose it might be grandfather's. Perhaps father made it for him long ago, and gave it to him as a parting gift when he took mother away to the town. If it's not grandfather's, it's the first real sign we've found of the fairy-folk. Will you eat the mushrooms now?"

"I can't, said Chanterelle.

"I haven't voice enough to shout," croaked Handsel, "but I have breath enough to play. Perhaps, if you have a tune to follow, you'll be able to sing."

So saying, Handsel sat down beside his sister and began to play on the little pipe. He had no difficulty at all producing a tune, but it was as faint as his voice if not as scratchy. It was pitched higher than any tune she had ever heard from flute or piccolo.

"It *must* be a fairy flute," said Chanterelle, anxiously. "All the stories say that humans must beware of playing elfin music, lest they be captured by the fairy-folk."

Handsel stopped playing and inspected the pipe. "I could have made it myself," he croaked. "Smaller hands than mine might have made it as easily, I suppose."

"Elfin music loosens the bonds of time, in the tales that mother used to tell," said Chanterelle, "and time untied has weight for no man . . . whatever that's supposed to mean."

"I think it means that while a fairy flute plays a single song, years may pass in villages and towns," said Handsel, very faintly indeed. "I only wanted to help you sing, Chanterelle—but now the dusk is falling, and the darkness is deepening. I couldn't see a bear by night, Chanterelle. I couldn't hurt his nose and eyes with pine-cones. If the bear comes back, it will gobble us up. *Are you sure you cannot sing, even if I play a tune?*"

"Even if you play a tune, dear Handsel," Chanterelle told him, "I could not sing a note. Even if you were to do what the man in the story did . . . "

"I never understood how that would work," Handsel said, his voice like wind-stirred grass. "On nightingales, perhaps—but how could it work on the luckless Luscignole, unless she were a nightingale herself? Will you eat some mushrooms, Chanterelle? I fear for your life if you won't."

"A she-wolf warned me against them," said Chanterelle. "I dare not—unless she comes to me again by night and tells me that I may."

Handsel would not press her. He set about his own meal quietly—but he was careful to show her that he had only eaten half the mushrooms he had gathered, and would save the rest for her.

* * *

When night fell, Chanterelle tried to sleep. She wanted to see her mother again, even if her mother had to come to her in the guise of a wolf. Alas, she could not sleep. Hunger gnawed at her stomach, so painfully that she soon became convinced that the bear could have done no worse. She tried to fight the pain, but the only way she could do that was to call up a tune within her head and the only tune she could summon was the tune that Handsel had begun to play on the wooden pipe which had somehow been left for him to find.

It was an old tune, perfectly familiar, but she had never heard it played so high. Chanterelle was afraid that it might be the key in which a tune was played that made it into elfin music, rather than the tune itself. At first, when the tune went round and round and round in her sleepless mind there was nothing but the sound of the pipe to be "heard," but as it went on and on it was gradually joined by a singing voice: a voice that was not her own.

Eventually, Chanterelle realised that although the sound of the pipe was in her head, conjured up by her own imagination, the voice was not. The voice was real, growing in strength because the singer was growing closer—but how could it be, she wondered, that the imaginary pipe and the real voice were keeping such perfect harmony?

Chanterelle sat up, and began to shake her sleeping brother, who responded to her urging with manifest reluctance.

"Let me sleep!" he muttered. "For the love of Heaven, let me sleep!"

"Someone is coming," she hissed in his ear. "Either we are saved, at least for a while, or lost forever. Can you not hear her song?"

The singer was indeed a female, and when she came in view—lit by the lantern she bore aloft—Chanterelle was somewhat reassured, for she was taller by far than the fairy-folk were said to be. The newcomer wore a long white dress and a very curious cape made from blood-red fur, flecked with large white sequins. She had two dogs with her, both straining at the leash. They were like no dogs Chanterelle had ever seen: lean and white, like huge spectral greyhounds, each with a stride so vast that it could have out-sprinted any greyhound in the world.

"*Bad* dogs," said the lady, who had stopped singing as soon as her lantern had revealed the two children to the inspection of her pale and penetrating eyes. "*This* is not the prey for which you were set to search. These are children, lost in the wilderness. Were you abandoned here, my lovelies?" As she spoke she looked down at Chanterelle. Her eyes seemed strangely piercing; it was as if she could look into the inner chambers of a person's heart. Chanterelle hoped that it was a trick of the lantern-light.

"We came in search of our mother," said Chanterelle. "Have you seen her?"

"I've seen no one, child," the lady replied. "I'm hunting a she-wolf which has plundered my bird-house once too often. I thought that Verna and Virosa had her scent, but it seems not. What are your names?"

"I'm Chanterelle, and this is my brother Handsel."

"Why are you whispering, child?" the lady asked, although her own voice was low, and her singing had been soft in spite of the notes she had been required to reach.

"We have no voices left," croaked Handsel. "Misfortune and too much shouting have taken them both away. Have you bread, perchance—my sister will not eat the mushrooms which grow hereabouts, because she fears that they have been poisoned by the fairies."

"It is not so," the lady said. "These old wives' tales do a deal of damage, and are best forgotten. I have bread at home, and meat too, if you can walk as far as my house."

"I can," whispered Handsel, "but Chanterelle cannot. She twisted her ankle while fleeing from a bear."

"Well," said the lady, without much enthusiasm, "I suppose I can carry her, if you can hold the lantern and my dogs—but you'll have to be strong, for they can pull like the Devil when they're of a mind to do so."

"I can do that," said Handsel.

The lady gave the lantern and the two leashes to Handsel, and bent to take Chanterelle in her arms. For a fleeting instant the warmth of her breath reminded Chanterelle of the bear, but it was sweeter by far—and the lady's slender arms were surprisingly strong.

"Who are you?" Chanterelle asked, as she was borne aloft.

"My name is Amanita," the lady said, turning around to follow the dogs, which had already set off for home with Handsel in tow.

"I hope your house is not made of gingerbread," murmured Chanterelle.

"What a thing to say!" the woman exclaimed. "Indeed it is not. Whatever made you think it might be?"

"There is a story about a boy named Handsel, who was lost with his sister in a wild forest," Chanterelle told her. "They found a house of gingerbread, and began to eat it—but the witch who owned it caught them, and put them in a cage."

"It's exactly as I said," the lady observed. "Old wives' tales are full of nonsense, and mischief too. I never heard of such a thing. Do you think I'm a witch?"

"You were singing a song," said Chanterelle, uneasily. "I was remembering a tune, and your song fitted the tune. If that's not witchcraft, what is?"

"You poor thing," said the lady, clutching Chanterelle more tightly to her, so that Chanterelle could feel the warmth of the blood-red fur from which her cape was made. "You've been sorely confused, I fear. Don't you see, dear child, that it must have been my song that started the tune in your head? Your ears must have caught it before your mind did, so that when your mind caught up it seemed that the tune had been there before. But you're right, of course; if there's no witchcraft there, there's no witchcraft *anywhere*, and that's the truth."

Chanterelle knew better than to believe *that*. She had heard too many stories in her time to think the world devoid of magic. She knew that she would have to beware of the lady Amanita, whatever her house turned out to be made of.

* * *

The sleep that Chanterelle had been unable to find while she lay on the bare ground, fearful of the bear's return, came readily enough now that she was clasped in Amanita's arms. The lady did not carry her quite as tenderly as her mother would have done, but the warmth of the red cape seemed to soak into Chanterelle's enfeebled flesh, relaxing her mind. In addition, the lady began to sing again, albeit wordlessly, and the rhythm of her voice was lullaby-gentle and lullaby-sweet.

In such circumstances, Chanterelle might have expected sweeter dreams, but it was not to be. This time, she found herself alone by night in a vast and draughty church—vaster by far than any church in the town where she had lived, let alone the village whose priest had advised them to search for their mother in the forest. Its wooden pews formed a great shadowy maze and Chanterelle was searching that maze for a likely hiding place—but whenever she found one she would hear ominous footsteps coming closer and closer, until they came so horribly close that she could not help but slip away, scurrying like a mouse in search of some deeper and darker hidey-hole. She never saw her pursuer, but she knew well enough who he must be, and what he must be holding in his gnarled and arthritic hand. She knew, too, that no she-wolf could come to her aid in such a place as this—for werewolves cannot set foot on consecrated ground, no matter how noble their purpose might be, nor how diabolical the schemes they might seek to interrupt.

When Chanterelle awoke, she realised that she was in a bed with linen sheets. When she opened her eyes she saw that the bed had a quilt as red as Amanita's cape, patterned with white diamonds as neatly sown as any she had ever seen. It was obvious that the lady Amanita was an excellent seamstress—which meant, of course, that she must possess a sharp, sleek and polished needle.

Bright daylight shone through a single latticed window the shape and size of a wagon-wheel. Handsel was already up and about, as he had been the morning before. As soon as he saw that his sister was astir he rushed to her bedside.

"Isn't this wonderful?" he said, gesturing with his arm to indicate the room in which they had been placed. As well as the bed on which Chanterelle lay it had a number of chairs, one of them a rocking-chair; it also had a huge wooden wardrobe, a chest of drawers, a wooden trunk and a tiny three-legged table. The walls were exceptionally smooth, but their grey surfaces were dappled with black and the curiously ragged shelves set into them were an offensive shade of orange.

"No gingerbread at all?" Chanterelle whispered.

"None," said Handsel, who had obviously recovered the full use of his voice during the night. "I'll bring you some bread. It's freshly baked."

Handsel left the room—passing through a doorway that was far from being a perfect rectangle, although the door fit snugly enough—before Chanterelle could ask where a woman who lived alone in the remotest regions of the Highland forest could buy flour to bake into bread. When he returned a few minutes later Amanita was with him, carrying a tray which bore a plate of what looked like neatly-sliced bread and a cup of what looked like milk.

Alas, the bread had neither the odour nor the colour of *real* bread, and the milk had neither the colour nor the viscosity of *real* milk.

"I can't," said Chanterelle, weakly.

"Of course you can," said Handsel.

"It's not poison," said the lady Amanita—but Chanterelle did not believe her.

"You're a bad fairy," said Chanterelle to Amanita.

"You're a silly fool," said Amanita to Chanterelle.

"This is pointless," said Handsel, to no one in particular. "We can't go on like this—and if we don't go on, how will we ever find our mother?"

"You won't," said Amanita. "This isn't like one of your stories, you know. This is the real world. Your mother never had the slightest hope of finding your grandfather, and you don't have the slightest hope of finding your mother. They'll both be dead by now—and you ought to count yourselves very lucky that you're not dead yourselves. You will be, Chanterelle, if you won't eat."

"Poor Chanterelle," said Handsel, who seemed even fitter and bolder today than he had when he drove off the bewildered bear, and was in far better voice. "Can't eat, can't walk, can't sing, can't do anything at all. How can we save you, little sister? What do we have to do?"

"Find mother," Chanterelle replied. "Leave me, if you must, but *find mother.*"

"He won't go on without you, Chanterelle," said Amanita. "If you won't get better, he'll stay with you until you die." *And after that,* she didn't add, *he'll stay with me.*

"Find grandfather," whispered Chanterelle. "Please leave me, Handsel. Find grandfather, because he can't find himself. The bell in the tarn can't toll, you see. Its chimes can't echo in his heart like the chimes of conscience, drawing him back to his hearth and home. Find mother, before she loses herself entirely. Find them both, I beg of you. If you love me, go."

"You'll regret it if you do," said Amanita to Handsel.

Handsel seemed to agree with her; he shook his head.

"One more day, Handsel," whispered Chanterelle. "If you'll search for just one more day, I'll eat something. That's a promise. Even if you fail, I'll eat—but *you have to try.*"

That argument worked, as Chanterelle had known it would. "If you're sure you'll be all right," Handsel said, dubiously, "I'll go." Even as he said it, though, he looked at Amanita. It was as if he were asking her permission.

Amanita shrugged her shoulders, whose narrowness was evident now that she was no longer wearing the speckled cape. "You might as well," she said, "although I'm sure that there's nothing to find. I'll lend you Verna and Virosa if you like. If there's anything out there, they'll track it down—but you'll have to be strong if you're to hold on to them."

"No," said Chanterelle, quickly. "Don't take the dogs. Don't take that little pipe, either. Your voice will be enough, now that you've got it back. Search *hard*—you have to find them today, if they're to be found at all."

Again Handsel looked at Amanita, as if for permission. Again, Amanita shrugged her narrow shoulders.

"Look after my sister," Handsel said to the white-clad lady. "If anything were to happen to her . . . "

"Nothing will," said Amanita. "She's safe here. Nothing can hurt her, if she doesn't hurt herself—but if she won't eat . . . "

"She will," said Handsel, firmly. "She will, if I keep my part of the bargain." And having said that, he left.

When the door closed behind him, Amanita looked down at Chanterelle for a full half-minute before she put the bread that wasn't bread and the milk that wasn't milk on the three-legged table. Then she sat down in the rocking-chair, tilting it back so that when she released it she moved gently to and fro. She never took her eyes off Chanterelle, and her brown eyes were exactly as piercing now as they had seemed by tricky lantern-light.

"That was very brave of you, my dear," the lady said, at last, "if you really believe what you said about my being a bad fairy."

"I do," said Chanterelle, "and I'm *not* a silly fool."

"That," said the lady, "remains to be seen."

* * *

Chanterelle tested her injured ankle by stretching the toes and turning it to the left and the right. The pain she felt made it evident that she still wasn't able to walk, and wouldn't be able to for quite some time. The pain nearly brought tears to her eyes—but the anguish wasn't entirely unwelcome, because it distracted her attention from the awful hunger that felt as if it were hollowing out her belly with a fork.

The fake bread and the fake milk were beginning to seem attractive, in spite of the fact that they were not what they seemed to be. Handsel had obviously eaten them, just as he had eaten the red-capped mushrooms, but Chanterelle couldn't be certain that Handsel was still what he seemed to be.

"I wish you would eat, my dear," said Amanita, after a long silence. "If you don't eat, you'll never recover your strength. If you do, you might even recover your voice. You mustn't let stories make you afraid—and in any case, you can see readily enough that my house isn't made of gingerbread."

Chanterelle put out a hand to touch the wall beside the bed. It was softer than she had expected, and warmer. It had a curious texture unlike any wall she'd ever felt before. It wasn't brick or stone, and it wasn't wood or wattle-and-daub.

"It's a mushroom," whispered Chanterelle. "The whole house is a gigantic mushroom. How did it grow so big? It must be magic—*black magic*."

"Magic is neither black nor white, my dear," said Amanita. "Magic just *is*."

"The witch in the house of gingerbread tried to fatten Handsel for the cooking-pot," Chanterelle observed. "She wanted to eat him. Bad fairies and witches are much of a muchness, in all the stories I ever heard."

"Did the witch succeed?" asked Amanita.

"No," said Chanterelle. "Gretel—Handsel's sister, in the story—put an old stick in the witch's hand every time she reached into the cage to see whether Handsel was plump enough to eat yet. The witch was near-sighted, and couldn't tell that it wasn't Handsel's arm. When the witch finally grew impatient and tried to cook Gretel instead, Handsel pushed her into her own oven and cooked *her*. Then the children took the witch's hoard of gold and jewels back to their father, so that they would never be poor again."

"I see," said Amanita. "I fear, dear child, that I am not near-sighted. Were I what you suspect me to be, you'd have no chance at all of escaping me. In any case, it would do you no good if you did bundle me into my own oven. I have no hoard of gold and jewels, and you have no father. Your brother told me *another* story, about a little girl with a marvellous singing voice, who lost the will to sing when her heart was broken—but she was found by the old man who'd kept her when she was a child, who knew the secret of making nightingales sing by day. You know that story, of course. You know how the old man made the nightingales sing by day. You know what he did to set free the little girl's captive voice."

"I know," whispered Chanterelle, fearfully.

"Well," said Amanita, "that's nonsense too. All you need to set *your* voice free is a little bread and milk."

"The bread isn't bread and the milk isn't milk," said Chanterelle. "The bread is baked from mushrooms and the milk is squeezed from mushroom flesh."

"That's true, as it happens," admitted Amanita. "As you've observed yourself, there's not much food fit for children growing wild in *this* part of the forest. There are insects a-plenty, and animals which eat insects, and animals which eat animals, but children can't hunt. Fortunately, the mushrooms with the red caps do make nourishing food. Handsel is as bold and strong as he ever was, don't you think? *He* isn't afraid to eat my bread and drink my milk."

"Handsel will find mother today," whispered Chanterelle, "and grandfather too. Then we shall all go home."

"Go home to what?" asked Amanita. She stopped the chair rocking and leaned forward to stare at Chanterelle even more intently than before. "To an empty foundry, which had failed long before the plague came and your grandfather tipped the unfinished church bell into the tarn? Do you know why no one can hear it tolling in the dark current, least of all its maker? Because it has no tongue! It cannot chime, dear child, any more than you can sing."

"Mother will know what to do," said Chanterelle, so faintly that she could hardly hear herself.

"When Handsel returns," Amanita told her, coldly, "you'll understand how foolish you are. Remember your promise, Chanterelle. When Handsel returns, you must eat and drink."

Having said that, Amanita got up and stalked out of the room, her white skirt swirling about her. The rocking-chair was thrown into violent motion by the abruptness of Amanita's abandonment, and it continued rocking back and forth for what must have been at least an hour.

* * *

Chanterelle tried to stay awake, but she was too weak. When she drifted off to sleep, however, the pain in her ankle made it difficult for her to sleep deeply. She remained suspended between consciousness and oblivion, lost in a wilderness of broken dreams.

She dreamed of mournful she-wolves and decrepit bears, of ghostly hunting-dogs which bounded through the forest like malevolent angels, of sweet-smelling loaves of bread which broke to reveal horrid masses of blue-green fungus, of cups of milk infested with tiny worms, of long ranks of club-headed mushrooms which served as cushioned seats for excited fairies, and of wizened old men who knew the secret of making nightingales sing by day.

When she woke again, the room was nearly dark. The patch of blue sky that had been visible through the latticed window had turned to velvet black, but the stars were out and the moon must have been full, for the room was not *entirely* cloaked in shadows.

At first, Chanterelle couldn't tell what it was that had awakened her—but then she realised that the door had creaked as it began to open. She watched it move inwards, her heart fluttering in dread because she expected to see Amanita.

When she saw that the person coming into the room was Handsel, not Amanita, Chanterelle felt a thrill of relief, which almost turned to joy when she saw the excited expression on his face. For one delicious moment she read that excitement as a sign that he must have found their mother—but when he came closer she realised that it was something else.

"Oh, Chanterelle!" Handsel whispered, as he knelt down beside the bed and put his head on the pillow beside hers, "You've no idea what a day I've had."

"Are you hoarse from shouting?" she whispered back, "or are you afraid of waking Amanita?"

"Amanita's not here," Handsel said, in a slightly louder voice. "She must have gone out again with those dogs of hers to hunt the she-wolf. I shouted myself hoarse all morning, as I knew I must, but no one answered. Then I stopped go pick and eat more mushrooms. Then I began to shout again, but it was no use at all. I had lost my voice again—*but I had gained my sight!*"

"You never lost your sight," said Chanterelle, faintly.

"I never *had* my sight, dear sister. I always *thought* that I could see, but now I know that I never saw clearly before today. I had never seen the trees, or the earth, or the air, or the sun.

"Today, for the first time, I saw the life of the trees, the richness of the earth, the colour of the air and the might of the sun. Today, for the first time, I saw the world as it truly is. I saw the fairy-folk about their daily business. I saw dryads drawing water from the depths and breathing for the trees. I saw kobolds churning the soil to make it fertile. I saw sylphs sweeping the sky and ondines bubbling the springs.

"Oh Chanterelle, you were right about the mushrooms—and yet so very wrong! The fairy-folk swarm about them, hungry for pleasure, and make them grow tall and red, but there's no *poison* in them. There's only nourishment, for the mind as well as the body. Those who eat of the mushrooms tended by the fairy-folk may learn to see as well as growing strong. You must not be afraid of eating, Chanterelle. You must not starve yourself of light and life."

"I *am* afraid," said Chanterelle, and shut her eyes for a moment. She knew that the sight which Handsel had discovered must be the *second* sight of which the stories told, which was sometimes a blessing and sometimes a curse. She had always thought that if either of them turned out to have the second sight it would be her, and she felt a sharp pang of jealousy. She, after all, was the one who could sing—or *had* been able to sing, before grief took the melody out of her voice.

When she opened her eyes again, Handsel was no longer there—or, if he was, he was no longer Handsel. Kneeling beside her bed was the strangest creature she had ever seen. It was part-human, having human legs and human arms, but it was also part-insect, having the wings and head of a hawk-moth. Where the human and insect flesh met and fused, in the trunk from neck to hip, there was a soft carapace mottled with white stars. Even in the dim light, Chanterelle could see that the colour of the carapace was crimson, exactly like Amanita's cape.

The huge compound eyes looked at Chanterelle with what might have been tenderness. The principal part of the creature's mouth was a pipe-like structure coiled like a fern-leaf, which gradually uncoiled and stiffened, so that the tip reached out to caress her face.

When the creature spoke to her, its words sounded as if they were notes produced by some kind of flute, and every sentence was a delicate musical phrase.

"The sweetest nectar of all is fairy blood," the monster informed her, "but the fairy-folk offer it willingly. Human blood is bitter, spoiled as anything is spoiled that is kept for far too long. Iron bells are hard and cold, and their voices are the tyrants of time. The bells of forest flowers are soft and beautiful, and their voices can unloose the bonds of the hours and the days. When humans go mad they usually become bears or wolves, but find neither solace nor liberation. The fairy-folk are forever mad, forever joyous, forever free. Children may still be changelings if they choose. While the true sight has not quite withered away, children may find the one true path. While the true voice is not yet lost, children may soar on wings of song."

If only the monster had chosen its words more carefully, Chanterelle thought, it might have contrived a melody of sorts—but she had heard the songs of the skylarks and thrushes that the city-dwellers kept in cages, and she knew full well that even they had little enough talent for melody. Nightingales, for all their fame, were merely plaintive.

Chanterelle shut her eyes again, and counted to ten. When she opened them the monster was gone and Handsel was himself again.

"What did you say?" asked Chanterelle, in a voice as faint as faint could be.

"I said that we might be safe and happy here," murmured Handsel, in a croaky voice that was not quite lost. "If we can only persuade Amanita to take us in, we might live here forever. She must be lonely, must she not? She has no husband, and no children of her own. She might accept us as her children, if we promise to be good. Wouldn't you like to live in an enchanted forest, sister dear?"

"I would rather find my mother," said Chanterelle.

"We have tried and failed," said Handsel, sadly, "and must make the best of things. Would you rather starve than eat? Would you rather go down to the valley, where no charity waits us, than stay in the wild forest and live as the fairy-folk live? You promised, did you not, that you would eat Amanita's bread and drink her milk, if I could not find our mother or our grandfather in one more day of searching? I have tried, and failed; I have lost my voice, but I can see. Will you eat, dear sister, and live—or will you break your promise, and die?"

"I will eat and drink in the morning," whispered Chanterelle. "If mother has not found us by then, I will eat Amanita's mushroom-bread and drink her mushroom-milk. That's a promise."

"I think you're foolish," Handsel said, "but I will settle for that." He stood up, and turned towards the door.

"Don't go!" said Chanterelle, although her voice was so feeble that she could not make her panic felt.

"I have my own room now," said Handsel, "and my own bed." *His* voice was growing stronger again.

No sooner was Chanterelle alone than the room grew noticeably darker. A cloud must have drifted across the face of the moon.

Chanterelle moved her injured foot from left to right and back again, and then she stretched her toes. The result was agony—but it was the kind of agony that chased sleep away, and delirium too. Her mind had never been sharper.

Because she had no voice, Chanterelle cried out silently for her mother and her grandfather. *If you don't come by morning,* she thought, with all the fervour she could muster, *you will come too late. If you don't come by morning, I shall be lost.*

In stories, she knew, such silent cries sometimes brought results. In stories, panic was sometimes as powerful as prayer. She prayed as well, though, in the hope that even if her mother and her grandfather could not help her, Heaven might.

As before, the pain could not keep sleep at bay indefinitely, but the sleep to which Chanterelle was delivered was shallow and turbulent.

She dreamed that she was running through the forest yet again, still pursued by the old man who knew how to make nightingales sing by day. All night long his footsteps grew closer and closer, until at last she sank exhausted to the ground and waited for the inevitable.

As before, though, the old man had no chance to complete his dire work. He was knocked flying by the paw of a bear, which then limped away into the forest with its ancient head held low.

When the old man attempted to rise again he was confronted by a she-wolf whose grey coat was flecked with blood. For a moment or two it seemed that the old man might try to defy the she-wolf, which was limping almost as badly as the bear, but when she showed her bright white teeth he thought better of it and ran off, in the opposite direction to the one the bear had taken.

"Thank you," Chanterelle whispered to the she-wolf.

"Don't thank me," said the wolf, sinking down beside her. "I can't help you. I can't even help myself." The wolf began licking at her wounds. Both her hind legs had been bitten, and her belly too. It was obvious that the hounds had almost brought her down.

"Who will help me if you cannot?" asked Chanterelle. "Must I trust in Heaven?"

The she-wolf stopped licking long enough to say: "Heaven is a poor ally to those still on Earth, else plague would have no power to consign us to damnation. Had you kept your promises, you'd be beyond help already—and those who are less than honest can hardly look to Heaven for salvation."

"Then what will become of me?" asked Chanterelle.

The wolf was too busy feeding on its own blood to give her an immediate answer, but when her fur was clean again she looked the child full in the face with sorrowful eyes.

"I wish I knew," the wolf said. "I can't even tell you the answer to your other question."

"What other question?" asked Chanterelle.

"Why the girl sang again when she was captured for a second time by the man who knew the secret of making nightingales sing by day. I don't know the answer. All I know is that there's no more joy in being a wolf than there is in being a bear. I have to go away now. If I stay in this part of the forest the hounds will have me for sure—and a wolf shouldn't have to live on mice while there are sheep in the valleys."

"Please don't go," begged Chanterelle, in a voice so weak as to be almost unheard. "If only you could save me, I think I *might* be able to sing again."

"Too late," said the wolf, as she disappeared into the darkness of the forest.

* * *

"Too late," said Amanita, as Chanterelle woke to morning daylight. "You must eat now, or it will be too late."

Amanita was sitting no more than an arm's reach away from Chanterelle's head, having drawn a chair to the side of the bed—not the rocking-chair, but one of the others. The white-clad woman was holding a bowl full of steaming soup, which had the most delicious scent. The soup was thick and creamy, with solid pieces of a darker hue half-submerged beneath the surface.

"Mushroom soup," said Chanterelle, very faintly.

"The best mushroom soup in the world," said Amanita. "No redcaps in *this* soup, I assure you. Not all mushrooms are alike, as you know. These are the very best. I had to hunt far and wide to find them for you, but I knew that I'd have to find them even if it took all night. Luckily, the moon was full."

"I don't want it," whispered Chanterelle.

"But you don't have any choice," said Amanita. "You did promise—and you promised Handsel too. You don't understand what's happening here. You don't understand who and what you are. When your father named you Chanterelle he thought it was a safe name for a nightingale, but he forgot the other meaning of the word. He knew that the highest string of a musical instrument was a chanterelle, but he'd forgotten that a chanterelle is also a kind of mushroom—the most delicious kind of edible mushroom. Memory plays these little tricks all the time, you see. You thought you were supposed to be a singer, but you were always intended for better things than that. All children are kin to the fairy-folk, dear Chanterelle, but only a few have the chance to cross over, to see the world as *we* see it, with the *second* sight. You have that chance, but you must seize it. You must welcome it, because the cost of refusal will be more terrible than you imagine."

"I can't," whispered Chanterelle.

"You must," whispered Amanita.

"Where's Handsel?" asked Chanterelle. "I must see Handsel."

"In the hope that he can seize me and throw me in my own oven, to burn me alive? In the hope that you and he can run away, laden down with gold and gems? Handsel can *see* now, my darling. Handsel will be my lover now, my darling boy, the sweetest of the sweet."

"I must see Handsel," murmured Chanterelle.

Amanita would not stand up, but she called out to Handsel to come and see his sister—and Handsel came. He stood beside Amanita, with his arm about her shoulder and his cheek next to hers.

"You must eat, Chanterelle," he said. "If you cannot eat, you'll never sing again."

"Can you not see that she's a wicked fairy?" Chanterelle asked of him, although her voice was so faint as hardly to be there at all. "Can't you see what she is?"

"I *can* see," said Handsel. "I never could before, but now I can. I never want to be blind again, Chanterelle. I couldn't stand it."

"The poor girl thinks that she's a nightingale," said Amanita, softly and sadly. "She can't believe what she really is, and she's starving herself to death because of it. But you know—don't you, darling Handsel?—how nightingales can be taught to sing by day. You know the secret. Tell me what the secret is, darling Handsel."

Chanterelle wanted to beg her brother not to betray her, but now she had no voice left at all. She couldn't utter a word.

"The old man trained the nightingales to sing by day by running hot needles into their eyes," Handsel said, calmly. "Afterwards, they thought eternal night had come, and that was their idea of Heaven—so they sang, and sang, and sang in celebration. When Luscignole first saw what the old man did she ran away, but that was because she didn't understand her true nature and her true destiny. She lost her voice when her heart broke, and the only way she could find it again was to learn to see as the nightingales see—and to find Heaven where she had never thought to look."

"Eat, Chanterelle," said Amanita. "Eat, and be what you truly are."

Chanterelle opened her mouth, and tried to scream, but no scream came out. Instead, a spoon went in, bearing a full load of the impossibly delicious soup.

Chanterelle would have swallowed the soup for sure if she had not gagged and choked, but she did—and the contents of the spoon were sprayed all over the bosom of Amanita's white dress, flecking it with grey and brown.

So astonished was Amanita that she dropped the bowl, and howled with anguish as the hot liquid flooded the thin fabric of her skirt.

Chanterelle, fearful for her very life, threw back the crimson coverlet that had kept her warm for two nights and a day, flew across the room to the open window, and was gone.

* * *

Some months later, on the first Monday after New Year's Day, Handsel and Amanita were walking in the wild forest by the light of the full moon. Their two ghostly hunting-dogs were beside them, neither needing a leash.

Amanita wore her favourite cape of blood-red fur, flecked with silver sequins. Handsel wore a fur cloak cut from the hide of a brown bear, trimmed along the edges with the silkier fur of a grey she-wolf. The body of the fur was a trifle mangy in places but the cape was warm in spite of the spoiled patches.

"How beautiful the sylphs are as they dance on the moonbeams," Handsel said, "freshening the air with their agility."

"Indeed they are, my love," said Amanita.

"I like the dryads even more," said Handsel. "They know the very best of elfin music, and they love to play their pipes when the wind blows. I was a piper myself once, and a plucker too, but I was never very good. One should leave the exercise of such arts to those who know them best."

"Indeed one should, my darling," said Amanita.

"There is another song in the air tonight, is there not?" said Handsel, pausing suddenly and cocking his ear. "There is another voice, even more distant and more plaintive than the dryad pipes. I have heard it before, but never by day and always very faint. What is it?"

"It is the song of a nightingale," said Amanita. "There *is* a way to make one sing by day, if you remember—but you would have to snare it first, and hold it very still while I worked the magic."

Handsel remained where he was for a moment longer, but then he shrugged his shoulders and resumed walking.

"What would be the point?" he said. "The poor thing cannot hold a melody at all."

PUBLICATION HISTORY

"Salome" was published in *The Dedalus Book of Femmes Fatales* ed. Brian Stableford, Dedalus 1992. "O For a Fiery Gloom and Thee" was published in *Sirens* ed. Ellen Datlow & Terri Windling, HarperPrism 1998. "The Last Worshipper of Proteus" was published in *Beyond 2* (June/July 1995). "The Evil That Men Do" was published in *Realms of Fantasy* August 1995. "Ebony Eyes" was published in *Horrors! 365 Scary Stories* ed. Stefan Dziemianowicz, Robert Weinberg & Martin H. Greenberg, Barnes & Noble, 1998 (as by Francis Amery). "The Fisherman's Child" was published in *The Penny Dreadfull* 10 [April 1998]. "The Storyteller's Tale" was published in *The Anthology of Fantasy and the Supernatural* ed. Stephen Jones & David Sutton. Tiger, 1994 "The Unluckiest Thief" was published in *Interzone* 60 (June 1992). "The Light of Achernar" was published in *The Last Continent* ed. John Pelan, Shadowlands Press, 1999. "The Mandrake Garden" was published in *The Magazine of Fantasy & Science Fiction* July 2000 "Chanterelle" was published in *Black Heart, Ivory Bones* ed. Ellen Datlow & Terri Windling, Avon 2000.

Printed in the United States
24544LVS00005B/417

9 781587 154089